ESCAPE TO CANAMITH

BookBullet.com
1300 W Belmont Ave Ste 20G
Chicago, IL 60657-3200

Editing by Elizabeth Irwin
Proofreading by Vanessa Fravel
Cover Design by Portfolio Creative Studio
Interior text design by James M

ISBN: 9781619843424

ESCAPE TO CANAMITH

Templeton's Ark

RICHARD FRIEDMAN

DEDICATION

To my parents, Edith and Morris Friedman

ACKNOWLEDGEMENTS

I'd like to thank my editor, Elizabeth Irwin, for her deft skill that improved the story and my sincere appreciation to Bookbullet.com and their proofreader, Vanessa Fravel, for all the assistance getting the book published.

Big thanks go out to my brothers. Lawrence is the wisest man I know. His guidance with the book began four years ago when he read the first draft of this story. Warren, a fellow author, taught me about the world of publishing and marketing. I can't wait to read his second novel.

A loving thank you to my children for supporting this endeavor. Special thanks to my wife, Debbie, for her encouragement, advice, and for keeping our household afloat during the countless hours I spent working on this book. I know you're my biggest fan.

A true Inspiration

One of my favorite books of all time is "*The Lorax*" by Dr. Suess. It was the first environmental story I ever read. I loved that the Lorax "spoke for the trees."

Two years ago I faced uncertainty about whether to continue the journey as a writer. I headed to the local library for motivation where I saw a book lying face down on a table, partially covered with newspaper. When I brushed the paper aside, I saw a copy of "*The Lorax*." My purpose was renewed.

I hope my eco-thriller inspires you to make a difference in this world.

CANAMITH COMMUNICATION DEPARTMENT

The deep blue cloth draperies peeled back from the middle of the wall and exposed the live image of Rex Templeton filling the white screen. He spoke in a clear, calm, and reassuring manner.

"Evening, folks. I thought I'd end tonight's weekly meeting and introduce you to the newest addition to our communications department. It's a video or news report that you can see on this monitor. I'd like to thank the communications staff for their hard work to make this information available to everyone.

"Our staff is constantly reviewing information from around the world and they're going to be showing you any pertinent information regarding what's happening outside these walls. If you look to the right of the screen, you'll see a green light. If that light is flashing, then you'll know a new update will be shown at the top of the hour.

"For those of you not working in the tunnels, the video link will be sent from the central communication server to your home monitor. Please make sure your system is tuned to the default settings.

"We're right on the edge of cataclysm. I need all to you to stay focused on your jobs. If you do that, we'll be okay."

CHAPTER 1

The flashing lights stopped when the rescue squad pulled into the emergency entrance of Sanderell Hospital. Doctor Willis glanced at Sophie's wound and shouted, "Get this girl on the table! Stat! Get that IV going. What's happened to this girl?"

Lila Jenkins jumped toward the doctor. "I'm her mother. We were at Malotte's Petting Zoo and it bit her! I think it got her femoral vein. Is she going to be all right?

"It's too premature to tell," said the doctor. "She's probably lost a lot of blood and we have to clean the wound. What bit her?"

"It was a billy goat."

"A billy goat? Interesting. Is she allergic to any medications?" asked the doctor.

"No. I mean, I don't think so. Please stop her bleeding!" Lila demanded.

The doctor ignored her impassioned pleas and focused on his patient.

"MOMMY!" cried the frightened girl. Her terrified face escalated her mother's anxiety.

"It's okay baby! The doctor is going take care of you. We're right here." Lila stroked her hand with reassuring confidence.

"Please, wait outside in the hall. I promise I'll find you as soon as she's stabilized."

Nurse Teel ushered the worried parents into the hall. Her hair was pulled back tightly into a bun and the force of the rubber band pulled on the sides of her ears, giving her an eerie, haunted expression. Staring at the clipboard, pen in hand, the nurse asked, "Please tell me what happened today."

Lila wiped away the mascara that dripped down the side of her face.

"We thought it would be fun to take Sophie, that's our daughter's name, to Malotte's Petting Zoo. It was pleasant and sunny today and then we—"

Nurse Teel interrupted.

"I thought that old place was closed. Mrs. Jenkins, please move ahead to the time of the injury."

Lila took a deep breath and began to explain what happened.

"Sophie approached the billy goat pen and she tripped. She tried to stop her fall by placing her arm on the wooden fence that kept the animals in their cages. Her arm cracked the wood and Sophie fell into the pen. One of the billy goats lunged forward and grabbed a chunk of her leg. She started screaming in pain right away. It was awful. There was so much blood, and I was freaking out. We called an ambulance and here we are. I'm telling you, that billy goat attacked her!" stated Lila.

"Hon, you can't say it attacked her," interjected J.J.

"I sure can! I was right there! I say it attacked her. I know animals better than anyone, and I can tell the difference between territorial preservation and aggression."

"I'd say it was scared and tried to defend itself."

"Whose side are you on?"

"Lila, this isn't about 'sides'. Nurse, I'm sorry, it's just that Sophie means everything to us, and if anything were to happen to her…" His voice faded to silence.

"Okay, I get the picture," interrupted the nurse. "I'll find you as soon as I hear from the doctor. Sophie's in good hands, I promise. You've been through a lot today. Please go to the family room. It's down the hallway on the right."

"Thank you. Let us know if you have any other questions," said J.J.

J.J. grasped his wife by the arm as they walked towards the hallway. He towered over her by almost a foot, but still managed to put his right arm around her shoulder to comfort her. There was nothing they could do in the waiting room do but sit and worry. J.J. stood up and tried to listen to the doctors working on Sophie's leg. He heard medical terminology he didn't like. Words such as "damaged" and "hemorrhaging" flowed down the hall. He tried to keep his spirits up. He faltered when he heard Sophie's ominous cries of pain.

"Come on, J.J., keep it together. I don't want to start crying again," begged Lila.

"I'll be okay. Did you see all that blood?"

"Of course I did! Who kept pressure on the wound until the ambulance arrived?"

"I know, I know, I feel so helpless. That's our baby in there." His pale expression didn't exude much confidence.

An hour passed.

Another man and woman entered the waiting room. The woman was distraught and her husband held her tight.

Lila whispered to J.J. "What happened to them?" J.J. shook his head.

The balding man guided his wife down on the couch. He lumbered across the room towards the Jenkins.

"Hi, I'm Donald Hunziger. That's my wife Denise on the couch. Our boy was attacked by our dog. It was the strangest thing I've ever seen. Our dog Bailey never growled at us one time in seven years. Today, little Ronnie comes down for breakfast…bam! Did you guys hear about the kid that was in here earlier? Horrible. Poor parents. You'd never think you'd have to bury your own kid."

"What happened to him?" Lila asked.

Denise interrupted.

"Donald…stop talking about that poor boy right now! You don't

RICHARD FRIEDMAN

know for sure that his pets killed him. That's probably just some
awful rumor. Come back here and leave those nice people alone. I'm
sorry; my husband talks a lot when he's nervous. Please forgive him."
Donald did as he was told and returned to the couch with his
wife. Lila shot J.J. a worried glance and cuddled up closer to him.
"No problem. We're all worried today. Our daughter got bitten at
a petting zoo. What in the world is going on?" she asked.
J.J. squeezed her hand. "I don't know. Can we just go back to the
World Health Summit and start over? I'll ask you out, you'll be coy
and standoffish, and then we fall in love and have a child someday,
we'll just make sure be avoid Malotte's. We'll take Sophie to a movie
or something. We don't even have to discuss Canamith until we get
married."
Lila wasn't impressed. "Just what you'd want to do, a man who
specializes in Oxygenates…you haven't been to a movie in ten years."
Mr. Hunziger couldn't help himself.
"Did you say oxygenetics? What in the world is that?"
J.J. didn't care to correct the man for his mispronunciation, or
discuss the entire gamut of his job with a complete stranger while
sitting in the waiting room of a hospital, but the momentary diversion
did distract his attention from Sophie.
"It's quite boring really. Think of it as using oxygen to help us
clean up the environment. I'm working with a company right now
that's installing gasoline storage tanks on the outskirts of the city.
We assist in renewable and alternative fuels and phytoremediation,
MTBE contamination, stuff like that…"
Hunziger fell quiet and turned his attention back to his wife.
J.J. moved closer to Lila and whispered in her ear, "He doesn't
have a clue about anything I just said."
The attempt to divert their attention from Sophie ended. Lila's
eyes welled up and she buried her head in J.J.'s strong body. He
stroked her short hair and tried to soothe her.
"It'll be okay, Lila…I promise."

4

"You can't make that promise. Let's hope the doctor comes out soon. The waiting is killing me."

One more hour passed. Finally, in the third hour, Dr. Willis appeared.

He hesitated for an instant as both sets of parents jumped to attention hoping the doctor brought good news.

He looked at the Hunzingers, and then spoke to the Jenkins.

"Mr. and Mrs. Jenkins, she's going to be fine. There was a lot of bleeding and we're going to have to keep her here overnight for observation. She should avoid vigorous activity for three weeks. It's going to take months for her leg to heal completely. I don't anticipate any long term damage to the nerves or the muscle tissue."

"Thank goodness. That's wonderful news," said Lila.

J.J. hugged Lila and then went to greet Dr. Willis.

"Thank you! Thank you so much!" said J.J.

"Mr. Jenkins, please!" said the doctor, pushing himself from the embrace. "There's no need to break my ribs. Save those hugs for your little girl. I gave her a sedative to help her sleep. It won't take effect for a few minutes. She wants to see you. We moved her to Trauma Room Three. This may sound odd considering what happened—she's one lucky girl. She was more fortunate than the teenager that was in here earlier today. He was attacked by a—don't listen to what I am saying. Go see your daughter."

"What about our son?" asked Mr. Hunziger.

"I'll be back with an update as soon as I have it. Sit tight, folks," said Dr. Willis as he departed from the room.

Lila and J.J. hurried down the hall, ignoring the doctor's comments and failing to say goodbye to the Hunzigers. Lila gasped when she saw Sophie's connected to a series of cables. One checked her heartbeat, another her blood pressure and temperature. The smell of fresh paint hung in the room. Blue tape outlined on the windows and doorways. The overflow of patients prevented the maintenance staff from finishing the trim work.

Sophie whispered to her parents.

"Mommy, that animal bit me. You told me they were herbidoors."

"You mean herbivores," said Lila, the beginning stages of a smile pierced the sides of her mouth.

J.J. tried to joke with the girl. "It bit you because you're sweet. We tell you that all the time."

Lila implored her husband, "J.J., please. Sophie, we don't know why it bit you. It's an animal, not a pet. Even at a petting zoo, an animal can make a mistake. It was an accident. The doctor says you should rest and daddy and I will be right outside in the hall if you need anything and the nurses will be in to see you soon."

"Mommy, stay!" the girl pleaded.

"Sophie, I'll be right outside the door if you need anything. Doctor's orders."

J.J. broke into the conversation. "I'll stay right here at the edge of the bed until you fall asleep."

"Okay," Sophie whispered those words and then faded and fell asleep a moment later.

J.J. winked at Lila and scooted to the bottom of the bed. Her heavy breathing returned to normal as the medication took hold.

The steady beeping of the monitors acted as a metronome, lulling J.J. into a catatonic state. He rose and went to the hallway where Lila was resting on a couch. J.J. caressed his wife's hand and gently pulled it towards him. The exhausted couple sat there wondering why their sweet girl had been subjected to this ordeal.

CHAPTER 2

Lila and J.J. headed down to the beach with Sophie. Her leg had healed sufficiently in two weeks for her to make the short walk from the Jenkins' backyard down the wooden pathway to the entrance of the beach.

The sun scorched the white sandy coast. The beach was filled with sun worshippers and employees taking excessive lunch breaks. The sound of the waves collapsing on the coastline met the squeals from boys and girls enjoying the day. Gulls made repeated diving runs for specks of food tossed away by careless families on a picnic.

Sophie played near the edge of the water. Her blonde hair was cut short like her mother's and hung an inch below her ears. The gentle breeze pushed it to the side. The lone remnant of her injury was a narrow red line where the wound was healing. Lila and J.J. hoped to minimize any long-term psychological damage from the incident. Lila spent time encouraging Sophie to understand her ordeal was rare and that the animal that attacked her was ailing and had been put down. The latter was true.

Tests could not confirm that the animal had been sick. All the standard examinations done on "Scoops", the billy goat that bit her, showed no abnormalities. Lila hadn't told Sophie that 317 other children had been attacked at petting farms and zoos in the last two weeks. The government shut down all of them, across the country, until further notice. The other victims hadn't fallen into the pen. In those cases, the animals appeared to be the aggressors and inflicted harm on the children without provocation.

Lila talked to the doctor who performed the necropsy on the animal that bit Sophie and the animal was found to have an inflated sodium level. That was typical for animals that were fed a diet of unsupervised food. Visitors regularly tossed food into the pen, refusing to follow the "Do Not Feed the Animals" signs.

As the Jenkins family played in the water, Lila peered out at the ocean. What Lila saw was unmistakable.

"J.J., look at that! There's so many of them!"

Huge plumes of water shot skyward from at least five hundred blue whales roaming towards the coast. The leading edge of the line of whales was several hundred yards away. The foaming whitecaps of the waves intermittently hid the beautiful animals. There was little doubt that the whales were coming closer to the shoreline with each turn of their majestic tails. They swerved back and forth, north a tad, and then south towards the beach again. Their motions were repetitive and worrisome to those on the beach...especially Lila.

"J.J., I wonder if this change in their migration patterns is due to the warmer weather. What if they are here because of a natural predator in the area? What am I saying? We're their only predator. J.J., this is crazy!"

"You say everything is explainable...start explaining."

A quick-thinking security guard had placed the call to the National Oceanic Department for support. Police cruisers pulled up to the beach. Two men leapt out of the car. More police arrived within minutes and they established a control line where the current tide trickled up the shore. Sunbathing was finished for the day.

The first policeman on the scene grabbed his megaphone and spoke to the crowd. His girth stretched the fabric of his shirt to new limits. His head dripped with sweat. With one hand he wiped his brow, with the other he bellowed for all to hear.

"This beach is closed. We need your cooperation. PLEASE! Gather your belongings and exit the beach at the North Gate. Let's go people. Move it along!"

The crowd of onlookers didn't want to leave. Instead, they inched closer to the water, trying to get a better glimpse at what was happening in the warm waters of the ocean.

This time the burly policeman spoke to the crowd in a tone that couldn't be ignored.

"People, I'm talking to ALL of YOU!!! Get your stuff together and get out of here! Now!"

This time they moved. Within minutes the beachcombers were gone. An ever-growing force of police assumed their positions.

"You too, sweetheart," barked the cop at Lila.

"Hey, don't call me sweetheart. I'm a science professor at Sanderell University and I'm not leaving!" Lila declared.

"I don't think so, lady. Orders are everyone clears the area, and that means you too," he said with conviction.

"That's okay, officer, she's with me." The new voice belonged to Lila's boss, Dr. Carlin Massey, Director of the College of Science.

The policeman shot Massey a nasty glare as Lila stepped closer to the older man.

"I get it now. I wouldn't have figured you two as a couple." He left them standing there without saying another word. Massey detested the inaccurate insinuation. A middle-aged man with an average appearance at the beach with a trim woman who was half his age would raise suspicion. They were not together.

Lila scanned the scene around her. The beach was awash with police. "Thanks, Dr. Massey, that was fortunate timing." Turning to her husband, she said. "J.J., you better take Sophie home. The police are correct. She doesn't belong here."

"I'm on it. I'll meet you at home. See you later, Dr. Massey." J.J. grabbed Sophie's hand and headed for the exit.

Dr. Massey turned to Lila.

"Lila, what are you doing here? Central Command notified me ten minutes ago. How did you make it? I mean, how'd you—" Lila cut him off in mid-sentence. She couldn't help notice that Massey was distracted by the cloth robe wrapped around her two-piece bathing suit.

"I live two minutes away. We came to the beach to relax. I'd hardly call this relaxing. It seems nothing is ever relaxing in my life."

Massey looked around and asked, "Do you know what is going on?"

"I don't think anybody does. The whales' migration pattern is in an entirely different part of the ocean. I've never seen pods this large. What did Central tell you?"

Massey rubbed his reddish-brown-gray beard with his fingers. His head had gone bald years ago. Tufts of gray circled his temples. The sun caused his eyeglasses to tint, making it impossible to see his blue eyes. He kept adjusting the placement of his glasses on his nose, a nervous habit that Lila noticed when her boss was worried.

"Well?" Lila asked again.

"Well nothing, and I can't talk here. Let's meet back at the office later tonight."

"That doesn't sound like 'nothing,'" Lila shot back.

Massey turned away and mumbled, "I'll see you later."

The pod of whales headed back out to sea as quickly and mysteriously as it had arrived.

Several policemen remained at the beach for security. An eerie quiet fell over the area.

Back at the house, Lila's head began to hurt. She couldn't exactly describe the sensation to anyone, not even to Dr. Bell, her primary physician. She didn't want to take the barrage of tests he wanted to run. She downplayed the frequency of the headaches. If Dr. Bell knew they occurred daily, he would admit her to the clinic for the whole gamut. Lila had no time for examinations. She needed to be with Sophie.

Her beautiful daughter was healing physically. Emotionally, she had become possessive of Lila and wanted to be near her mother at all times.

CHAPTER 3

Canamith Village was located high atop the mountain ranges of the West Coast. The people of Canamith knew of the blue whales at Sanderell Beach. They had televisions, radios, computers, and other modern conveniences. Stories of whales visiting close to the shore didn't scare the people of Canamith.

Canamithians were content to farm the land and sell their products in Sanderell. This income sustained them and allowed their leaders to purchase the supplies required to build and stock the tunnels. Each child was raised to study the ancient texts and learn the ways of the village from birth. The citizens of Canamith respected the planet and the creatures that inhabited it.

They spent this night gathered by their spiritual leader, Rex Templeton.

He stood five feet, nine inches tall. His striking handsome looks cut a dashing figure wherever he went. His hair refused to turn gray, helping him look younger than his real age of 58. Rex had raised two fine boys, and one girl.

Rex stood at the podium and raised his right arm straight over his head, which indicated to the assembled throng of 453 people that he wished to speak.

"I have had the honor of being the High Priest for the last 33 years. I have survived the death of my wife, and the shame of my daughter leaving the village. We will honor our ancestors by fulfilling our sacred vows, abiding to the words inscribed in the Holy Tablets.

The work on the tunnels of the Saviors is almost complete. Tonight I stand before you and tell you that there is little time remaining to finish our preparations. I want all of you to double your efforts in the next few days. You have your assignments…the Elders will be around to check on your progress and assist you as needed. Goodnight."

The maximum number of people living in the village at any given time was 455 residents. This number was derived by the ancient writings that told the villagers precisely how many people could live in the tunnels.

Rex's eldest son Buck watched the proceedings carefully. His goal was that someday the people would be listening to him. Buck sensed a significant change in his father over the last six months. He couldn't pinpoint the date of the change. Buck attributed the change to the pressure of completing the tunnels.

Rex called his two boys into his private chambers as the mass of people dispersed.

"Buck, Mathis, we need to have a serious discussion."

"I had a hunch you were up to something," said Mathis.

"I am sure that you and your brother have wondered who will replace me."

"We have lots of time to worry about that, father," said the younger son, Mathis.

"Not as much as you think. I've enacted the Emergency Protocols, which allow me to select my successor without the customary selection process. I will appoint one of you as the next Chief Elder. You won't be assuming all of your duties right away. Continuity is important in this village. It's vital to establish your authority immediately. We don't want the Village sensing indecision on my part. Choosing is difficult. Each of you has characteristics that I'm proud of. I couldn't let my emotions dictate this important decision.

"Let's take a walk in the garden. Perhaps in that idyllic setting I may find the wisdom to use the right words. I've already made my choice."

The men moved into the lavish gardens that filled the courtyard. Buck was twenty-nine years old and Mathis, age twenty-seven. Both were physically fit, of solid resolve, and of kind hearts. But neither had chosen a wife. Four years earlier Rex told the boys that they shouldn't marry until after the tunnels were completed.

Mathis struggled with that arrangement. Buck's charm was more in his mannerisms and quick wit, rather than high cheekbones like his brother. Both boys were trim and tall. Mathis, without putting much effort into it, had a more muscular frame. His rugged features and genealogy made him the prized bachelor in the village.

They sat down on a tan bench that wrapped around the oldest tree in the village, the same spot where Rex's own father told him many years ago of the responsibilities that he would face someday. Rex sat back on the bench, and closed his eyes. The minutes passed. Buck and Mathis knew their father wouldn't be dissuaded from his decision.

"Boys, please give me a minute or two alone."

The boys walked out of their father's earshot and discussed the pending choice.

"I'm the one who should be chosen," insisted Mathis.

"I disagree; I'm better suited for the job. I'm more like dad than you are," said Buck.

Mathis resented the comment. "That's easy for you to say. If dad picks you, the entire village is going to treat you like a king for the next 40 years."

"That's if I can handle it."

"You'll handle it. You have many of dad's traits and that sickens me."

"There's a compliment. Dad sickens you. Is that what you mean?

"What I was trying to say is… oh, just forget it," Mathis said, trying to soften his harsh words.

"The village men say your personality is like mom's. That's not a bad thing."

"It's not bad if you're a woman. I barely remember her," said Mathis.

Buck put his arm around his younger brother and spoke from his heart. "She was a wonderful person and she loved you. I thought you were her favorite. She joked that it was because you were the baby of the family and you needed more attention than anyone else."

"I don't know if I've been insulted by my dead mother. I'll trust that you didn't mean it that way," said Mathis.

"Brother, sometimes I want to pummel you into the ground."

"Try it and learn what it's like to get pounded by your baby brother."

Buck laughed. "Sorry, after dad chooses me, I'm going home. Got a lot to do, you know, safeguarding the Village takes a lot of work."

"Don't count your chickens, big brother."

Now they were forced to sit and wait. This singular choice by Rex would carve each young man's future for decades to come.

Rex lost his daughter years ago to the outside world. That event shook Canamith to the core. People didn't leave Canamith. When the oldest child of the Chief Elder left it almost cost Rex his position. The Elders were the high priests of Canamith that led spiritual rituals and ranked a notch below Rex. They debated whether Rex should be replaced.

Weeks of meetings and discussions ended with Rex keeping his role as Chief Elder. His reputation was buoyed by his zeal to finish the tunnels. His determination never wavered and his guidance helped the village through the lean years when the crops were devastated by drought conditions. He persevered over the problems in the air filtration system too.

Now it was time to choose which of his children would lead their people when the tunnels were sealed. Rex waved his hands and motioned for the boys to return.

"I have given this much thought. I've been thinking about this day for years. The journey to the lead this village will be difficult.

I've chosen Buck. Mathis, there's no point in second-guessing my decision. There is too much work to do. When I'm gone and laying next your mother in the ground you can sit and discuss my decision. Mathis, you will fulfill your duties and assist Buck. Goodnight. I love you."

The old man ran his hands over the thick brown hair of each child and let his fingers gently slide down the back side of their heads. Rex walked away. Neither son said a word while Rex was within earshot, but once he was gone, the debate continued long into the night.

CHAPTER 4

Two hours later Lila, J.J. and Sophie left home to buy groceries. Lila had a few hours to kill before she needed to return to the college for her meeting with Dr. Massey.

When J.J. pulled into the parking lot of the grocery store, he couldn't believe the size of the crowd. "You'd think it was a holiday with these big crowds."

"It's not that. It's the president. He was on the television while you were giving Sophie a bath. He is concerned that the contamination problem is driving up the price of wheat. He explained how the wheat traders started a buying panic yesterday. The price of a bushel of wheat doubled overnight. This triggered a *bigger* panic, and now people are acting as if we're running out of food."

"I heard the contamination problem wasn't considered severe."

"It's not. Dr. Massey and I were invited to the Council of Domestic Food Processors meeting almost two weeks ago. Remember? I couldn't go because of Sophie's injury. Dr. Massey went and told me he spoke with executives from three major food suppliers and they couldn't explain why the wheat was growing shorter and taking longer to develop. We've had the same amount of rain, more or less, anyway."

Lila watched the crowds gather outside the front doors of the supermarket.

A robust lady in a blue dress and bad shoes was yelling at the boy placing her groceries in her car. Her deep baritone voice was uncommon for a woman. "You listen here, kid! I paid a lot of money for those potatoes and you dropped them all over the parking lot. I don't have time to go back and get new ones, damn it."

The skinny kid smiled at the lady and said in a stern voice, much more mature than Lila expected, "Lady, I don't give a shit about your potatoes! I hope you grasp this concept. I quit. I don't need this stupid job." He ripped the queer hat off his head and sent it sailing like a Frisbee.

When "Ned's Super Grocer" cap landed on the windshield of the Jenkins' car, J.J. overreacted and turned the car too abruptly, and the front right tire hit the curb.

"Dammit!" yelled J.J.

"Easy, honey. It was a hat, not a bomb," noted Lila.

J.J. parked the car. He checked the tire for damage and found none. They went into the store and saw long lines stretching from the checkout counter past the frozen food aisle, a distance of fifty feet from the registers.

"Should we even bother to try?" puzzled Lila.

"I don't know. Hold on, I'll ask that guy over there," said J.J.

The Government announcement had started a run on the food supply. People were scooping up every bag of rice, wheat product, cereal, canned food and bottled water in the store.

"Lila, it's insane here," said J.J.

"Yeah, I'm getting a bad vibe. Let's try Thompson's."

They grabbed Sophie's hand and scrambled back to the car and headed down the street to Willie Thompson's Quik Mart. Old Man Thompson ran a small store specializing in organic food at reasonable prices.

When they arrived at Thompson's, tempers were flaring and people were yelling. Three men in their twenties ran out of the front door. Each of the men was carrying two large packages. The tallest of the men was muscular, with short black hair cut close to his head. He wore a thin black tee shirt that hung down to his hips. He held a semi-automatic rifle in his right hand. His lackeys were in close pursuit. One of the men laughed aloud and drew Lila's attention. The two made direct eye contact as J.J. circled for a close parking spot.

"Drive!" shouted Lila. "Drive!"

J.J. accelerated. Lila shouted at Sophie in the back seat.

"Sophie! Take off your seat belt and get on the floor! Hurry!"

"What's wrong, mommy? You tell me to wear my—"

Lila screamed at her daughter. "Just get on the floor!" Sophie started sobbing as she took her position on the floor of the vehicle as ordered.

As J.J. drove toward the street, Lila saw Willie foolishly attempted to stop the thieves from pilfering his goods. His whiskbroom was no match for the gun. Lila heard gunshots ring out. Willie crumbled to the ground, blood oozing out of multiple entry wounds.

"J.J., they shot Willie! He's down, oh J.J., get us out of here!" Lila squawked in near hysterics.

J.J. hammered the gas pedal to the floor and made it to the main street. A single gunshot ricocheted off the "No Parking" sign next to them.

"Lila! Call the police! Quick!"

Lila used her mobile phone and pressed the button that immediately summoned the police. She heard the "click" of her call being answered.

"Hello. I need to report a—"

Lila stopped when she heard the dispatch officer.

"Hurry! That man could be dead any minute," J.J. prodded. "Lila?"

Lila pressed the speaker button, so J.J. could hear what was going on. A female voice responded. "You've reached the Sanderell Police Department. Due to the large volume of calls, all operators are busy. Please be patient and we will be with you as soon as we can. Please do not disengage the call if you are experiencing an emergency."

When a live person responded to the call, the Jenkins were close to their driveway. Lila described what they'd witnessed as best she could and the dispatcher promised to send an ambulance and patrol cars to the scene.

Sophie was bawling when they reached their driveway.

"It's okay. We're home now," J.J. said.

Lila lifted Sophie and carried her into the house. "It's okay, baby, mommy's here. We're okay now." She rubbed Sophie's back and gave her a small kiss on the side of her head.

"I'll take her to her room. Let's get an inventory of our food supply. We may have to barter with our neighbors. You know Mr. Gordon is going to want all our beer."

"Trust me. You don't want anything from his pantry," stated J.J. "Let's take it one step at a time. You get the shopping list. I'll get Sophie to sleep."

CANAMITH COMMUNICATION DEPARTMENT

Update #66

Major theft reported

Residents of the sleepy West coast town of Benhapel awoke today to reports of a substantial theft last night at the warehouse belonging to Meredith Food Supply, the town's largest employer. Local authorities said that the building was "picked clean." When police departments got to the store, a note was taped to the front door. It read: "Sorry …food crisis looming…gotta stock up." Witnesses said dozens of large trucks were seen leaving the area heading north towards the highway.

CHAPTER 5

The adventure at the grocery store rattled their nerves. J.J. turned on the television to see if the Thompson murder made the evening news. Lila poured herself a stiff drink and J.J. guzzled down the last of his cold beers in the refrigerator.

Nearby, Sophie played with colored paper and glitter crayons. She loved the way the pink ones sparkled in the light. The crayons were a gift from J.J.'s sister Kate to help pass the time during recuperation. Sophie drew mermaids, unicorns and princesses. There were no pictures of billy goats.

J.J. scanned the television channels until he found the National News Network.

The attractive woman on the television was adjusting her auburn hair. She was unaware that the camera was recording her every move. When she realized the camera was on, she feigned a smile and began her report. "This is Jennifer Brown reporting from Sanderell Beach. Earlier today, this popular beach was shut down indefinitely due to the sightings of hundreds of whales roaming the coast of Sanderell. Local police wouldn't comment on the situation other than to say that residents were not in immediate danger. However, the beach does remain closed. Let's show you the footage taken earlier today by our National News Network Cameras."

"Look!" shouted Sophie. "There's mommy!"

"Hey, babe, you are the best looking professor on the beach," boasted J.J.

"Oh, great," muttered Lila in her sarcastic tone, "I'm as white as a ghost. Look at my arms!"

"The sun doesn't shine inside a laboratory," said J.J.

The television showed exactly what the Jenkins' had seen in person. Then the tape switched to the video shot by the network helicopter crew.

The reporter continued speaking while viewers watched the tape roll. The helicopter's blades in the background gave his voice a staccato sound. "What we're watching is from high atop the drama on the seas. This reporter has never witnessed anything like this. We're going to replay the last few seconds in slow motion for you."

What the Jenkins clan and millions of other people saw was an overhead shot of hundreds of blue whales. They appeared to be pushing containers towards the shore with the skin directly above their baleen plates.

The telephone rang and Lila grabbed it right away. "Hi, Dr. Massey, it's me. Yeah, I'm watching it. No, I don't think they're pushing the barrels. That doesn't make any sense. Don't believe everything you see. I'm sure there's an explanation for how it looks. I understand, I'll be there right away. Bye." Lila hung up and turned to J.J. "That was Carlin. The staff is gathering right away. I told him I'd be there. I think we're in for a long night."

"Mommy, don't go," cried Sophie.

"Baby, it'll be fine. Daddy has you all to himself and he'll stay in your room until you fall asleep."

"You go ahead and save the whales. I'm taking Sophie to her room and I'm going to tell her the best bedtime story ever."

"Promise me. The best ever," agreed Sophie.

"Ever," said J.J.

Reporter Jennifer Brown continued her story. "Scientists speculate that the whales have altered their usual migration patterns due to the unusual weather in this region. I spoke earlier today with Dr. Carlin Massey and I asked him one question.

"Dr. Massey, could this change in migration patterns help prove that the warming of the planet may be factual and not the ranting of those aligned with the 'Save the Planet' movement?"

"I don't think it's fair to suggest that the unusual actions by these whales constitute a condemnation of our society or how we've dealt with the rising global temperatures. We shouldn't rush to judgment. When we have a better grasp of the situation, I'm sure you'll be the first to report it," said Dr. Massey.

The view returned to a live shot and she continued her report.

"Off camera, I pressed Dr. Massey on the crisis. All he told me was the image of these containers would be reviewed by many parties using the footage provided by our network and that he anticipated enhanced satellite imaging technology would be able to offer a better answer in the coming days. This is Jennifer Brown reporting live from Sanderell Beach."

CANAMITH COMMUNICATION DEPARTMENT

Update #77

Death at sea

"…Three whaling ships capsized today in the choppy waters of the ocean. The ships disappeared off the radar early this morning.

"The captain of one of the lost ships, *The Webster*, noted in his final ship entry that large whales surprised the crew by hitting the ship from underneath. The hulls of the ships were breached and began taking on water. The damage could not be contained and the ships were lost, taking at least two hundred men down to their watery grave…"

CHAPTER 6

At 8:00 PM, Lila rushed into the college faculty parking lot and hurried by the security guard stationed by the iron gates of the parking area.

"Hey, Professor Jenkins, slow down!" shouted the guard.

Lila ignored him. Her mind was racing with ideas.

The security guard at the front of the building recognized Lila and opened the big glass doors as she was fishing for her faculty pass. She hated that picture. It was taken a few hours after oral surgery and the right side of her mouth was swollen to twice its usual size. Massey had suggested that she re-take the picture to avoid any future security problems. It wouldn't be a problem as long as Whittaker and Finch, two long-time guards of the main science building, remained at their jobs. The identical twin guards had been employees of the college for the last twenty years.

Finch was on duty tonight. Lila hardly acknowledged him as she hurried past the startled guard on this night, forgetting to say her customary greeting, "Hi, Finch Bear." That was the nickname she gave him because he reminded her of a bear. His thick beard covered more of his face than any other person she had ever met, except for his twin brother. His thick build was draped in the dark brown school security coat. The matching brown pants didn't provide much contrast, hence the bear reference. The majority of people couldn't tell them apart. Lila found that Finch smiled easily and her cheerful greeting was designed to determine which twin was working, not an indication of how happy she was to enter the parking lot.

Lila rode the elevator to the fourth floor. A few steps to the left and she entered lab room three, her own personal hideaway and the room she called home when she wasn't with her family. She spent countless hours in this room that she knew each piece of chipped paint, crooked nail, worn seat covers and the precise location of her years of research. Each year of study was safely stashed away in an ever-growing row of filing cabinets stuffed to the brim with science papers and computer discs.

As a professor she taught several classes each week. "All Things Explainable" was her favorite motto. She stamped "A.T.E." on her students' papers that she deemed worthy of such exemplary work. Lila's version of an A+.

Lila switched on the computer that connected her to the school's main database. Moments later, Aldo Gorrell entered the room. Sweat poured down his neck.

"Good, you're here," he puffed. "I was beginning to think you weren't coming."

"Typical graduate assistant, giving me grief and the night is young. Won't Dr. Massey teasing you all day be enough to satisfy your bruised and battered ego? You would not believe the day I've had today. First the beach, and then we went to the grocery store and we saw Willie Thompson shot. I've never been that scared in my life, and oh, poor Sophie, she was inconsolable when we reached home. I think Willie's dead. Then I saw the television report. It's gonna be a long night. I see you brought coffee. Thanks," said Lila.

"You saw a man get shot? Tell me what happened?"

"It doesn't matter now. It's too horrible to discuss. I'm trying to put it out of my mind. Did Dr. Massey tell you anything?"

"Nothing much, I think I have more valuable information than he does."

"What do you mean?" replied Lila.

Aldo combed his thin multi-colored hair with his fingers. His shirt hung outside his jeans. That was his usual attire. The tee shirt had the name of a rock band on it.

"Who is Train Wreck?" asked Lila.

Aldo smiled, pointing down at the image of five guys on his shirt. "These guys are great. You'd love them. Three guys that play guitar and an unbelievable drummer. The keyboard player is blind. They have a recent hit. It's called 'You Rev my Engine all Night.'"

"Nope, can't say I know that one." Lila tastes in music were stuck with the mellow twelve string guitar sounds created years ago and she didn't care for modern music.

Lila gulped down her coffee. The black steaming hot liquid felt soothing going down her throat. She sat back in the swivel recliner that her J.J. bought her last year for their anniversary. Aldo scooted his chair to within a foot of hers.

Lila's left eyebrow rose half an inch as she waited. "I'm listening."

"Okay. Here goes."

Aldo flipped open his computer and opened the file labeled "World Incident Report." He began to read aloud.

"Item one," said Aldo. "'*Over a thousand coal miners were killed today when a fire burned out of control in one of the world's largest mineshafts. Local firefighters had no chance of extinguishing the blaze. It is the worst single-event tragedy in the long history of mining. Mine officials were meeting to determine how the fire started. One local councilman said that the fire started when an oxygen line exploded at the mine entrance.*'" Aldo interrupted himself, "I didn't even know that many people could fit in a mine shaft." He didn't wait for a reply. He pressed on.

"'*Local Authorities were surprised by reports that local fisherman said two-thirds of their boats returned back to the dock empty. Seventy-two of the seventy-nine registered fishing boats stated that even with optimum conditions, their boats returned with less than two percent of their customary catch. The remaining seven boats claimed to have had*" moderate success. *The captain of the vessel Taz's Wonder said in an earlier report, and I quote, 'I've been fishing the waters of this sea my whole life, and I've never seen such a thing."*

"You're not impressed. There's more. *'The Federal Department of Transportation reported that six tanker trucks careened off the road and exploded. The ensuing colossal inferno killed four of the drivers immediately. Two others were rushed to local hospitals and remain in critical condition. Three bystanders were also killed in the explosion. Eyewitnesses of two of the crashes said that the drivers of the trucks were waving their arms around the cabin in a frantic motion. No other details are available at this time.'"*

Aldo continued. "*'Wire reports today say that animals attacked 500 people in the nation's capital. Domesticated animals were listed as the culprit in most of the attacks. Unsubstantiated reports said that horses, raccoons, and cats were mentioned as the aggressors too.'*

"*'Police dismissed the reports, saying that in a large city that falls within the normal range. Speaking under the promise of anonymity, one police spokesman did admit that 500 is indeed a large number of reported incidents, but views the day as a 'statistical abnormality'.'* Professor Jenkins, 500 is a big number. I bet you dogs were biting people. Listen to this one…

"*'Thousands of sheep have died from an unknown source. The herd was in perfect health one week ago, but a large number of them died in the last six days. The Center for Disease Control Administration has dispatched a team to review the disaster. It is too early to ascertain what happened. The director of the Sheep Bureau has not ruled out foul play. Scientists are heading to the region to begin their internal investigation into the matter.'* Do sheep really need a director?" asked Aldo.

Lila stared at the ceiling. She saw a new spot on the ceiling tile that showed water damage from the room one floor overhead. It was Professor Whitcomb's classroom. He was continuously doing outlandish things with water in his freshman "Hydration" class. Her attention went back to Aldo.

"Those poor dead miners. That's awful news, Aldo."

Standing in the doorway, Dr. Massey interjected his own opinion. "Nicely done, my boy. You've discovered the news wire." He continued as he inched closer to the duo, carrying a large briefcase. "In here, a spot typically reserved for budget information, classroom assignments, and the rest of the humdrum events that go on at this institute of higher learning, I've had material sent to us from the Capitol. There's a briefing in the conference room. This is hush-hush stuff, no phone calls, leaks to friends, etcetera... Mr. Gorrell, your intentions are noble, however, if you think that these sorts of things don't go on all over the world then you have more to learn than I imagined when I hired you. By the way, I hired you with the full blessing of the lady sitting next to you. Remember, ten minutes... don't be late!"

Dr. Massey turned and left the two as silently as he entered.

"What a jerk!" said Aldo.

Lila didn't like his tone. "Aldo!"

"I'm sorry, Professor Jenkins, gimme a break! All he does is ride my ass each time I see him. Just once it would be cool if he said to me 'good job, kid', or 'keep up the outstanding work.'"

"Aldo, I'm waiting for that day myself. You picked the wrong college if you think that day is coming," said Lila.

Eight minutes later, Lila and Aldo strolled into the conference room. They grabbed seats at the end of the cherry wood table. The windows in the room started at the floor and continued to the ceiling. This created an abundance of natural light during the day. The university window washer wasn't a big fan of the design. The room was used for weekly staff meetings. Five stale donuts remained in the cardboard box from yesterday's meeting. Smears of raspberry jelly clung to the opening of the napkin dispenser.

Dr. Massey consumed his lunch in this room when he could. He scarfed down his food in front of his computer on most days. Dr. Carlin Massey was not a popular man among his peers. He knew one way to run a department, and that was to enforce a sense of strict discipline with a little bit of humor tossed in. Dry humor.

He appreciated Aldo Gorrell's skills. He respected his knowledge and long hours of work for little pay but didn't think Gorrell was mature enough to handle the position of Head Research Assistant. The clothes, that fuzzy stuff growing on his chin and the humor were the reasons Massey wasn't convinced Aldo would grow into a full-time faculty position with the University. Lila had persuaded him to give the kid a try.

Everybody knew Massey's achievements in the scientific community. Anyone interested in animal behavior had several volumes of Massey's books on their shelf. His books were frequently used as the definitive source for all levels of students ranging from age seven, *Animals and Me*, to the College Freshmen bible, *Massey's World of Animal Behavior*, to the casual fan, *Animals: An A to Z Compendium*.

Dr. Massey cleared his throat. The men and women in the room understood that meant that the boss was ready to begin. Among those attending the meeting on this night were Lila and Aldo; Dr. Emily Goldman, the Chief of Staff at the Center for Treatment of Diseases; and Dr. Roberto Morales, noted bestselling author. His fields of interest included morphology and cytology. He had left the college two years ago on sabbatical that sent him crisscrossing the country promoting world health issues and hawking his best-selling books at retail locations close to the schools. He could be found occasionally sharing herbal tea with Lila in the Student Union Center. It maddened the university staff that nobody knew where Dr. Morales was or what he was doing. If there was a problem, he would invariably show up to assist Lila and Dr. Goldman, and when the crisis was solved, he disappeared as quickly and quietly as he had arrived.

Jenkins, Goldman, and Morales were known as the "ABC" gang. "A" represented Lila Jenkins' knowledge of the animal kingdom; "B", a slight twist on Goldman's status for knowing "Bugs", as in germs; and Morales earned the "C" for the study of cells. Together, the "ABC" gang had solved many national problems during the last five years.

Dr. Massey sat at one end of the table, a tall glass of ice-cold water next to his ever-present yellow notepad and his ten-cent pen. Dr. Massey began. "At 1300 today, a large pod of whales was seen close to Sanderell Beach. I was summoned by the local authorities to review the incident and provide any expertise to those in charge. I bumped into Professor Jenkins at the beach. Imagine her nerve, trying to enjoy time with her family."

Nobody was in the mood for laughter.

Dr. Massey continued. "At 1400, helicopter pilots flying over the whales captured these digital images. Initial reviews were inconclusive. The Government Satellite Imaging System realigned their coordinates to the beach. Their results were astonishing.

"As we sit here tonight, teams of hazardous materials handlers are sifting for clues on the beach. It remains off limits to all citizens. Authorized military personal are maintaining their surveillance of the area. They believe the satellite photos prove that the whales are pushing large containers towards the shore. I'm an expert in many fields, but I don't claim to understand this cetacean behavior." That comment drew a small chuckle. "These barrels, or containers, have been resting in the same spot all day.

"Within the last thirty minutes, I've conversed with the governor, who has speculated, and I emphasize, *speculated* that these barrels may be from the Western Border Nuclear Power Plant located 200 miles away. Early indications are that these barrels were scheduled to be stored in the Mountain Storage Facility twelve years ago. It's not clear what the barrels contain. Maximum efforts are underway to determine the precise material we're dealing with."

"I'd love to get some whale DNA if that's possible, Dr. Massey," piped Dr. Morales.

"I'll see what I can do that. I'll call the Command Center and see if anyone is patrolling near the pod. Great idea," replied Dr. Massey.

"I'm glad I don't live near the beach, that's a disaster area waiting to hap—" began Dr. Goldman.

Lila stopped her cold. "I live a few hundred feet from there!" she said. "I've got to get my family out of there!"

"Please, Professor Jenkins, I understand your concern. We can't start a panic because a few barrels of goo rolled up a few hundred yards from shore. You can't move out of town!" snapped Dr. Massey.

"I can't say I blame her, Dr. Massey," said Dr. Morales.

Aggravated, Dr. Massey wiped his perspiring brow and said to Morales, "I was hoping for assistance, doctor."

"You want me to believe it's 'goo?'" said Lila.

Massey was not going to hear any of it. "Lila, we'll address your situation in a moment. Now, as I was saying: these barrels, nobody knows exactly what's in them. It wouldn't be fair to assume the worst. The Director of the Nuclear Plant has been notified. Unfortunately, he's only been on the job for six months. The previous director, a fellow named Rothschild, died months ago. By the way, he died skiing, for you conspiracy theorists. Yes, I'm talking to you, Mr. Gorrell.

"The Federal Government wants to remove these barrels as soon as possible. They must confirm the barrels are watertight and can be removed safely. There is a concern on the part of the government that if they send in a team of retraction experts, their team may be attacked by the whales. Our job is to offer guidelines to the government as to why the whales are near these barrels. We must provide substantive information to help them. I must tell you that time is short. If the government decides to remove these barrels, and I'm sure that they will, and if the whales interfere with their efforts, the whales will be destroyed without hesitation. This would have an enormous effect on the species. This pod of whales is the single largest one we've ever seen and it could take generations for the population to recover. We have less than twelve hours to solve it. We're down to eleven hours and twenty-two minutes. I'm going to open discussion to the floor for suggestions. Don't be shy."

The astonished experts sat quietly in their seats.

Lila rose from the table and started to make her exit.

"Professor Jenkins! Stop!" shouted Dr. Massey.

Lila was half way down the hall when Massey caught up to her.

"Lila, this is when your leadership is required more than ever!"

"This is when my daughter needs me more than ever!" she replied without the respectful tone she normally used with Massey.

"I understand. I apologize for not mentioning the barrels earlier. But personal feelings shouldn't interrupt your obligations to the school. More importantly, your duty to your country, and, in an odd way, your duty to those whales, who will be reduced to heating oil if we can't think of a way to help them stay out of the way of those government idiots."

"Five-thousand barrels of heating oil would go a long way towards meeting our energy independence. That's a good yield for one day," cracked Lila.

Her sarcastic retort failed to amuse him. "Please, come back. As soon as I hear definitive news about those damn barrels, I'll tell you. I promise."

Lila grudgingly turned direction, grunted, and walked back towards the room.

"I swear, if I ever learn that you know what's in those barrels, I'll—"

"You'll what? Are you threatening me?" he asked in amazement.

Lila realized her error immediately. "No, of course not. I apologize. I don't know what's come over me. I have a splitting headache..."

Dr. Massey cleared his throat again. "We're under a lot of pressure. Let's get back in that room and put our collective years of experience to use."

"Fine, let's go to work. I'll be there in a minute."

Lila slipped into the ladies' room and used her mobile phone to call her husband. She knew disclosing information was against policy, but she was way beyond the point of rules and regulations. J.J. answered as Lila finished checking the stalls for other people.

"Hello?" said J.J.

Lila whispered into the telephone. "Hi, it's me. I can't talk long. Get some clothes packed. You must take Sophie to your sister's house."

"Lila, what are you talking about? Is it the whales?"

"It's more than that, trust me. Get ready and go. Tonight! I'll call you later. I love you and Sophie, now please—go."

"It sounds like you're overreacting. Sophie is sound asleep and I mean—"

"Listen to me! I'm serious and I've got to go too! Just do it. Even mild-mannered Dr. Goldman wouldn't stay in this area and she never panics. Wake Sophie and get out of there. I'll call you when I can." She closed the phone and jammed it deep into the front pocket of her pants.

Lila washed her face, unable to remove the remorse she felt for the uncomfortable position she was in. J.J.'s sister Kate would be angry with the unexpected company. That would be dealt with later.

She returned to the conference room where the group of brilliant scientists worked long into the night trying to determine the cause of the erratic whale behavior. They reviewed water temperature, weather anomalies, and any type of scientific evidence that would have led them to any conclusions that evening. The end results were the same. The staff failed to produce any reasonable explanations for the whale activity earlier in the day.

CANAMITH COMMUNICATION DEPARTMENT

Update #94

Animal clinics close

Monroe Delevan, Director of the Association of Emergency Veterinarians, issued the following statement to the media:

"I'm disappointed to announce that due to the high number of euthanized dogs and cats, hundreds of our outstanding clinics have been forced to close. There simply isn't enough business to sustain them any longer. I urge people to stop killing their beloved pets while the scientific community establishes the reasons behind recent canine and feline behavioral problems.

"We also request people to stop kicking their animals out of the house. The number of feral cats and wild dogs has quadrupled and forcing local municipalities to spend vital resources dealing with animal control instead of helping our fellow human beings."

CANAMITH COMMUNICATION DEPARTMENT

Update #127

Local folks go on killing spree

"…Local citizens ignored the governments call for calm, and armed militias roamed the city of Portos and shot at anything that wasn't human.

"By the time police were able to stop the slaughter, the streets of Portos were filled with dead dogs and cats, birds, squirrels and raccoons…"

CHAPTER 7

J.J. followed Lila's insistence that he abandon the city and flee. He called Kate on his cell phone as he sped down the highway.

"Kate, hi, it's J.J. Yeah, I'm fine, sort of. Remember those late nights when we were kids and we wished we were older and we could take a drive and go get food in the middle of the night?"

"J.J., it's late. Get to the point," said Kate.

"Yeah, right, sorry I'm calling you this late in the evening. Did I wake you?"

"Of course you did!" Kate snapped. "It's close to midnight."

"Sorry. This couldn't wait. Lila insisted that Sophie and I leave the city tonight. It must be about the whales down by the beach."

"J.J., why are you calling me?"

"We're coming over. We'll be there in a couple of hours. I'll fill you in on what I know when I get there."

"Let me guess…Lila thinks? Or is it Lila says?"

"Why do you get like that?"

"I don't trust her. That's nothing new, little brother."

"I wish you'd give her a chance to see the warmer side to her. She's a brilliant scientist and a wonderful mother."

Kate wasn't impressed. "The key's in the same place. I'm going back to sleep and pray this was all a rotten dream."

"It's not a dream, sis."

"Whatever, see you soon." Kate slammed the phone down.

"That went well," said J.J. to a dial tone.

He spent the next three hours navigating the winding roads adjacent to the ocean from Sanderell Beach to Kate's quiet suburban town of Taylorville. J.J. flashed back to the hour prior to his wedding while he drove. He had tried often to smooth over the contemptuous relationship between Lila and his sister Kate.

His sibling knew little about Lila's former life in Canamith. An hour before their oceanside wedding, Kate, nearly as tall as her brother, towered over Lila and led her aside to question the wisdom of the wedding. "I have serious reservations concerning your relationship. I hardly know you. You could be a crazy lady trying to latch on to my kid brother for all the wrong reasons. I love him with all my heart. When our parents died, I made a vow to look after his best interests and I don't think you are in his best interests."

Lila grew angry at the insinuation. Drawing up to her full five feet, Lila had shot back. "Kate, we may never be best friends, but I can assure you that I'm crazy, all right. Crazy in love with your brother. I've been vague. I have my own reasons for that. I won't be coerced into telling you anything. Trust me when I tell you that I love your little brother. And you should stop thinking of him as your kid brother and see the man he's become. We're getting married and I expect you to deal with it."

When J.J. pulled into his sister's driveway, Sophie was sound asleep. He carried his daughter to the front door. He found the key and tried to open the door without disturbing his older sister.

Kate was standing in the foyer, groggy eyed and not looking too happy with the situation at hand. "This better be good," she snarled.

"Nice to see you, too!" retorted J.J.

CHAPTER 8

Lila scanned the contact list on her mobile phone. She pushed "call" and listened for the connection. She hadn't called the number in years. The phone rang once and a young man answered. She was 125 feet from her office, but spoke in soft tones. Massey wouldn't be pleased to hear her on the telephone.

"Hello."

"Hi, Buck. It's Lila. Can I talk to dad?"

"The prodigal child calls home. How long has it been? Two years?"

"Over four years, if you want to be accurate."

Buck wasn't impressed. "Have you saved the world? Do you want to know how I am or do you want to talk to dad?"

"I'm sorry, Buck. I'm in a hurry and I wanted to talk to dad. It's important."

"I'm fine, thanks for asking. If you're calling here it must be important. Dad's in a meeting with the Elders. You recall those meetings?"

"That's one of the reasons I left. The ancient scrolls, I remember. Please tell him that it's urgent I speak to him right away. Please tell him that I called. Do you remember my number?"

Buck scoffed at the suggestion. "Yeah, sure, I dial it daily and hang up. I don't remember it. I'm sure dad has it. By the way, while I have you on the phone, you know you broke his heart when you left. I guess you had your reasons."

"Buck, we've been over this a thousand times. I didn't call to get into an argument with you or get a guilt trip. You, Dad and Mathis are wasting precious time. You have one life. Do you think the planet will explode because the 'Elders' gave somebody a warning a thousand years ago?"

"We got that warning 2,000 years ago."

"See, that's my point! Things happen for specific scientific reasons, Buck. There's a scientific reason for everything we experience. Following ideology that stipulates divine intervention prior to a disastrous series of events is absurd. I choose to live for today. How many lives would have been wasted if the people on the planet had decided to follow your path?"

"That's not the point. The Elders knew that people wouldn't believe. Don't you recall reading 'The Great Divide'? It was never their intent or belief that everyone would listen. What mattered was that *our* people listened, and outside of the daughter of the wisest man in town—that would be you—we all stayed here. We stuck to our obligations and will die here knowing we have lived a noble life. I don't apologize for that."

"You shouldn't. You've consumed any spare time I had tonight. Tell dad to call me. We have the same stupid argument when we speak, and you wonder why I don't call? Goodbye."

"Goodnight to you too, sis."

Lila slipped back into the meeting and tried to stay positive. She interjected, "There must be a scientific explanation for this."

"There is," said Massey. "I'm afraid it'll be too late for the whales. I want each of you go back to your offices and search for answers. Let me know if you have any new ideas. Perhaps we'll have better luck coming up with ideas on our own. We're certainly not having much luck this way."

Lila went back into her office. She turned the computer back on and logged into the Internet site "ScienceNow", a website devoted to developments in the world of the scientific community. Lila hadn't dismissed Aldo's reports earlier in the night as coincidence, as Massey had done so matter-of-factly. She typed the phrase "anomalies in the world today" in the search box and forty-three items populated the screen.

She scrolled the list, and each article was stranger than the next, starting with the first report where the east coast police had found marauding packs of grown men hunting down squirrels and killing them. She was floored when she read the rest of the story.

When captured by the local authorities, the leader of the men reported he had personally seen squirrels working together to chew a hole in his cable line. When the man called for service, he was told that he was one of 1,300 customers complaining of an identical problem and the estimated time for his repair would be four weeks. This prompted the man to gather a "posse" to eliminate the cable-chewing critters.

She spent the next hour reading equally inexplicable accounts from around the country, each of them indicating that animals have instigated attacks. When she was done, she sighed, shut the computer down and stared out the windows, wondering what her father was doing at this exact moment.

CHAPTER 9

Rex clutched the phone to call his daughter back. He longed to talk to her, but was too stubborn to verbalize it. He felt compelled to return her call. Maybe she was calling to seek permission to return to Canamith? She hurt him when she left the village years ago. Lila was the first citizen of Canamith to leave. She disappeared fifteen years ago to attend college and get a formal, advanced education. Rex knew that there would be repercussions within the village. His position as Chief Elder had been challenged, and he worried that his sons would be ostracized by their peers, a fear that came to fruition several years later when the boys were approaching manhood.

Rex seldom communicated with Lila after Sophie was born. It tore Lila apart that Sophie didn't have a relationship with anybody on her mother's side of the family. But Rex and Lila had made their decisions and they were sticking to them.

Rex waited for his daughter to answer. He choked up when he heard her voice. He regained his composure and sounded as casual as if he was discussing the weather with a neighbor on a steamy summer day. "Hello, Lila, I heard you wanted to talk to me. Go ahead."

"So much for the warm greetings, Daddy. I'm glad to hear your voice anyway. I miss you."

"If you miss me, move back home." He cringed with these words, angry that he allowed her to get under his skin so quickly in the conversation.

"Dad, please don't start. I called you because I'm worried that the ocean is full of poison and I wanted to warn you. I've spent my life studying these types of scientific anomalies and the biotoxins they produce. This one has me concerned."

"And what exactly does my little scientist propose I do?"

"I think you should get out of town for a few weeks. I'm concerned for the health and safety of all of the people in this area. There is hazardous material in the ocean by Sanderell. The village is close to the beach, too."

The silence on the other end lasted eight seconds and then Rex tried to implore his daughter to understand his views. "Lila, you may be worried, but I'm prepared for what is coming. Our water originates from mountain run-off. No, my dear daughter, I'm not going anywhere. I have nothing to fear. We are making the final arrangements to seal the tunnels. Perhaps *you* should leave town?"

"Here we go with the tunnels again. Anyway, dad, I thought I'd try one more time. It's clear you're not going to listen to anything I have to say," said Lila, her voice rising half an octave. "There's a rational explanation for what's going on and I'm going to prove to you that I made a wise decision to go to school. By the way, why close the tunnels now?"

"I can't discuss that with you. You're an outsider now. If you had stayed, you would be hearing all the details soon enough. I would be comforted knowing that you, your husband, and that granddaughter of mine would be safe. You have chosen to live your way, and if you want to run to the hills, or the woods, or wherever, I wish you the best, but I'm not going anywhere. I think you know that. As I said, why don't you come home?"

Lila's voice rose in desperation.

"Daddy, this is important! Think of Mathis and Buck. They're my brothers and—"

"As I recall, they were your brothers when you left here, too! You didn't seem concerned with their health back then. They're men now and they don't need you. Thanks for the warning, but it's misplaced. You need it. You have limited time to save your life. In a matter of a few days or weeks you will be on your own."

"Daddy, I have a home here with J.J. and Sophie in Sanderell. Although at the moment, neither of them is here, they're with J.J.'s sister. That's beside the point."

"As you wish. I'm not leaving here. There will be a place held for the three of you until we seal the door, and then I probably won't see you or talk to you again. That pains me. There is nothing else to say."

"I suppose not."

"Then I think we're done. Goodbye, Lila, I love you."

Click. The telephone line went dead.

Rex was crestfallen when the call ended. He had played his best "father knows what's best for you" card and it failed. He reflected on his life had Lila chosen to stay in the village. His dreams lasted a moment. This was not the time for self-indulgence. There was work to finish.

CHAPTER 10

Last spring, Rex knew he needed to prepare his replacement. A new Chief Elder would take over his responsibilities when the tunnel doors closed. He hiked with the boys to the banks of the Larousse River. The river was named in honor of former Chief Elder Garrison Larousse. The river provided an assortment of fresh fish and tranquil scenery less than half a mile from the village. Fifty feet across at its widest point, the water was unspoiled by pollution. The banks of the Larousse were a frequent spot for families to celebrate weddings and special occasions. The view from atop the mountains looking down at the river was picturesque. That vista provided a panoramic view of the mountains, the sky, and the clear water below. The two-hour climb to the top of the mountain was grueling.

On that sunny day of last year, Rex had taken the boys up the mountain with a specific goal in mind. He didn't tell them the purpose of their journey. He woke them early, excused them from their daily chores, and whisked them away. Rex told Elder Braham to handle any problems that arose and under no circumstances, short of catastrophe, to bother him. The trio trudged up the trail at a quick pace, pushing to reach the top of the mountain by early afternoon. A break at lunchtime offered Rex a chance to rest his weary legs. He debated the wisdom of stopping at all; his legs didn't recover as quickly as they once did, and stopping for too long might cause them to cramp, and prevent him from finishing the ascent.

"Dad, this is high enough for now. Let's take a break," said Buck.

"No, thanks, let's keep pushing," grumbled Rex.

"Oh, come on, Dad, you're dying here. Give it a rest," begged Mathis.

"Okay, you win, a short rest. These bones aren't what they were. Years ago, Ethan White and I used to climb the mountain for amusement. I think he broke his ankle one year, and we never did that again. I thought his father was going to kill him. You know, he thought that injury cost him chance at being selected Chief Elder. Way back when I beat him in an agility test, he blamed his mountain injury for his inability to navigate Creekstone Pass. That footrace didn't cost him being selected Chief Elder. There were many reasons for that. He's not a good person. You'll see that for yourself someday. I didn't come here to talk about ancient history. My relationship with Ethan has been strained ever since. I don't think he ever got over the disappointment of not being selected Chief Elder. That business with his son and Lila didn't help either. By the way, if anything ever happens to me, keep your eyes open. Ethan may be lurking in the weeds. Mathis, aren't you friends with his youngest boy?"

"He's a good guy. He used to follow me like a puppy dog until he married the lady who works in the Oxygen department."

"It's his sister that wants you, Mathis. That girl would do anything for you," said Buck.

"What's this?" said Rex, surprised by this revelation.

"Dad, the whole village knows it. Mathis is too dumb to see it. I mean the girl is beautiful, smart, and totally worships him," jested Buck.

"Hey, who are you calling dumb? I'm not the one who nearly drilled a hole in my hand the other day."

"You moved the piece of the wood."

"Boys, that's enough," said Rex. "I didn't mean to start a quarrel. I'm not the kind of father to tell you whom to love. When your mother died, and your sister left, my heart hasn't been open to find another to love. There was one woman in my life. It's time for this old

50

man to get back up that big hill."

"Dad, you sure you want to keep going?" asked Mathis.

"Help me with the bag and let's go," replied Rex.

Buck grabbed his father's pack and put it over his own pack, making his twice as heavy. "No arguments, dad, I've got it." Rex was not used to hearing his son talk that way, but he didn't protest.

The climb ended a half-hour later. The temperature dropped as the three men scaled higher into the sky. A brisk westerly breeze cooled their skin. The view at the top of the mountain was as breathtaking as Rex had remembered.

"Nice view," marveled Rex. He didn't wait for a reply. His own observations gave him the satisfaction that couldn't be matched by his son's admission that this was a special place indeed.

"Dad, this is great. It's been too long since we spent this much time alone with you. We used to come here often," said Buck.

Rex's broad smile revealed a handsome set of teeth, unblemished by his years.

"Buck, you think I have an angle, don't you?"

"I do."

"This time I don't. I wanted to be with you. I'm not sure how many times we can come back here and I wanted at least one more trip here with the two of you. There's much to do and I fear we won't be able to get back here for a while. Is it wrong to bring you here?"

"Dad, it's great. I'm wondering why the sudden change of heart?" said a perplexed Mathis, who was not buying the "dad wants to spend time with us" line.

"You boys know the pressures of my position. We've discussed it for years."

"Dad, you talked to us, not with us. You know, without mom, it would've been okay if you had been more—"

"More what?" Rex exploded with anger. His reaction was out of character. His demeanor changed from calm to furious in an instant. He pressed on. "Did you crave more love? The older women in the village took you under their wings and helped you. Your aunts served you dinner on Sundays while the Elders held meetings. I brought you a token gift from my trips to Sanderell. Do you realize how ungrateful you sound?"

"Dad, please calm down. Don't take this personally. You don't get it. You're still talking about you, and your sisters, and your Elder meetings, and your trips. All we're saying is your life revolved around your obligations to Canamith and I guess that's fine. I respect what you and others have done for us and what we'll do for future generations. I'm talking about two boys and one dad. That's all." Mathis's eyes were red, but he refused to let his father see him cry. He turned away. He sighed, faced his dad, and said, "Dad, I love you. I love Canamith. I'll live here my entire life and I'll die here. Can we please enjoy today?"

There was an awkward silence for a moment as the three men sat quietly watching the incredible vistas before them.

Rex broke the ice with his opinion on the previous conversation. "Perhaps you will be blessed to have children and have the pleasure of those children being as rude to you as you have been to me. Remember this moment. Keep walking."

Mathis nearly challenged his father. Buck reached out and covered Mathis's mouth before a sound could be heard.

"Save it," said Buck. "Remember what you said? Let's enjoy the day."

Rex broke the tension later when he identified several different types of birds at considerable distance, with the naked eye.

"The body may be shot boys," he said, "but I can see as clearly as ever."

Mathis whispered to Buck, softly enough that Rex could not hear, "His tongue is pretty sharp too."

On the return trip to Canamith, Rex led them along a path that the boys had never seen. The beginning of the path was grown over by shrubbery. A small tree with oversized leaves grew on one side of the path and a vast field of wildflowers was on the other side.

"See that, boys?" Rex pointed to the path. "Your great-grandfather helped build this path many years ago. Hardly anyone else even knows it's here. This was the trail that led previous generations to the original work site of the water containers. When I've had a particularly rough day, or need a break from the pressure of the village and the tunnels, I rest my head right here, on this big rock, and watched the sunset. If this were the last sunset I ever saw, and if I watched it from here, it would be fine with me. The mountain water runs a fraction to the left of this part of the mountain that juts out from the big section of trees. Years ago, I recall it was during the early development of the containers, a new path, the one you've seen down the mountain closer to the city, has replaced this more dangerous path. The new way was their Plan B. I wanted you to understand the history of where you live." He grabbed the boys by their shoulders and repeated his lifelong lesson to them, "Like I always say—"

And before he could finish his sentence, both boys joined in the banter.

"You must have a Plan B." They chuckled a bit and kept walking.

"Go ahead and laugh if you must. I've heard stories that the original entrance to the tunnels was started here many hundreds of years ago. In fact, not far from this exact spot, right over by the collection of large rocks stacked next to the edge of the mountain. A small seismic shift caused the Elders to abandon that site and build the one we know today. It was never finished; I heard they came close. It was deemed too dangerous. The new entrance and the bulk of the tunnels are built much lower down on the mountain."

"That's great, Dad," said Buck. "Come on, Mathis, race you down the hill!"

The boys fled quickly on foot, much to the chagrin of their father, who continued to yell at the boys to slow down until they were out of earshot.

CHAPTER 11

Rex met his future wife years ago at one of the traditional Sunday dances that the village scheduled to get the young men and women together. The young adults worked hard and when it was time to unwind, the fun began. They danced, they sang, and sometimes romance filled the air. Sara had kept a watchful eye on Rex. He never paid much attention to her. Sara was not the type to throw herself at a man. If Rex Templeton was as smart as Sara thought he was, he would come to see what other men in the village grasped immediately. Sara Goodmote was the prize of the village.

When Rex figured out what he was missing, he swooped in and two months later the two were married in a beautiful ceremony in front of the Larousse River. One year after that the happy couple welcomed their first child: a girl they named Lila.

Sara doted on Lila, as new mothers do, and the two of them spent hours huddled over books and on nature walks in the gardens.

Sara would ask her child, "Will you ever stop asking so many questions?

Lila's response was direct and to the point. "When I am smarter than you, mommy, I will be the smartest one in the village."

"I'm sure you will sweetheart," said her proud mother.

Sara and Rex had a baby boy six years later, which they named Buck, in honor of Rex's grandfather, and then two years later, Mathis was born.

Rex and Sara were overjoyed with their trio of kids. Sara pushed Rex to complete his next task as leader of the village. He was the hopeless romantic. Rex enjoyed surprising Sara with a bouquet of fresh flowers from the fields surrounding Canamith. He scoffed at his friends who chuckled about his standing in the marriage, taunting him that Sara was the real leader of the village. In fairness to Rex, he was as clever as she was and together they made a terrific pair that benefited the entire village.

Sara Templeton never ventured from Canamith and Rex had begged her to come on his next business trip. He knew there were risks when any of the villagers left the safe confines of home and went to Sanderell, but wanted Sara to meet his friend and Army veteran Donald Taft.

Taft's highest level of schooling was the year he spent at Sanderell Community College. He knew all the world leaders by name, and could tell you their political strengths and weaknesses. If you asked him about a particular war, Taft could describe particulars of the key skirmishes, where the troops were positioned, what weapons were used, what weapons should have been used, what the outcome was, and how that outcome affected that region of the world. Taft couldn't describe the pasteurization process, but he was no military thug either. He was an above-average public speaker and had the type of personality that allowed him to mix with civilians too.

Rex met Taft several years earlier as he searched for a reputable company to do business with. Taft's family owned a distributorship that sold many types of products in the region. Canamith's plan of action necessitated supplies from various industries for the village. The people of Canamith were known for making beautiful wool rugs and a system of bartering was arranged. Every three or four months, Rex hauled several carts of wool rugs down the mountain in exchange for items previously agreed to.

Rex never imagined that this would be Sara's only trip to the city.

They met Taft at their pre-arranged lunch spot. The two men greeted each other with firm handshakes and smiles as they stood in front of a little restaurant named Chambers Café. It was the kind of place where you could find an entree on the menu that pleased even discriminate tastes. The men agreed to bring their wives on the next trip. Taft didn't think that the two ladies would have much in common. Rex insisted that they meet anyway. Taft surprised Rex when he arrived at the restaurant with his wife and daughter.

"It's a pleasure to finally meet you, Colonel Taft," said Sara. "I've heard a great deal about you."

Pointing to the other adult woman, Sara said, "You must be the lovely Elizabeth. Rex told me how beautiful you were from the picture he's seen. You're even prettier in person."

"Why, thank you. One minor correction," said Elizabeth, "it's General Taft now."

"Almost, dear," interjected the blushing Taft. "I should know if the appointment comes through within two weeks."

"That's exciting news for you. I'll consider it a done deal and call you General," said Rex. He stuck out his right hand and gave the general another hearty shake.

"Thanks, Rex. I guess if you stay in the military long enough, anybody can get a promotion."

"Does it come with a big fat raise?" asked Rex.

"I'm afraid the government doesn't care too much if your wife has a penchant for the latest in fashion or jewels or luxurious handbags. Funny, I can lead thousands of troops into battle and nobody questions my choices, at least not to my face. The minute I mention reducing our credit card debt, Elizabeth ignores me. She does make up for it in other ways."

Taft didn't explain what those "other ways" were. Rex understood them to mean sex, especially when Elizabeth smacked her husband on the hand and Allesandra turned her head away from the four adults and mumbled, "I shouldn't have let you talk me into coming with you."

Rex hoped that the talk would drift back to the promotion instead of the lowbrow humor Taft found amusing.

"I bet you earned those medals," said Sara, noticing the array of medals pinned to the crisp uniform of the soon-to-be general.

"That's kind of you, Sara. That's enough talk about me. I wanted you to meet our daughter, Allesandra. We didn't want to leave her alone. She's never met anyone from Canamith before, and she—"

"No need to explain. It's a pleasure to meet you, young lady. As for meeting people from Canamith, I don't know what you've heard. I promise I won't eat you!" Sara rubbed her stomach and laughed.

Allesandra was old enough to know when someone was joking. This time she was unsure.

Her mother bailed her out before it became uncomfortable. "Darling child, she's kidding."

"Mom," exhaled the daughter, "I'm not seven years old anymore. I hate when you call me that."

"I'm sorry," said Sara. "That's a little village humor for you. I should be more careful with people I eat—I mean, meet!"

Laughs were abundant, as Sara had broken the tension of the moment. Even Allesandra cracked a smile. Her body language showed her disdain for the company. Four adults and one kid meant that the teenager was due for a long afternoon.

"Let's find seats," suggested Taft. He removed his hat, leaving an indentation in his closely clipped brown hair.

Rex examined Taft and then raised his head slightly to a pinch above his shoulder and gestured with his fingers that it would be prudent for his friend to place the hat back on the head. Taft picked up on the clue and nestled his hat back on his head.

Sara missed Rex's hand motions and hadn't spotted the ring around Taft's hair. She stared at the gift-wrapped package that Elizabeth was holding under her left arm. They found a table that sat six, and Elizabeth placed the package on the empty chair. Each table in the restaurant was covered in a series of satellite pictures taken from airplanes flying over Sanderell. Individual stores were too small to distinguish. The beach was pristine and small white caps hit the shore in a haphazard pattern. The water turned azure as the image headed off the coast.

"Rex, do you have a pen I can borrow?"

"Yeah, hold on a second." Rex reached in to his left chest pocket, took out a pen and handed it to his wife.

"That'll do. Thanks."

Sara wrote down the number "fifteen-seventeen" on the napkin lying on the table.

"Fine." said Taft. "I'll bite… what's with the 'fifteen-seventeen'?"

"I'll bet you lunch that the picture on this table was taken between fifteen and seventeen years ago."

"I don't get it," said Rex. "Sara, the general is probably not a betting man and since when did you become interested in gambling?"

"It's an innocent little wager," declared Sara with a devilish smile.

"Rex, you don't know everything. I'd never deny the young lady her wish," answered Taft smartly. "You're on, lady."

Sara flashed a big grin and said to her new acquaintance, "It's not gambling if the odds are tipped heavily in favor of one side of the better."

Sara spotted their waitress. An older woman with creaky knees approached the table.

"Pardon me, ma'am," said Sara, "are you Mama Chambers?"

"Dear, there isn't a Mama Chambers. The boss made up a marketing slogan for the advertising campaign. I'm just old. My real name is Belinda."

"Oh. Can you tell me when this picture was taken?"

"Which one, dear?" asked the waitress.

"The ones on the table tops. The view is from way up high."

"Gosh, let me think. I started here twenty years ago and these

59

tables weren't here then. Let me see, I'd say fifteen years ago. Hold on a sec, it was fifteen years exactly because if you peer closely you can see my red car in the parking lot. I had purchased that old gas hog right before fuel prices shot through the roof."

"I guess lunch is on me," said Taft. "That was quite a first impression, Sara. How'd you do it? Lucky guess?"

"Not a guess, General Taft."

"Almost General," he interrupted.

"I wouldn't gamble unless I was certain of the results. It was easy. You can tell by the clarity of the water. From our view in the Mountains, we have a view that resembles the ones taken by the airplanes. There's a beach near us and when I look down at Sanderell I can tell that the water hasn't been that clear in fifteen years. You may not notice the changes because you see the water every day. I observe the beach occasionally. Have you ever watched a child grow up? You don't notice how your own child grows fractionally each day. When you see a cousin or a niece every few months, you tend to notice the changes. We don't get those chances in Canamith; it's such a small village. There are intervals when the children go unnoticed, and then you look up and realize how big they've grown."

Taft smiled at Rex, who was beaming with pride in regards to his wife's ability to make such a strong first impression with his old friend.

"That's a real lady you've got there, Rex," said Taft.

"Don't I know it," answered Rex.

Sara slapped her menu on the table.

"Hey, boys, let's order food. Food tastes better when I'm not paying for it!" Sara laughed at her own joke and scooted her chair closer to Rex. She draped her right arm over his shoulder and gave him a little squeeze.

"Belinda! Two meat loaf specials for the men and...the lady will have?" Taft tapped his fingers on the table while Sara decided.

"I'll have the salad with diced chicken, your house dressing on the side please," said Sara.

"Sounds good for me and Allesandra too. Make that three salads please." chipped in Elizabeth.

Belinda limped through the swinging wooden doors and put the order into the new computer system that brought Chambers Café into the modern world of food service.

Sara kept her eye on the gift.

"I see you're eyeing the gift wrapped item?" said Taft.

"I am a little curious. May I be so bold as to ask what you bought your wife?"

"It's not for me," declared Elizabeth. "Oh heavens, the general would never buy anything for me. That's not his style. He gives me the money and I pick out what I want."

Taft didn't care for his wife's claim and turned to Lila. "It's typically more expensive than a gift I would buy. This is for you, Sara. I was going to give it to you when lunch was over. Go ahead. Open it," said the trim Army vet.

"Thank you! That wasn't necessary," blushed Sara.

"Come on, don't be shy," answered the General.

Sara grabbed the package and gently tried to remove the olive-colored paper.

"Sara, please, rip it open. We don't have all day," said Rex.

"Rex, please don't be rude. If the general and his wife went to the trouble to wrap it, I want to unwrap it nicely, thank you very much." She started gently, and then ripped open the rest of the paper with the panache of a street brawler.

"You call that gently?" said Taft with irony.

Her face lit up when she saw the cover. It read: *Living Off the Land* by Ryan Gates.

Sara skimmed the book, smiling as she thumbed the pages, from the first bright white one to the last of the 300-plus-page collection.

"What is it?" asked Rex.

"It's a cookbook! The recipes are made with produce we grow in Canamith. Thank you both. That was thoughtful of you."

"Glad you like it! You know, your husband and I don't see eye-to-eye on this whole 'tunnel' thing. I want him well-fed in case he's right. I trust there's a page or two in that book that he will enjoy. Rex says you can really make a mean dinner."

"That's kind of him to say. I do rather well for a mountain girl!" She laughed out loud at her own joke and then continued, "Thank you, again, and I'll treasure the gift."

Sara and Elizabeth chatted while they ate. Rex and Taft discussed what supplies Rex wanted to procure at their next rendezvous. Allesandra sat with her handheld device and headphones, focused on the latest top hits.

When lunch ended, the five of them went for a walk down the boardwalk to stretch their legs and burn off some of the calories. Rex ignored the group of rowdy teens that could be heard, but not yet seen by anyone. The teens came down the east side of the boardwalk. As they made their way closer to the general and his guests, the tallest of the teenagers shouted,

"Hey, fuckface, why aren't you out killing somebody today?"

Taft's training taught him to ignore comments from civilians. This was different. An uneasy sensation developed in his stomach. Allesandra was scared. You could see that in her green eyes.

Taft tried to calm her. "Easy, baby, daddy won't let anything happen to you. These boys are trying to rile me up, that's all."

Taft glanced at the teen and chose not to reply to his comments.

Rex and Sara had never heard those vulgar words before, and although they didn't know what a "fuckface" was, they did know how to interpret alarming intent when they heard it. Sara positioned herself slightly behind Rex, who placed his left arm in front of Sara as a measure of protection.

Allesandra tucked in close to her mother.

The teens came closer, and when they were within arm's length of the general, the bulkiest teen removed a knife that had been hidden from view and attempted to stab the general.

Taft spun to his left and avoided the sharp blade. The attacker turned to face the general. Taft grabbed his wife and daughter with his left hand and pushed them to the ground, while his right hand found his pistol and he fired a shot into the chest of his assailant. The boy stumbled backwards and hit the ground.

Allesandra screamed and covered her face. The punk had hurled his last insult. His wound was terminal. While blood flowed from his wound, another gunshot rang out.

The second gunshot wasn't from Taft's gun. One of the other teens had responded to the general's shot with one of his own. The poor kid had no business holding such a powerful weapon in his small hands. He couldn't have been more than sixteen years old. The bullet struck Sara in the stomach. She doubled over in pain; dark red liquid spilled from her midsection and covered the book that Taft had given her minutes earlier. The white pages of the book absorbed the first few drops of blood and then the sand crystals turned red. Sara stared at Rex in disbelief. It took Rex years to forget the look in Sara's face as she tumbled to the ground, blood flowing out of her. Rex rushed to her side and screamed for help.

Taft had turned and fired a second shot, this one a direct hit in the middle of the back of Sara's assassin. He fell forward, his face planting with a thud on the paved parking lot. He didn't move again.

"Elizabeth?" yelled the general.

"We're okay!" cried the general's wife. She clutched her daughter and tried to stop her from shaking.

Taft pressed several buttons on his mobile phone and within a minute the sound of sirens could be heard. The rescue team arrived on the scene and Rex feared the worst. Valiantly, they put pressure on Sara's wound as blood continued to leak out. Rex held Sara's hand as she was put in the ambulance. Taft followed them in his truck as the rescue vehicle and staff attempted to save Sara's life. They whisked alongside the Boardwalk, past a collection of frightened on-lookers and then rushed to Sanderell Hospital, where she died later that day.

CHAPTER 12

Buck spent the next two weeks learning in greater detail how his descendants built the tunnels in Canamith. The Elders spent this time discussing his future role in the village. The books that Buck studied were written over 2,000 years ago. The Ancient Ones believed that terrible danger was ahead. They couldn't predict the exact date. The Chief Elder would determine when world events dictated sealing the tunnel doors. It might happen in their children's lifetime or in another ten subsequent generations. The Scriptures couldn't predict what day or year the right time to seal the tunnels. To anyone paying attention, the world around them was making that point crystal clear. The time approached.

Seven days before the closing of the tunnels, the Elders began their council meeting. This timetable was noted in the scriptures as "The Last Week of Man" and "The Beginning of the End."

Prior to this gathering, Buck had a mild suspicion of what was to come of the world. An Elder named Braham had come to his house early that morning. The sun was cracking over the peaks of the mountains in the east. Glistening streams of light danced on the tall trees that had been covered in snow until a few months ago. Fresh water ran from the mountaintops and entered the village at a slow, steady pace. The spring thaw had been heavier than usual this year and the water diverted into special overflow containers located on the eastern side of the village.

Each container was meticulously hand-crafted directly into the walls of the tunnels. The main pipe that brought the water into the container was sealed within the solid rock. A series of aqueducts brought the water inside the tunnel. Once there, the water ran down the entire twenty-two foot shaft of the container. There was enough fresh water in these containers to last the village for two years. Underground reservoirs would supply additional water if needed.

Waste removal was coordinated with special pipes that ran down underneath the tunnels to a geothermal stream that led away from Canamith towards the ocean. There was a back-up plan completed by Rex twenty-five years ago. It consisted of a series of pipes that ran the length of the tunnels to a vast waste receptacle. It wasn't the perfect way to fix the problem, but at least it was a plan. Rex Templeton always had a back-up plan.

Buck and Mathis scarfed down their breakfast of eggs and toast and were discussing the topics of the day when an older man approached from the southern end of the village.

When Buck saw his dark blue robe he realized this wasn't a social visit.

"Good morning to two of the finest young men in the village," said Elder Braham. He was given the task of teaching Buck the responsibilities that would be placed on his shoulders in the coming weeks. Braham had been handsome in his youth—many years ago. Too many second helpings of his wife's stuffed chicken and cheese dinners, and his unfortunate battle with decaying teeth, made the once comely man look older than the sixty-three years.

"Morning, Elder Braham," replied the boys in unison.

"Come with me, Buck. We have much to discuss."

"I understand," said Buck.

"I guess I should find somewhere else to be, huh?" said Mathis.

"Don't be downhearted. You will fulfill your future in Canamith someday. Be patient, your moment will come," said Braham, as he watched a discouraged Mathis walk to the center of the village.

The Elder Braham and his new apprentice headed to the holy site of the tunnels. Buck's father was in charge of the village, but neither son had ever considered trespassing on this holy shrine. Buck was escorted into the building as if the entire place had been constructed for him. He hesitated at the entrance point and Braham ushered him onward.

"Come, dear boy, there's no use in pretending you don't belong here. You've got as much right to stand here as I do, perhaps more. Come now, there are no evil monsters in there ready to attack. When the others see you, they should see you are secure in your forthcoming journey."

"Others?" Buck said, startled. "How come my first visit in here can't be with just you? You're adept at keeping me calm. Even my dad makes me a little nervous; sometimes he scares the living you-know-what out of me. His legacy is impossible to follow."

"You shouldn't *try* following his legacy," said Braham. "You must create your own. I've had many conversations with your father and I assure you he is confident that you can handle it. If the leader of the village says you are the one, than the rest of the Elders will believe it. Remember that nobody is expecting miracles from you. The true miracle of the village is the long and arduous task that brought us to this point. We're close to achieving what our ancestors knew could be done. Comparing when this process started to the time when it will be completed can be measured in practically the blink of eye." Braham gave Buck an exaggerated "blink" of his own to belabor the point.

"I get it. Nice and easy. Any last minute words of wisdom?"

"Yes, don't speak unless spoken to. Funny, that's what I used to say to my kids. Be yourself and you'll be fine. Pretend you've done this every day of your life. Walk in and introduce yourself to everybody. They know you."

"Yeah, I get it," said Buck. "I've been raised on meetings, secret chambers, you name it, and I've seen it."

Buck entered the holy site with his head held high. Buck and

Braham came upon twelve men standing silently in a semicircle. The men were wearing ceremonial robes that flowed down to within two inches of the ground. A six-inch strip of white fur near their necks softened the bright blue of the robes. A purple flower adorned the fur and imparted a lovely fragrance.

As Buck came closer, the smell of lilac filled his head with warm memories. His mother had pressed lilac flowers in her perfume jar. When Buck was a young boy and had a nightmare, he'd run to the bedroom where Rex and Sara slept and leap into the middle of the bed and hold his mother close. The scent of flowers helped calmed him. There was always a fresh bouquet of flowers in the corner of the room. He hadn't thought of those flowers in years. In the time of bereavement following Sara's murder, Rex cut fresh lilacs and placed them in his room. They stayed there for the seven-day mourning ritual that was customary for the village.

Buck was unaware of such details when Sara died, and when he surprised his father with more flowers on the eighth day, Rex snarled at the boy, extracted the flowers from his grip and crushed them in one hand, saying, "No more flowers."

Filled with the images of the fractured pieces of flowers in his head, Buck forced himself to return to his current role of student and realized he had better stop daydreaming.

If Buck appeared incapable of this new position in the village, doubts would be cast at Rex's decision-making process. Buck was not going to let that happen.

"Who dares enter this holy place?" said a voice from the crowd.

"Good morning, Elders. I am Buck, son of Rex Templeton." In unison the group gave him affirmation with a nod of their heads.

Rex went to him. "Sit down next to me and prepare your mind for the first step in this long journey. You can't accomplish the task we have put in front of you until you understand all that we know. Your knowledge of the history of our people is limited; that's about to change."

Buck shifted his weight from side to side. He wasn't too keen on hearing his knowledge was "limited". He tried not to show any displeasure and repeated the phrase "stay calm" to himself.

His father continued, not noticing that Buck's concentration had drifted.

"Two-thousand years ago, our ancestors were given instructions in this room how to prepare the tunnels for our survival. Your grandfather stood in this exact spot and placed his hands on me, giving me the responsibility to become head of the village and continue the obligation we have to the rest of our people."

Buck nodded his head in agreement. He had heard this mantra throughout his youth. He wondered what other secrets of the village were shrouded from him.

The Elders marched Buck over the green meadow that had crept up alongside the Crooked River. The road wound down a hill not much more than 75 feet until they stood next to a series of large buildings. Entrance to these buildings was prohibited to non-tunnel-building citizens in the village. Buck had walked past these structures a thousand times, but had never entered the hallowed area. The Elders and those chosen to work on the tunnels had full access. The tallest of the structures was a thirty-foot, two-story dwelling that housed the sacred texts of the ancestors. Adjacent to the tallest buildings were two shorter ones that maintained the village offices. The exterior of these buildings seemed ordinary enough, but each structure had a secret door that led to the special chamber where the Elders would meet and discuss philosophy or interpretations of the ancient texts. The original ancient scrolls of parchment had been copied many times. The first manuscripts were still housed there. If you didn't live in the village, you wouldn't know there was any life within these rocks. The stone surrounding the buildings hid the entire the structure.

At the end of the pathway within the secret chamber of the tallest building there were three huge rocks. Each huge rock weighed at least sixty tons, and stood twelve to fifteen feet tall. Elder Braham led Buck to the front of the largest of the boulders.

"Put your hands on the rock, Buck. Watch me," said Braham, holding his hands in an out-stretched manner that made his fingers look frozen in one position.

Buck followed Braham's lead, but held them out directly in front of him instead of placing them on the rock.

"On the rock, Buck, don't be alarmed. It won't hurt you," said Braham. He showed Buck again, this time the young man placed his strong hands directly on the spot.

Buck's fingers rested comfortably on the cool rock. He viewed the Elders and noticed their eyes were closed in prayer. One by one the Elders lined up behind Buck. Without electricity or the sound of hydraulic lifts, the massive boulders began to shake. Buck started to remove his hands.

"Be still, Buck, don't move," said Braham.

The largest of the stones to the left of the group began to retreat into the side of the hill. Inch by inch, foot by foot, the heavy slab of rock moved until the gap reached fifteen feet wide.

Rex found his place at the entrance of the two rocks and reached out to the group.

"This is the moment that our ancestors prophesied and the reason that our people have spent an eternity toiling. The Great Tunnels of the Saviors are ready for final preparations. We have chosen the one to lead us into the new world that awaits us. Now, Buck, enter the tunnels."

Buck felt trepidation at entering the tunnel, but he kept his gait purposeful as he strode down the illuminated path. Small bulbs lit the passageway. The ground was soft under his shoes. Not crunchy or gravel-filled as he expected. As the last of the Elders passed by a light, it would blink twice, and then go dark. Buck and the Elders followed the path for several minutes.

Then, they turned one long corner and had reached the center of the tunnels.

The cavernous central section was illuminated beyond what Buck could have ever believed possible. The ceiling rose some 150 feet and eight corridors radiated from it. Writing filled the walls. The writing appeared fresher where the letters soared skyward to the spiral-shaped ceiling. A golden hue glistened from the letters. The inscriptions closer to the floor showed more age. The original gleam was worn over a dozen times by moisture and oxygen. As Buck peered closer, he could see the letters formed names.

Braham nudged Buck and whispered. "Impressive, huh?"

"Impressive? This is unbelievable! I've heard about this place my entire life. I wish Mathis could see this. The names on the wall are a sight to see. Is it a list of all the people who have lived in the village?" asked Buck.

"No, those people who spent their lives working in the tunnels so the rest of us could benefit from their meticulous labor. Each name was hand carved and polished with gold. As you can see, many of the names have been partially eroded. We can repair those when we arrive."

"Arrive?" said Buck.

"I said arrive, and we will be living here soon enough."

"Are you saying that my grandparents and their parents are listed on these walls?"

"Some of them are here. If all goes well for you, there will be ample time to read their stories."

"What do you mean if all goes well for me?"

"You have a big job ahead of you, and I'm sure you'll do fine. Let's not speculate on any negatives. Remember, Rex Templeton doesn't make mistakes, and he chose you. I'm sure you'll be fine. Let's keep moving."

The group passed the main chamber of the tunnel. It led to a hallway that had many paths, or branches, to choose from. Each path was large enough for four men to walk abreast. These branches led to the different sections of the tunnels. Buck gazed up at the walls of the tunnels. Each coarse rock was smoothed over by loving hands.

Buck's head remained on a swivel as he tried to gather in the splendor and rich history that the tunnels represented.

They turned right at the first opportunity and that hallway was sprinkled with more writings. These walls were filled with stories written hundreds of years ago. They were imprinted into the granite and stone walls so future generations would have the chance to revel in their achievements.

Each story encompassed a spot on the wall nine feet high by two feet wide. Buck imagined the person sitting quietly, marking their moment in Canamith history, knowing that someday the person reading these tales might be a future offspring. Fancy etchings with beautiful penmanship filled the walls. Buck glanced at one section and saw stories about famine, floods, earthquakes, fires, meteorites and war bore a tearful footnote to yesteryear.

"Don't be alarmed, Buck, the corridors have stories of love and beauty too," said Braham.

Buck and the entourage pressed on another hundred yards down the hallway to another chamber, this one half the size of the main chamber. This vast opening was divided into twenty, perhaps thirty, individual "family" units that would give a semblance of privacy to the people who would eventually occupy this dwelling.

Buck approached one the units and saw the family nameplate located on the frame of the door. A glass frame had been placed into the wall of the unit, and a slip of paper was placed inside the frame. Braham escorted Buck into one of the units. The name on this residence read "BRAHAM."

The Elder extended his left hand and pointed to the 400-square-foot quarters that Braham would be soon be calling home.

"Please, Buck, enter my new home," said Braham half-joking.

"It's humble, as you are, Elder Braham," said Buck with the perfect amount of respect, not sarcasm.

"Dear boy, it's not the dream house I envisioned for my retirement."

Braham plopped down on the larger of the two beds that were

in the room, and sighed, "Buck, I'd like you to imagine the effort that led to this day. There is nowhere else in the world that had the commitment to complete a project of this magnitude. These beds, these walls; can you imagine carving these rooms out of the rock? This is my new… house, or residence, or whatever you want to call it. A more fitting description would be 'my accommodations.'"

"I think it'll be fine," said Buck. His words sounded optimistic, but internally he envisioned the stress of the entire village living within these walls and that didn't sound appealing.

Buck scanned the room next door saw the name "Orrick" on the door.

"Who's Orrick? I don't recall seeing him around the village. I know everyone," asked Buck.

"Don't be so sure of that. You'll find out."

The group left the family area and followed a second path to the eating quarters.

Tables, each about forty feet long and built out of stone, rose three feet from the ground. Space on either side of the tables had been carved away and another long narrow swath of the ground slightly hollowed out. This made a perfect place to sit at the tables without the cumbersome requirement of chairs. The entire village could sit together at once. This spot doubled as the main meeting room when the Elders spoke to the village or when the entire community gathered for special occasions.

The rear of the room led to another pathway. Buck followed the Elders into what was clearly the kitchen. Dozens of bowls, pots, serving pieces, containers, spoons, forks, knives, and a host of various kitchen utensils filled the vast wall of shelves that ran the entire length of the kitchen. Three sliding ladders were affixed to the top and bottom of the shelves to help facilitate the easy transportation of items stored on the top shelf. There were several other hallways to visit. Braham ignored those and took Buck to the Room of Elders.

Buck froze in his tracks. He barely heard Braham speak. "Buck.

We're going to give you time alone in here to see the pictures and look at the names of the people that helped make this day possible. I'll be back in a few minutes."

Braham and the others left Buck to stare at the history of the place and let the emotions seep into his soul. Faces were etched into the stone, and under each one, a hand-written paragraph. It was the Village's lasting tribute to previous generations.

Buck snugged close to the wall on the left, careful not to miss a single person. When Braham returned, he was astonished to see what little progress Buck had made.

"Come on, Junior Elder Buck, you must pick up the pace. You'll have years to sit in here and read everyone's life story."

Buck pointed to a picture of a man on the wall, his face fading with each passing year.

"See that man? He's my great-grandfather. I was named after him. They said he was smartest man in the village…not a bad guy to be named after, huh?"

"Not bad company. They'll be plenty of time to tell me all about him. Let's go, there's more to the tour."

CHAPTER 13

While Buck learned the past, Mathis planned for the future. He was crushed by his father's choice. Whether that decision was right or wrong, he didn't care. Mathis was overcome with disappointment. Even his oldest and closest friend couldn't lighten Mathis's spirits on this day.

"Mathis, are you crying?" asked Jeremy White.

"Jeremy, hi. I was… ah… getting dirt out of my eye."

"What? Is that some Buck in your eye?"

"Very funny. Is there a reason you came by? Or was it to make me feel worse?" Mathis asked.

Jeremy saw Mathis fighting back tears. He didn't push it.

"Do you want come over to the shop and check out the girls?"

"No, thanks, buddy, I'll pass. Today's not my day."

Mathis was standing outside his house when two birds landed near his feet, pecked at the ground for a moment and flew away as quickly as they had arrived.

He shouted at them.

"Sure, you two can go anywhere you want. I must stay here and guard the tunnels. Jeremy, did you ever wonder how different our lives would have been if your dad was picked Chief Elder instead of mine?"

"Nope. Never. Can't change what was. Visualize the future. Don't look back. That's what Lucas and I always said. If Lucas kept looking back, all he'd see is your sister and that would not have been a healthy choice. You know my dad isn't happy about our friendship. Your family drives him crazy. I can't handle his resentment. One day we had it out and I told him I won't let him dictate who my friends will be."

Mathis was surprised. "Thanks. That means a lot. I could use a true friend today."

Jeremy and his brother Lucas were brought up in a household filled with anger and jealousy. Their father, Ethan White, lost the battle that determined whether he or Rex Templeton would be the chief Elder years ago. Lila broke Lucas's heart when she left while the two were dating. It had appeared that marriage was eminent. Her departure ended any chance of that. Lucas quickly moved on with his life and sought another to marry. His father did not handle her departure with equal passivity and it became another notch in the grudge belt that Ethan had for Rex Templeton.

People familiar with Lila knew of her love of science and the thousands of books she maintained in the village library. Nobody could have predicted that one day she would leave the village. Buck and Mathis were children when the girl left and villagers didn't speak of her much. The Templetons seldom talked about Lila. Rex might have gotten over the trauma, at least on the outside, were it not for power hungry Ethan White.

Long before Rex was elected the Chief Elder, he was known only as the offspring of Marcus Templeton. He and Ethan White were the two logical choices to select for the new Chief Elder of the village. Rex was the odds-on favorite. His dad was the reigning chief and that gave him a huge advantage. There was years of history and future responsibility that came with the title and birthright wasn't enough to hold the prestigious title of Chief Elder. Marcus had to insure a fair way to choose the next leader. The committee to elect the new Chief Elder consisted of five men. The winning candidate would need a majority vote. When the ballots were counted and the new Elder decided, the committee agreed privately to announce that the results of the vote were unanimous. There was vigorous debate and arguments between them. The committee was justifiably concerned to announce a split in the vote. A statement that one candidate won the position by a "three votes to two votes" split had the potential to wreak havoc with village morale. The last split vote occurred over a hundred years ago. This modern day contest had the potential to be closer than anyone would have thought possible a few years earlier.

The competition to select the new Elder was divided into three parts. The first section consisted of physical strength. Ethan should have been an easy winner. An old mountain climbing injury thwarted his best effort.

The half-mile obstacle course was designed to challenge the men's muscle, and their brains. A series of short runs led the contestants into a myriad of mazes. The path was blocked at certain locations by large, heavy boulders. Ethan had trouble with this part because his leg couldn't sustain the effort required to maneuver through the terrain fast enough and ultimately led to his defeat in this challenge. Rex knew that one victory didn't secure his spot at the top, and this proved all too true when Ethan edged Rex in the second of the tests. That contest pitted the men in a series of tests that pertained to the history of the village. Ethan won by a single point, remembering the exact order of previous Elders dating back 500 years. Rex missed the correct sequence of leaders once, inverting Elder Meredith and Elder Burgeson. A small misstep for sure, but Ethan had placed them in the correct order. The margin of victory was slim, but still his victory. This set the match at a tie and each contestant was told to wait for the results of the Elders vote. That would determine the winner.

Rex sat on his favorite green bench, surrounded by his friends and supporters as he awaited the news.

"I had my chance to win on my own merits, now I must sit and wait for the Elders to choose my fate. If selected, I will not let other people put me in that position again, I'll figure out a way to beat them to the punch. I'll be better prepared for the challenges ahead," said Rex to his friends.

A man shouted from the back of the crowd. "This is how it should be decided. You are clearly the people's choice and the Elders will choose wisely. You are best suited to guide us into the next and perhaps final phase of our obligations."

"The Elders know best and I respect their wishes," said Rex.

Twelve hours went by. Rex tossed and turned in his bed, failing to land in a restful sleep as the Elders discussed the merits of each man.

Rex awoke to find his fathers hand resting on his forehead, his face ashen, lips dry, and a tear coming from his left eye.

Rex tried to interpret his father's stare. "I didn't get it, did I?"

"On the contrary; the Elders have chosen you," said his father.

"Then why do you look despondent? You should be proud and happy for me."

"Proud? Indeed. Happy? That's difficult to say. As Chief Elder, you will be hard-pressed to find happiness. You'll find satisfaction in knowing you have fulfilled your job. There is much to do and I'm afraid not much time to do it."

In another part of the village, Ethan White was learning his fate too. Outwardly, he accepted the decision of the Elders. Inside he teemed with disappointment.

When the messenger left Ethan's house, the frustrated Ethan turned to his wife and said, "Rex may be Chief Elder, but I vow to make his life miserable whenever I can."

Ethan's wife was not interested in hearing the details of her husband's plans.

"Please don't turn this into a personal vendetta. He didn't choose against you. The Elders did that."

"You heard what I said," said Ethan, and he slammed the door and rushed out into the night to reflect on what his future could have been.

CANAMITH COMMUNICATION DEPARTMENT

Update #151

Family Found Killed

Forest Ranger Donald Jamison began the press conference.

"Last night, a family of six was killed in a remote campsite located 120 miles outside of the capital. Mr. and Mrs. Walter Richardson and their four children were killed in an overnight attack. The parents were found near the fire pit, and the boys, Clinton, age 12, Clarence, age 9, Cooper, age 6, and Christopher, age 4, respectively, died in their cabin. Evidence collected at the scene indicates a bear killed the family.

"Myself and several members of my staff spent several hours searching in the vicinity of the campground earlier this morning, and came across a large black bear. We trapped the bear and then it was destroyed. The tourist season starts tomorrow and we want to assure visitors that the area is safe.

"I'd like to remind everyone that this is first death in the campground in twenty years. Our deepest condolences go out to the Richardson family and their friends."

CHAPTER 14

Lila and the rest of the staff at the college regrouped in the morning. None of the staff questioned why she was wearing the same clothes from the previous evening. Lila used the toothbrush she kept in the back of her bottom right drawer for the third time in the last nine months. A quick wash under her arms and a refresh of her makeup and she was ready to go. Her overnight work sessions diminished in frequency last year, but she maintained a stash that included toothbrush, toothpaste, deodorant, and feminine hygiene products just in case. Like her father, Lila believed in backup plans.

Dr. Massey greeted Lila with a quick smile and opened his mobile phone. Lila followed him to his office but Massey was unaware, or didn't care. He sat down at his desk and spun the brown leather swivel the chair away from Lila while he placed his call. His voice was hushed and all Lila could hear was, "I understand. Do what you must. That doesn't mean I like it."

Aldo came in seconds later and whispered into Lila's ear. "Man, I can never get here before that guy," pointing to Massey. "How are J.J. and Sophie?"

"They're fine. I talked to them when they reached Kate's."

"What do you mean talked to them at Kate's? Didn't you see them at home?" he asked.

"I didn't go home. Please don't tell Massey. He'd be angry with me. I slept here for a few hours. That cushy chair of mine isn't comfortable at four in the morning. It felt like there was a metal pole stuck up my backside. When I woke up, I flicked on the news and saw nasty stuff going on out there. I understand Massey gave you grief about your 'World Incident Report', but the news coming over the ticker is downright scary. I have to run those by Morales and Goldman."

Massey finished his conversation. He still clutched the phone in one hand. He sat stoically for a moment and glanced at Lila and Aldo. Doctors Morales and Goldman entered the room laughing; their smiles faded when they saw the pained expression on Massey's face.

"I'm afraid I have distressing news concerning our whales. They're dead. The government killed them early this morning."

Gasps of anguish rose from the group. Lila slammed her hand down on the desk, sending her beverage flying on the cold marble floor. The hot liquid spilled out of the cup.

"This is inexcusable. It's a crime, I tell you, a damn crime!" shouted Morales.

"Can we get those samples you were requesting?" said a rather stoic Dr. Goldman.

"Emily, please!" said Morales. Using her first name was uncommon, but he was too upset to use his formal training.

"I'll check on the tissue samples for you, Dr. Goldman," said Massey. "This is a national travesty. I finished speaking with General Anderson at the Coastal Control station a minute ago and he gave me the news. The whales were 'neutralized' as he put it. I'd like to 'neutralize' him. Damn it!"

Lila was busy cleaning her coffee spill and asked, "Why didn't they give us the hours they promised?"

"Anderson said the situation changed and they hadn't heard from us. They went ahead with Plan B."

"Great," said Lila, "another man in charge with a Plan B. I wonder if he knows my father."

Gorrell raised an eyebrow at Lila. "I don't think you've ever mentioned your father."

"I have my reasons, trust me."

Massey continued. "The general told me that they have removed all the barrels and they don't believe there is any danger to the community at this time."

"That's a laugh. You want to eat the fish that have been swimming around in that hazardous waste? I don't," said Dr. Goldman.

"Anderson told me that our ABC group was selected to represent the college in the capital. We're going there to review the strange behaviors going on in the world. I'm afraid I haven't been completely forthcoming with any of you, and for that, I'm sorry, but I've been sworn to secrecy for several months and unable to discuss any of this with anybody. The whales are a recent and dare I say the largest example of what the government is referring to as an 'episode'. There have been numerous smaller events that the government's been trying to deal with and keep out of the media. Traditional steps to understand these odd behaviors and episodes haven't worked out."

"How come I wasn't notified?" asked Lila, perplexed and disturbed to think that government bureaucrats were bypassing people at her level.

"You weren't singled out. The top government scientists have requested our help. It doesn't matter when they asked. The point is that they have asked now. Let's not confuse the message and messenger. This was not my choice. I was told in a clear and direct manner that I was forbidden to discuss this with anyone. That means you, Morales, Goldman, or the parking lot attendant. That was the then, and now, due to many factors, the government has chosen to go in another direction. They want our help and I informed them that we would be willing to jump in and help wherever we can. I know I can count on your support."

Aldo was silent. Lila sat fuming while Goldman and Morales stared out the windows.

"I need to know. Are you in? Or out?" asked Massey.

"Count me in, Dr. Massey. I wouldn't turn down the chance to learn more about what's happening," said Lila.

"Count me in too," said Morales.

At the Applegate School of Medicine, where Morales ran the Cytology Department years ago, he parlayed his education into a million dollar a year job as the CEO of Cell-Techular, the industry leader in the growing field of studying organisms at the cellular level, specifically understanding if those cells were cancerous. Morales sold his cell-testing equipment around the world and his patented equipment treated more than seventeen different forms of cancer.

His unique way of looking at problems was his greatest strength. People looked at a forest and saw trees. Morales asked: "What is behind the forest?" or "What is below the forest?" Morales was always making notes, or speaking into his portable audio device, allowing him to review his notes at a later date.

Lila drove Dr. Massey crazy with her own checklists and notebooks full of scribbled notes. She was a perfect match for Morales. The two of them sat next to each other making lists.

"There's no ABC without me. You know I'm in," said Goldman.

"Mr. Gorrell, I'm extending an invitation to you too. We'll need somebody to manage assorted details. Can you handle that?"

Aldo sighed.

"Dr. Massey, I'd have to cancel my dates with the cheerleading squad, but if the country is calling, then I'm in."

"Your humor fails again to strike a chord with me. How Professor Jenkins is able to tolerate your lack of grace is beyond my comprehension," smirked Massey.

"I'll work on that, Dr. Massey." Drops of sweat ran down the back of Aldo's neck. He grabbed the dirty towels from Lila's spill and gave his neck a quick wipe.

"I received the overnight wire reports. I must tell you, Mr. Gorrell, I may have judged you too harshly when you tried to bring these issues up to my attention. It seems that the episodes that we've reviewed are reaching treacherous levels. That's precisely why the government is asking us to convene at the capital to discuss this problem with scientists from around the globe. Aldo, I apologize, and I will try to listen respectfully in the future. There, I said it. Now don't tell a living soul that I apologized to you or my entire reputation will be washed away in an instant."

"Don't worry. I'm not saying a word," Aldo chuckled. "They wouldn't believe me anyhow."

"I took the liberty of packing up the computers. Our plane leaves in one hour. Any questions?" He didn't wait for any and continued, "Excellent. We'll meet downstairs in thirty minutes. I realize that doesn't give you much time to prepare, but do the best you can. Things are happening quickly and we haven't a moment to waste."

"Thirty minutes!" declared Lila. "I must talk to J.J. I'm not even packed."

"Dear old Dr. Massey has thought of everything. I tracked J.J. down and filled him in on the plan. He was not pleased with me. I've sent staffers to your house and had them make a quick emergency wardrobe run for you and it will be waiting for you at the airport. Mr. Gorrell, I had the pleasure of speaking to your parents early today. Nice people. I'd like to meet them one day. They indicated you prefer not to fly. That's unfortunate. There's no choice for this trip. Your mother wanted to know if you would be flying on an empty stomach? Anything the other passengers and I should be wary of?"

Humiliated Aldo mumbled, "I'll be fine. I always get sick when I fly. My mom says I shouldn't eat before I fly."

"That's nonsense, young man. There's your problem."

Massey picked up his mobile phone and pressed a series of buttons.

"Not to worry, Mr. Gorrell, I've ordered food that will be waiting for us at the airport. I requested a meal that will stick to the walls of your stomach. I suspect hot pancakes and syrup will do the trick."

Lila dismissed herself and called J.J. from the other room to fill him in on her sudden departure.

"Yeah, babe," said J.J., "Dr. Massey told me you had to leave in a hurry. He called right after I spoke to you earlier. He said it was a national emergency. He sounded concerned, but he always sounds like it's the end of the world when he calls here. Are you sure it's a great idea for you to get involved at the next level?"

"Yes. You know the ABC Squad. We can't say no to the president. Massey said he asked for us specifically. I'm getting up to speed on events happening today. I'll call you when I get to the capital. How's my baby girl?"

"She misses her mommy, I can tell you that."

"Please tell Kate thanks for her help. I love you, J.J. Kiss Sophie for me, okay? Bye for now. I'll call you as soon as we land in the capital."

CHAPTER 15

There wasn't much conversation during the short drive to Sanderell Airport. The driver raced through town in fifteen minutes to make it to the waiting private jet, and on the tarmac. The engines purred, anticipating full throttle. The wings of the twelve-seat plane glistened in the morning sun.

"Ready, Professor Jenkins?" said Gorrell.

"Ready, Aldo. I love to fly. When Man figured out how to travel vast distances at incredible speed, it changed everything," said Lila.

"I'm glad you're all happy. I'll guzzle down a few shots of alcohol and fall asleep until the plane lands," said Aldo.

"Massey would love that. A drunken teacher's assistant ready to begin his biggest assignment ever? That's a great idea, Aldo. Why don't you suck it up, sit down and try not to look as though your breakfast is going to land two seats in front of you?

"Thanks for the moral support. And I thought Massey was tough on me? He's a dream compared to you!"

They both chuckled as Aldo helped Lila into the aircraft's narrow opening.

Lila plopped down in the window seat of row three.

"Is this seat taken, young lady?" said Dr. Massey from the rear of the cabin.

"Please, be my guest. Are you ready to sit on the same plane with the 'flying puke machine?'" asked Lila.

"You mean Aldo? He'll be fine. He sure loved that breakfast. I filled him up with pancakes, syrup, juice, you name it."

"Aldo? What were you thinking?" asked Lila.

"I don't know. Dr. Massey told me to eat it. So I ate. I figure if I puke, then I can blame him for stuffing all that food in me, and if I don't? Then maybe I've got this air sickness thing figured out."

"There's no way you're sitting behind me! You better keep those relief bags close at hand."

Two hours later, as the airplane was gliding through the three hour flight to the Capital, Aldo's breakfast made a full and complete arrival in a brown paper bag, and parts of row two, seats A, B, and C.

"Oh, man, that food smelled better when you ate it than it does now!" said a disgusted Lila.

"Thanks for trying, Dr. Massey, but I think your plan needs tinkering," said Aldo, now turning several shades greener than his Caucasian skin usually looked.

"Go get washed up, Aldo, we'll be landing soon. You can't meet General Taft looking like that."

Morales and Goldman were sitting in the rear of the plane. They spent the entire flight with their laptops on, energetically filling notebooks with ideas.

Massey seized this opportunity to use the Captain's microphone to talk to his team of experts.

"There's too much cabin noise for me to talk to all of you without screaming. This way I know you'll be able to hear me." Massey read aloud the reports about dogs turning on their owners and biting them. Many dogs were set loose from their homes and formed roaming packs that were terrorizing neighborhoods. This provoked retaliation and dogs were hunted down and killed. There were stories of panic in third world countries that faced a crisis due to lack of potable water. Meteorologists predicted wetter and colder weather in the coming months. This would cripple the Midwest's ability to harvest enough corn to meet supply. And lastly, Massey read the growing concerns of parents whose children were succumbing to diseases because previously capable antibiotics no longer stopped strains of bacteria.

Dr. Goldman stuck her two cents worth into the conversation. "I've been screaming for years about the overuse of antibiotics in pediatric medicine, but my calls fell on deaf ears. I was horrified to read the actual number of childhood deaths far surpassed the number that had been reported through traditional government reporting agencies. I believe the data was altered to avoid a panic. Now it's time to panic."

Massey continued. "There were challenging problems at water filtration facilities on the east coast, and several other plants throughout the world. Insects have damaged four nuclear power plants across the country. There were reports of enormous flocks of birds flying into a hydroelectric plant. The damage caused a six month delay in the completion of the facility."

Massey summed up his talk with more depressing news. "There are problems with the water, problems with the food supply and problems popping up all over. The President is counting on us to come up with ideas that can fix one, or all of these issues, and fast, before panic takes hold. If you've ever seen a group of panic-stricken people, let me tell you, it's not a pretty sight. It's kill or be killed when it comes right down to it. Neighbors will fight neighbors for the last morsel of food if it means their child will eat that night. I'm not saying it'll come to that, but that's the road we're headed down, and it's ugly. Professor Jenkins, you're the animal expert. We need you to decipher why the animal kingdom is off-kilter. Morales, you can tell us what's going on at the cellular level. What changes have occurred to these animals? Dr. Goldman, we're counting on you to help put all the pieces together. The President told me that we'd be working with a Mr. Drake once we get to the capital. I don't know much about him. He's not a scientist. Communications is his deal. How that fits in to what we're doing, I don't know and I don't care. The President said to work with him. Please don't tell me what a jerk he is. Keep him busy, find a project to keep him out of your hair and that way I can tell the President he's part of the team. That's it for now. I've passed out a number of pieces of literature for you to read while we finish the flight to the Capital. I appreciate your attention."

The pilot greeted the cabin in a cheerful voice. "Good morning, fellow flyers. We want you to enjoy the ride. That even goes for our youngest passenger today. That would be Mr. Aldo Gorrell. The flight attendant has mentioned that you've spent a considerable amount of the flight in the bathroom. I expect you're feeling better. We started our descent twenty minutes ago. We should be landing a little ahead of schedule. The tailwinds were kind to us today and the weather is ideal. Perfect flying conditions. The current temperature in the capital is sixty-seven degrees with winds from the west of eight miles per hour. Relative humidity is forty-four percent. Dr. Massey tells me you guys are coming to save the world. We could use it. Good luck. Lock your tray tables and please return your seats to their upright position. That's it for now."

"Wonderful," said Aldo. "We have a pilot that makes fun of me. I wish he would just fly the plane."

"Aldo, try taking a few deep breaths and I think you'll feel better. That used to help me when I had to listen to the story of The Great Divide every year back in Canamith," said Lila.

"You're from Canamith? No way! How come you never mentioned it?"

"It didn't seem important until a few days ago."

"What is The Great Divide?"

"It's the story of Canamith. We weren't allowed to hear all of it. Allegedly there are secret writings that I'll never see."

"If the writings are secret, how do you even know they exist at all, or what they said?"

"Aldo, that's one of the reasons I'm sitting here with you and not sitting on a stone chair back in Canamith. The Great Divide was a book written thousands of years ago that told the story of how long ago my ancestors lived amongst the world in cities that resemble any place you may have read about in history class. The story is retold to children every spring."

"I never knew that. I was told that the people of Canamith have historically lived in the mountain regions."

"You were misinformed. I hear that all the time. I never speak of it because I'm not their greatest spokesperson. I don't correct people when I hear that stuff. People in Canamith live in houses. Not fancy ones. Did you think they lived in tents or huts?"

"You hear a lot of rumors. What's the story? Come on, spill the beans."

"This stays between me and you. I've discussed this with J.J. and I'll tell Sophie when she's older, and of course, Dr. Massey knows where I'm from. I'm telling you now so have a better understanding of why I'm so adamant about solving this crisis with science, not faith."

"Yeah, I get it. That explains a lot about that whole 'everything is explainable' thing you have going."

"As I said, years ago, our people lived among the world. There was a strong Chief Elder back then, I don't recall his name, and he believed that mankind was headed for a catastrophic ending. He led his followers back into the mountain region and began living away from the rest of society. As years went on, interaction with the world became less frequent and the people of Canamith were shunned. The people in Canamith live a much simpler life."

"Didn't you have electricity?"

"Of course we did. Everything in Canamith is measured with its effect on the planet. That was okay with me, but the overwhelming feeling in the village was that mankind was doomed and the village was building a contingency plan to survive the disaster. I desired a more challenging intellectual existence and I knew that would never happen in Canamith. That why I left there and came to Sanderell.

Once I left, there was no going back home. I could never go back to that simple lifestyle, and I wouldn't have been accepted back anyway. They believe I would contaminate the village. It's silly. I can respect the customs and rules of any place that I've traveled. I never wanted to go back and live in that mountain setting without the advances of technology to make my life better, or at least what I perceived was better. I'm sure my dad would vehemently disagree with the sentiment that I live better than he does, and well, there you go. I'm here with you, and they're living in the mountains, building tunnels as a 'Plan B' in case something goes wrong."

"You mean wrong like this?" Aldo said, pointing to his notebook filled with hundreds of events from throughout the world detailing bizarre events of destruction aimed squarely at man and his crops, his ships, and his stranglehold on the planet.

"Yes, Aldo, wrong like that. There's a logical explanation for that stuff and I'm not heading back to a cave in fear."

"I need to throw up again."

Aldo excused himself and ran to the bathroom.

He stayed in there until the captain insisted that everyone get in their seats for landing.

The warning lights located by the passengers' heads flicked on as the smell of smoke wafted through the cabin. The fasten seat belt automatically turned on while two attendants sped through a series of checklists.

Aldo scurried back to his seat as the aroma hit the back of the plane.

"I smell smoke. Shit!" he yelled.

Lila grabbed his arm and pulled him close to her.

"Keep calm. It's probably nothing."

As Lila spoke, emergency lights flickered on the floor of the airplane. The lights alternated in a manner that passengers looking down would see arrows pointing to the closest emergency exit.

The airplane took a sharp turn to the left and sent Lila leaning into

Aldo. Her seatbelt kept her from falling into his lap. Aldo gripped the armrest so tight that his fingers were as white as his face. The airplane then overcompensated and swung back the other way as the pilot fought for control of the plane. Overhead compartments flew open and carry-on luggage hurtled at innocent targets. A laptop case with a medium-sized computer struck one passenger in the head. The plane began to steady and Lila could see the runway in the distance, off the right side of the plane.

The captain came on the intercom and informed his terrified passengers of the plane's status. "This is captain again. We're within a mile of the runway. There'll be one more big turn coming up. We'll be coming in fast. I'll have you folks down on the ground in a minute. I'd like you to assume emergency landing positions."

The smoke inside the cabin dissipated, but Lila peered out the window and saw smoke coming from engine three, closest engine to the cabin. There were two engines on the left side of the plane, and two on the right. She couldn't see what was happening with engine four because Aldo was in the way.

The plane dipped and a retching sound came from Lila's right. Aldo had vomited. The runway was ahead of them and the captain came back on the intercom. "Prepare for landing." There were no reassurances.

Lila recalled the Emergency Instruction Card located in the front seat pocket that she had seen all her life. She never imagined needing to recall the instructions… something about tucking her head between her legs as far as she could reach. She thought that was foolish. If she was going to die, then she wanted to see how it was going to happen. Instinctively she tucked her head away again, preparing for the impact of the plane smashing into the ground.

The captain had to using all his aeronautical skills to keep the airplane aloft. A grinding sound now reverberated throughout the cabin.

"What's that?" asked Aldo.

"It's got to be the landing gear," said Lila.

In a matter of a few seconds, the airplane's wheels smacked the ground, forcing the plane upward for a moment, and then back down to the ground. The airplane sailed past the gates at a high speed. They stopped 200 yards shy of the end of the runway. The emergency slide automatically opened and the passengers slipped from the plane. A majority of the passengers were unscathed, but a few of the crewmembers had noticeable wounds and received prompt attention from the emergency medical team.

Massey gathered his team at the base of the slide. He counted heads with his finger and was pleased that everyone was accounted for and, other than slight discoloration of Aldo's clothes, the parties appeared intact.

"Welcome to the Capital," said Massey.

CHAPTER 16

The bustling airport was full of businessmen heading from the Capital to destinations throughout the world. Planes took off and landed every minute, filling the air with the constant rumble of jet engines ripping through the sky.

Taft and his assistants were there to meet the weary travelers.

"Welcome, Dr. Massey, Dr. Jenkins, and you must be Mr. Gorrell. You folks certainly know how to make an impression. I trust your landing on the way back home will be less dramatic. I'm General Taft, and say... Gorrell, you look a little peaked."

The staff studied the general with amazement. Hadn't he seen their near-death disaster minutes earlier?

"Excuse me, Gen. Taft. We practically crash-landed here. Do you think we can have a few minutes to gather our thoughts?" asked Dr. Goldman. She wasn't over the stress of the landing.

"You're Dr. Goldman?"

She nodded.

"Doctor Goldman, let me tell you a thing or two about rough landings. Four years ago my pilot was shot dead right in front of me and the co-pilot picked a dreadful moment to have an anxiety attack. I had to land the plane myself. Would you care to hear the story how I crossed a river with enemy fire coming at me from both banks?"

"What's your point, general?" asked Goldman.

"Doctor, in moments of complete chaos, you must continue to

move forward, and that's exactly what we're going to do right now. Gorrell, how are you feeling, lad?" asked the general.

"I'm fine, sir. Perhaps a bit of that famous airline tummy, you know how it affects certain people. It was a bumpy ride, especially the landing." Aldo shot Lila a look, but she wasn't in the mood for laughter.

"Not me, Gorrell... stomach made of iron." The general patted his mid-section. "Too bad it's like my personality. If you don't believe me, ask my wife."

Aldo didn't speak.

"That was a joke, son," said the general.

Aldo feigned a smile. He was tired of being the brunt of everyone's jokes. Aldo noticed that Dr. Massey appeared perturbed. It was the face of embarrassment for his young assistant.

"I'm all right, sir. I'll grab the luggage," insisted Aldo.

"No need. It's in the limo. Why don't we get out of here and get to the hotel.

The group walked back to the black stretch limousine. General Taft led the way, keeping himself a few paces ahead of the rest.

The group of Massey, Lila, Goldman, Morales, Aldo, the general and his assistant entered the armored vehicle and sped away from the airport. An Army convoy escorted the group to the exit. Aldo looked out of the rear window and flipped the bird to the entire airport property.

Forty-five minutes later they were ushered into the capital's priciest hotel. The government had commandeered the building for the entire group of scientists from every country participating in the crisis. Massey, Jenkins and Gorrell were given suite 212. It featured three separate bedrooms, a small kitchen area, a living room area, and two bathrooms. The trio went to grab a quick lunch prior to the mandatory meeting scheduled for thirteen hundred hours. Aldo had regained his appetite and was ready to eat. Goldman had room 213, and Morales 215.

Taft greeted all the guests at an informal opening session that was designed to get the group comfortable with their new surroundings. Taft grabbed the microphone. "My name is General Taft and I'll be your host while you're guests in this facility. I'm not going to get into any details this afternoon. I want you folks to get a full night's rest. Tomorrow, we'll start early. We're in for a long day. I'm leaving documents for your review. These packets contain your security badge, important telephone numbers, etc…don't lose this stuff."

All parties present in the room acknowledged him in various forms of confirmations.

Massey, Lila, and Aldo met in their suite a few minutes after dinner. Lila tried to reach J.J. by telephone. The entire telephone network was out of order and she couldn't reach him.

Massey turned the key to the heavy wooden door and locked it. Then he clicked the dead bolt. Nobody was coming in without permission from Dr. Massey, who took this opportunity to fill in his roommates with new information.

"I have additional news about the situation back in Sanderell. I was told by an undisclosed source that the deceased man, Mr. Rothschild, was in charge of the Western Border Nuclear Power Plant Storage Facility where the nuclear waste was presumed to be held. My source also told me that Rothschild was way over budget and about to lose his job. So what does the idiot do? He farms out a tanker full of toxic nuclear waste to small-time fishermen, who were more than willing to take the barrels of waste into the middle of the ocean for a handsome sum of money. You may recall the story about the ship called *The Falcon* that sank during the storm a few weeks ago. All hands were lost, as were the hundreds of barrels of toxic waste and inexplicably, those were the barrels found in Sanderell. The barrels were on the damned *Falcon*.

"You mean 'damned' liked 'cursed', or just 'damn'?" asked Aldo.

"Does it matter?" Massey snapped.

"I guess not, I was wondering, that's all," said Aldo, his voice retreating.

"How long was Rothschild illegally dumping waste?" asked Lila.

"Nobody knows for sure. There's an ongoing investigation and it appears that he was dumping waste for years. This explains why he was given a multi-million dollar bonus for coming in under-budget three years in a row, at least until this year. It also helps explain large areas of the ocean being declared 'dead zones'. The consequences are incalculable. Remember that we'll be dealing with a lot of emotional people tomorrow. As an example, at least now we know why the barrels of toxic waste were close to shore. They weren't pushed 1,000 miles to shore by angry whales. These barrels were a few miles out to sea when the ship sank. Underwater currents helped push the barrels a little closer to shore."

Lila interjected, "I tell my students that there is a logical scientific explanation for things and now perhaps people will stop thinking the whales brought these barrels from the depths of the sea to the beachfront."

"Then why are we here? They could have issued a two-sentence press release and been done with it. We've seen the reports. There's more than toxic waste to deal with," said Aldo.

"Simple: the problem out there today and what could potentially develop in the future can't be addressed in a press release. We need real solutions, not a cosmetic face lift with the same old 'We're going to have to do something about it sometime' speech that the political parties stream out there at election time. The world is facing disastrous consequences. There's a lot more at stake than a few hundred dead whales."

Lila could sense another headache starting to develop. This one was above her left eye. She used the ball of her thumb to rub the affected area in a slow, circular rubbing motion. The steady pressure eased the pain a bit.

"You all right, Professor Jenkins?" asked Aldo.

"I'll be fine. It's a headache, not a toxic waste dump. I want to go back to this Rothschild character for a moment. Let's examine his background."

Aldo flipped through his color-coded charts of people, places and disasters. "I've got that. Hold on a sec… right here. Here it is. See; all the people are color-coded blue."

"Aldo, what can you tell us, not show us?" interrupted Massey.

"He was in way over his head. He used to work in the telecommunications field and then somehow landed this huge job at Western Border. He has—er—had assets in the millions. He earned a substantial amount of money from his job at DCE Communications. They did a lot of work with the government. Lots of no-bid contracts that brought them under surveillance from citizen groups and government watchdogs, etc…but nothing ever came of it, and eventually he left DCE and went to work at Western Border. He was married briefly, then divorced, never had kids or heirs to spend the money. Too bad for them; I could use it."

"That's enough commentary, Mr. Gorrell," fired Massey.

"The investigation is ongoing. My guess is this guy's been a dirty bastard for years and he killed himself to avoid public embarrassment. Who wants to be known as the cause for the single largest nuclear waste dump in the history of the planet? That's a lot of shit to have on one's head, huh?"

Dr. Massey concurred with Gorrell. "As you eloquently described, that's a 'lot of shit'."

Lila chipped back in with her two cents. "The guy was dirty, but that's not even half the story. If the world is in the middle of chaos, it's not all because of this guy Rothschild. Let's keep the goal of why we're here in mind, shall we? What can we do to help turn the tide and get things back to normal? Rothschild may help explain what happened at Sanderell Beach…What about everything else?"

"Agreed," said Massey. "Let's review our notes from General Taft. That may give us fresh ideas to bring to the meeting tomorrow. Why don't we review our documents, get some sleep, and we'll meet in the morning, say, fifteen minutes before the meeting?"

Massey, Jenkins, and Gorrell went to their respective rooms and spent the next several hours looking over a myriad of calamities, deaths, and scenes of destruction throughout the world that bordered in the bizarre, the weird and unexplainable.

CANAMITH COMMUNICATION DEPARTMENT

Update #233

Chemical Spill Kills 3,400

Poisonous gas seeped out of the Dragarian Chemical Company last night. The northeast wind blew the chemicals over the shantytown of Reedville. Residents had little chance against the odorless Methyl Isocynate. The dead are being stored at a local refrigeration plant until proper burials can be performed.

There has been no formal explanation for the leak, but Dragarian officials have confirmed that tiny holes were found in many of the containers along the eastern side of storage building number seven.

CHAPTER 17

The grand ballroom of the Capital Hotel encompassed the entire second floor. Hastily converted into a working area for the conference, the hotel staff had put up partitions allowing representatives of each country to work together without distracting the group next to them. Massey and his group were discussing things quietly in their cubicle when a voice echoed from the loudspeaker.

"Attention. Attention. Will the representatives proceed to the General Assembly meeting room in five minutes. Five minutes, please."

General Taft sat at the head table. Senator Leary and Dr. Massey sat on either side. Lila and Aldo sat at an adjacent table. The rest of the head table had other notable scientists. Lila recognized the top two viral experts in their field: Dr. Jonathan Carmen and his wife Dr. Gracey Lubitz. They sat at a nearby table with the world-renowned geneticist Brian McDivitt, and Roger Drake, who garnered fame and fortune as the world's most acclaimed telecommunication expert. Dr. Goldman and Dr. Morales sat with Massey, Lila, and Aldo. The room was filled with the best that academia had to offer. Each guest in the hotel was given an update on the world's disorder that morning.

Massey gathered his staff for a quick talk before the meeting started.

"General Taft didn't make a great first impression, but he rose to his lofty status by leading the Armed Forces to victories in the war against terrorist factions seven years ago. His clever use of force, computer technology and sheer guile were key elements that put a big dent in the terrorist network. The general told me that satellite imaging from our landing, in conjunction with the recordings from the black box in the airplane, confirmed that several large birds flew into engine number three and caused our mishap."

Massey continued, covering the rest of the head table. "I met Mr. Drake once or twice. He was instrumental in developing the computer systems that linked computer technology and the international telecommunications network. The advances in communications under Drake's leadership at the government's Technology Department pushed the science of telecommunications ahead years faster than any of his peers had thought possible. Establishing lines of communication will be important. We've got to set up the network configurations too. Drake is the man you want on your side. He has contacts throughout the modern world and has access to a vast set of resources that can cut through red tape. He has carte blanche to use whatever connections he has to assist us."

General Taft grabbed the microphone. "I want thank you for coming on such short notice. I'm confident the accommodations are to your liking. Please keep your credential badges with you at all times. It will get you anywhere in the hotel. The restaurant is staying open day and night. Computers are available in Conference Rooms A, B, and D. We've linked up the hotel database with the International Computer Communications Station. This will allow you to log into your computers in your country. I want to thank Mr. Drake and his staff at DCE for getting the systems up and ready. The entire room was synched up within minutes of my request. I think you'll be amazed at the resources you have at your fingertips. If there is anything that you need, don't hesitate to ask. Everybody on my staff is wearing these bright green lapel pins. It'll make it easier to find one of my people. You'll be able to find technical support here at any hour of the day. Let's move on.

"Each of you has a blue notebook. In it you will find a complete listing of the attendees at the conference. It's an incredible list of talented people. You'll find a brief synopsis of the crisis, as it stands today, on page one. Events are happening rather quickly these days, and if anything changes, and I'm sure it will, you'll be notified as soon as possible. It will take the hard work and dedication of all of us to solve this problem and I suggest we begin right away."

A modicum of applause rang throughout the room. A flurry of activity was about to begin.

Taft motioned to quiet the crowd by raising his long arms high in the air.

"You can see the 'status monitor' on the wall. Mr. Drake, is it ready? It is? Thank you. The monitor will keep you abreast of any incoming video feeds we receive from international and national news sources. They'll be transferred immediately to the data collection devices in your bag. That's a clever device, Roger. Thank you again for supplying those on short notice."

The monitor was approximately fifteen feet high and twenty feet wide.

"If you take a look to the left side of the monitor, you'll find several clocks that give the correct time across many time zones. You don't want to wake your spouse up in the middle of night."

A small chuckle and nodding heads greeted that remark.

Lila and Aldo watched Taft handle the crowd with aplomb.

"He can be firm when required, but he knows when to ease back on the throttle," said Lila.

Aldo agreed. "I betcha there aren't a lot of men who could step into this situation and keep their cool while the world is heading into madness."

Taft continued, "If you look on the right hand side of the screen you'll find a GPS system that will enable you to find any of your constituents and their exact location in the hotel. Each of you has your own coded number key card with a GPS tracking identification number embedded into the card. If that number on the screen is red, that indicates that you have left the perimeter of the building."

"Some of you have excursions scattered around the city. Dr. Massey and his famed ABC team are headed to the zoo. Dr. Stitt and his team are going to the hospital later today. Finish your business and then head straight back here. Please remember to return to the hotel as quickly as possible. Our resources are stretched to the max. This is the one place we can guarantee your safety."

Aldo whispered to Lila, "Oh, like the guarantee to get us here in one piece? We almost died… he can't guarantee squat."

Gen. Taft continued. "We've set up hospitality suites on floors two, four, and six for your comfort. Please, if you need to take a break, visit one of those areas for a few minutes. I think that covers the basics. If you have questions, and I'm sure you will, let one of my staff assistants help. Like I said, we've got computers, printers, maps, phones, and scanners, whatever you want. At this point I'm turning the meeting over to Dr. Carlin Massey, our distinguished animal behavior specialist. Dr. Massey, it's all yours."

A round of applause greeted Massey as he approached the podium.

Massey prepared his notes, reviewing them to make sure they were in the proper order. That gave Lila enough time to nudge Aldo.

"Did you read the biographies of people in this building? It says in there that Drake was from DCE. Drake and Rothschild? Working together? We should dig deeper into that relationship."

Aldo blistered away on his computer, searching for articles from his giant database that linked the two men.

Massey's voice interrupted his work. "Thank you, General Taft. Hello, ladies and gentlemen. The bizarre incidents started two years ago. At first, it was a few unusual events happening here and there. More recently, animals have been accused of premeditated attacks on man and our infrastructure. Disaster has worked its way around the globe. We've been unable to explain to the general public what is happening. They're afraid to leave their homes. Absenteeism is up twenty-five percent at work and thirty-three percent in the school systems throughout our country. These numbers are increasing daily and are a common problem throughout the world. Hospital admissions are up eighteen percent, and on and on. We must prevent a worldwide panic. We cannot have a population gripped with fear. We've seen the beginning stages of it. We must act quickly to preserve the flow of energy and food. Disruptions in a few key segments of our economy could mean a worldwide calamity of epic proportions. As an example of what we're dealing with, I'd like you to please focus your attention to the monitor. Mr. Drake, please start the video presentation… As you can tell, we're watching a horse race."

The monitor showed a slightly grainy film of the third race at an unnamed racetrack. At the halfway point of the race, the horses formed into two distinct groups. The four leaders bunched together, and led the second group of fillies by three or four lengths. A horse named Lucky Lady stole the lead by a nose and then threw her jockey. The miniscule man came to rest on the muddy turf. The other leading contenders followed suit and hurled their jockeys from their mounts. The trailing horses were close behind and stepped on the fallen men.

A groan went through the hotel as the crumbled bodies of the jockeys lay mangled on the ground. The videotape stopped as the camera zoomed in tight on Lucky Lady.

Lila turned to Aldo and whispered, "I could swear that horse was smiling."

CANAMITH COMMUNICATION DEPARTMENT

Update #264

Rampaging Animals Claim 38 Lives

Thirty-eight people were killed yesterday while they were watching the annual wildebeest migration in the grassy plain states.

Witnesses said that ten sightseeing buses were flattened during the annual movement of the black wildebeest. Numbering close to half a million animals, wildebeest migrations have been observed for years without incident. Scientists that spoke to the National News Network say the wildebeest is not an aggressive species and there are no records of such attacks previously.

One witness described the scene: "It was horrible. Those animals are huge and they made a low, groaning sound and some of them were snorting as they rampaged through us. They rammed right into the side of the buses! Can you believe that? Our bus tipped over and the next wave of them trampled over us. I climbed under the seat for protection. The man next to me got a hoof right in the stomach, tore him open…went right through him. I'm sure he's dead."

CHAPTER 18

The forty members that made up the conference participants buckled down to the work at hand while gulping down fresh muffins and coffee. While the video monitors and press reports rushed in from around the world with more devastating news each hour, Massey's group veered from their job at hand and began arguing about science and faith.

Lila loved to discuss these matters. Nettled by her peers' inability to see her point of view, she continued to drive home the scientific point of view with Dr. Goldman.

"But, doctor," Lila said, "we've had problems before. We've had great minds sit down and discuss them until we establish a clear, concise cause for the crisis, then man adapts his technology and resources to fix the problem. I don't see where 'faith' or 'belief' comes into play."

"Professor, do you think it always works that way?" countered Goldman. "How do you explain the miracles that are reported on the news? I've seen television reports where a child is found alive after being buried in the rubble of a flattened building for days. Or when a horrific storm sweeps in and sends debris flying everywhere and the wind picks up a small baby, and tosses the poor innocent youth upwards and then hurtles the child down to the ground and the child lives, sometimes without a scratch. Do you think science can explain that?" asked Dr. Goldman.

They drew a crowd as they traded ideas and philosophies. Neither woman allowed herself the possibility of being incorrect.

"Dr. Goldman, I understand what you're saying, but isn't it more likely that if you, and please forgive the ghastly analogy, but you were the one to bring it up, isn't it possible that if you place enough babies in the path of storms of the magnitude that you described, once in a while, using the scientific method, or as I would say, 'All Things Explainable', that one baby would survive? And out of ten of those babies, one might be fortunate enough to withstand the storm, the debris field, and come through without a mark on his or her precious little derriere?"

"Professor, I can't deny you the possibility that your scenario could occur…I choose not to believe it would happen that way. It's too much of a reach, even for me."

"Dr. Goldman, do you give credence to the thought of a 'higher power' protecting the child we described?"

"Absolutely, professor. Failure to allow that possibility is as foolish as you insisting it must be explainable. I'm not saying which one of us is right. I'm giving you another viewpoint for you to look at the world through. I'm a woman of science myself and I can accept that there are many forces in the world. Science is one of them. What about love? Is that science? You don't have to be raised by the intelligentsia to understand these concepts. Millions of people are clinging to their faith and praying for us to help them. What if we made an announcement that we are stumped? No solutions. Good night everyone and good luck. You better have a couple of hundred cans of food in your pantry and a few thousand gallons of water stashed away somewhere too! Oh, and you better not get sick, because you won't be able to find a doctor anywhere, and your medications will not be available anymore either. Can't we consider 'prayer' a viable choice in this desperate hour?"

"That's a bleak picture you painted, doctor," said Dr. Morales. "Do you think that's where we're headed?"

"That's an unequivocal 'yes'. If we can't stop the degradation of the food supply, the rest of my message is moot. You can't live if you can't eat," replied Dr. Goldman.

Lila was unfaltering in her beliefs. She shook her head. "No. No. No. I'm not buying your argument. You can't sit here today and make those doom and gloom predictions based on today's information. I'm telling you—I'm telling all of you—there's a scientific reason why this is happening! And we're going to figure it out. My daughter is counting on me. Do you know what Sophie asked me as I left the house?" Nobody ventured a guess, not even Aldo, although Lila expected one of his poorly timed attempts at wit. She pressed on without waiting. "She said, 'Mommy, I want to be a mommy someday. Do you promise you can fix the world?' I'm determined not to let my kid down. I don't know about the rest of you. You have the right to your own opinion about my views or Dr. Goldman's, but I didn't fly here to discover the best solution we can come up with is to pray that a higher power 'spares us' because he or she thinks we're worth saving. If there is a higher power, perhaps that entity has instilled in us the knowledge to fix this. I'm counting on myself to do the best I can. I'll take a little help from anywhere, but my ship sails with the belief that we *will* fix this, not the man or woman up in the sky."

Dr. Goldman looked at Lila with disdain. "I guess we'll have to wait and see what happens."

"Folks, I'm sorry to interrupt the discussion." Taft made his way into the area: clean boots, pressed uniform, and tightly fitted cap, complete with decorations of valor earned from conflicts with other humans, not nature.

Drake stood and grabbed the General's hand and gave it a firm squeeze.

"General, we're going to do our best," said Drake. "We won't let you down. I'm flattered that you've included me in this prestigious ABC team of yours from the west coast. I anticipate being a vital cog, as the 'D' in the group will make things happen."

Lila, Goldman, and Morales weren't aware that Drake assumed he was part of the team. When Drake said that he was the 'D' in the group, it showed his unfamiliarity with their accomplishments.

"I trust you all slept well?" asked the general. He didn't break his thought to listen or look for an answer and pressed, "I'm glad to see we're here ready to go. Very well then, finish your breakfast and I'll be in touch during the day." He held up a folder. "Here is your briefing for today. Call me if you find out anything interesting or make any breakthroughs."

"Absolutely, general. Right away, sir," said Drake.

The general exited the building and hopped back into his truck. The large blue envelope that Taft had set on the table waited for someone to open it. Every member of the team stared at the envelope like it was the check from an expensive restaurant and nobody seemed too interested in picking it up. Drake, the oldest member of the team, was still contemplating grabbing it when Morales swept in. He chuckled a bit when Drake's lame half-hearted attempt to grab the package came up empty.

"Ah, Mr. Drake, let's hope your mind is sharper than your reflexes."

Dr. Massey made two loud attempts to clear his throat before speaking.

"Pardon me, this dang throat of mine. I see we have disagreements. I'd prefer we set our different philosophies aside and work as a cohesive unit."

Nods from around the table gave Massey his opening. Morales hadn't opened the briefing package and decided to hand it over.

Massey grabbed the envelope and carefully opened the top, then pulled out several sheets of crisp paper neatly placed in a clear plastic binder. He reached in a second time and found a duplicate copy. "I guess the powers that be don't have much confidence in us not to misplace the original. They must know you, Aldo."

Lila shot Aldo a glance of reassurance, but Aldo had grown used to the insults. He barely blinked.

"Joking, son," said Massey, trying to cut the tension, but it didn't work. "At 10:00 a.m., the transport vehicle takes us to Capital Zoo for a review of animal behavior and study of collected tissues. It's already a few minutes shy of ten. I have a feeling it's going be an interesting day at the zoo."

CHAPTER 19

Four weeks ago, the screeching of the tires pulling into the zoo would have sent guests fleeing for safety. The park had closed two weeks ago. A skeleton crew maintained the bare essentials to keep the animals alive. There was no direct interaction with any of the animals. Food was tossed into the cages from a safe distance and zoo officials forbade entrance into any cage, for any reason. Flowers once decorated the pathways between habitats. The fragrance permeating in the zoo today was feces and urine emanating from the cages.

The first stop for the team was the chimpanzee habitat. Six months ago, the entire living quarters of the chimps were transferred from the southern part of the zoo to the northern end. Several of the oldest chimps had stopped eating. They were gaunt and their odds of survival were slim.

Lila made the first observation. "A move from one side of the park to another may not seem like much of a change. Humans change habitats from time to time. We move to a new apartment, or a new house, or even move the furniture around in the house we're living in, but for these animals, some of them had been living in the same spot for years, and it can be traumatic. The sights, the sounds, especially the smells of their old habitat are gone."

Aldo forgot the suggestion about not speaking much and blurted, "My grandmother had a heck of a time adjusting to her retirement home. She lived in her old house on Blanche Avenue for forty-six years."

"That's right, Aldo. Older people are especially sensitive to a change in their living areas, or their habitat."

Drake rolled his eyes with boredom and then stole a glance at his wristwatch. Lila chose to disregard him and continued. "There are new sounds, smells, the view of the rest of the zoo is different, everything has changed, and it's not surprising that these older chimps require time to adjust to their new setting."

"I agree with, Professor Jenkins. It can take time… but according to the report we received, even the younger animals are acting with peculiarity," said Goldman.

Lila nodded. "That's because they are taking their cues from the elders in the group. Our species acts in a similar manner. How often do you see an old person who has lived in their home for decades and after you ship them off to an assisted living dwelling and they lose their zest for life? They seem depressed, and when their children come to visit, they're despondent on their way home, wondering if they have done more harm than good by moving their loved one. It's the same thing in the animal world. Somebody had a great idea to move these animals, and now look at them."

"That's true, but what about the rest of the zoo?" asked Dr. Goldman.

"I guess that's why we're here," said Lila. "To try and figure it out."

Morales peered around the grounds. He raised his right hand and blocked the sun from distracting his view of the area.

"It's beautiful," he said, "but it's all wrong. It's too quiet. The animals aren't making any sounds. Listen."

The team sat still while a minute passed without a sound. No birds, no elephants, no people.

They loaded into the zoo tram vehicle, and toured the green, lavish grounds, but none of them had ever visited a zoo that was this quiet.

They passed the lion habitat. One of males, lying on his side, his mane matted down with dirt, opened one eye and sat motionless as the group went by.

"Keep driving," said Aldo. "He looks hungry!"

"Don't worry. We're not stopping till we get to the lab. That's where I am expecting to review the tests I requested from the staff here," said Dr. Goldman.

As they entered the laboratory, one of the zoo assistants greeted Dr. Goldman with her requested materials. "Thank you. Hey, guys, I'm going to find a quiet spot in the back of the building somewhere and review the documents."

Morales got to work aligning his portable microscope to take a peek at the slides the zoo had prepared for him. "Hey, wait a minute, doc, let me come with you. I'll be quiet as a… hey, I'll be as quiet as this entire zoo!" Morales joined Goldman and that left Drake hanging around looking for a task.

"I'm afraid this is not my field of expertise," said Drake. "I'll give it go. Whatever you need, please, just ask."

Massey cleared his long-suffering throat. "Mr. Drake, you're an invaluable member of this team. Why don't you take a walk around the park? We'll be here for a while studying various animal behaviors. Can you get a sense of how the animals are acting differently using your communication skills, not the technology side of it, but the human side? We tend to look at everything as science and everything must have an explanation. Correct, Professor Jenkins?"

"Definitely; you know my motto: 'All Things Explainable'. I couldn't think of a better test of that theory than right here."

"My point, Mr. Drake, is that precisely because you are a man of technology, not science, at least not science in the manner in which we refer to it, you bring a refreshing view of the situation."

"Thanks for the vote of confidence, Dr. Massey. I'll do that. Do you mind if I take your assistant with me?"

Aldo looked up, shocked.

"Any objections, Aldo?" asked Massey.

Aldo thought about his answer for a millisecond. "No, sir. I'll be happy to show him around. I grew up not far from here. I know this park like the back of my hand. Tell me what you want to see and I'll lead the way. I think the layout of the park is the same as I recall from my youth—except for the chimps."

"Thank you for stating the obvious, Aldo," mocked Massey with more than a touch of sarcasm.

Massey called out to them as they prepared to the leave the safety of the room and head outside. "Gentleman, don't you want to take the security guard with you?"

"Nope, I think he's outside in the truck. Let him be," boasted Drake, acting the part of the macho man he aspired to be, but seldom was.

"Maybe we should listen to the doctor, Mr. Drake," said Aldo. "You know we're not invincible out there."

Drake rendered Aldo's point moot when he grabbed the young man by the arm and the two made a quick exit out the door.

CHAPTER 20

"I loved coming to the zoo when I was a kid," said Aldo. "We used to get one day off a year from school to come here. That was a treat. I'd stare at the lions for an hour. They never moved. I used to make funny faces and try to get them to acknowledge me. They never did. The zoo was so loud back then. Today, I don't hear anything."

"There used to be people here. It's a ghost town now," said Drake.

They headed north fifty yards to the newest attraction called "Wolves of the Wild". The buildings were covered in a brownish straw material designed to look old. There was nothing "wild" about the wolves living in this area. Three of the four-legged creatures could be seen sleeping by the water station. One of the wolves poked his head up for a moment when he saw them scoot past the wooden slotted gates protecting the two parties from direct contact. The other animals didn't acknowledge the visitation and kept sleeping. The sign at the front of the habitat indicated that there were six wolves. Aldo thought they must have been hiding inside one of the structures.

Gorrell and Drake slid past the wolves and into the oldest section of the park. "Monkey Island" was a ridiculous name and design for the small howler monkeys. They were banished to the far end of the park because of their aptly placed name. Their howl-like sound carried over long distances in the wild. Here, in the park, large sound dampening devices were strategically placed to disperse the noise. While the visitors were near the monkeys, however, the sound could be deafening. This single feature of the "howler" annoyed even ardent animal lovers. When the crowds thinned over the years at this spot of the park, management had become slipshod in maintaining the habitat. Brown and red howlers spent their time sitting around waiting for action.

"Not much happening here," said Drake.

Aldo saw the despicable conditions and shook his head in disgust. "I bet they would give up those big voices for a few acres in a rain forest."

Drake stopped. He snapped his head around, scanning the area.

"What's wrong?" asked Aldo.

"Something…. I can't put my finger on it. It's an odd sensation, like we're being watched."

"We are, Mr. Drake, by dozens of little monkeys."

"No, not them. Something else," he said with force. "It's out there." Drake waved his hand towards the middle of the zoo, in a northwest direction.

"Let's get back to the group. We don't have to achieve hero status today. I learned a valuable lesson."

"What did you learn?"

"I learned I'm more comfortable in an office environment. Come on, let's pick up the pace. This place is freaking me out."

The two members of the team left the monkeys and were heading back down the same path that had brought them in front of the wolves. As they cleared the wooden gates, Drake stopped short.

"Hold it. Don't move, Aldo."

"What's wrong?"

"It's the gates. The middle pieces are gone. These animals could leap right through that opening. Remember, we saw four of the six wolves. Let's go slow and keep quiet. If those two other wolves are out here, I wouldn't want to be us right now."

"Haven't years in captivity diminished their hunting skills?"

"Perhaps, but an animal is still an animal. There was a reason they closed this place and it wasn't because people weren't buying tickets or little Billy's third grade class cancelled their annual field trip. You want to get real up close and personal with a wolf and ask if he'd like to tear a hunk of your flesh out of your leg?"

"I see your point."

Drake gently lifted his foot an inch or two off the ground and then cautiously brought his rear foot forward and placed that foot down gingerly. Drake looked like he was stepping on an egg but trying not to break it. Every few steps, one of the men would miscalculate the ground beneath them and step on a wayward twig or branch that had haphazardly blown astray from the rich brown-mulched woods. The grounds crew was sent home two weeks ago, and with nobody to tidy up the park, pathways and walkways beneath were starting to show signs of neglect.

Snap. Aldo's left foot met the center cross-section of another branch.

"Shhhh! Be careful, man!" whispered Drake.

"Sorry, I thought I had it cleared."

Drake's pace increased as they left the front of the wolves' area and saw the final turn in the road that would take them back to the laboratory.

The next sound they heard was unmistakable. The cry of a howler monkey resonated all the way to the walkway. This was no ordinary cry. It sounded strangled. This monkey let out a low grunting gasp of monkey sound and then a gurgling sound followed. Then silence. Then the shrieks of the entire group of monkeys carried all the way back to the lab.

As Aldo and Drake made the last turn, they saw Lt. Branley rushing at them.

"Look out!" he yelled.

Aldo turned and saw two wolves running full speed no more than thirty yards behind him and gaining fast with each stride. Aldo turned back towards Lt. Branley and hustled, arms flailing back and forth, feet slightly pointed outward while he covered the path with increasing fear. Drake kept losing ground to the four-legged creatures that were designed for one purpose: chasing prey. Drake and Gorrell were now within fifty yards of the lab. Neither man had the speed to outrun the wolves. Each animal, with their tongues shifting from one side of their mouths to the other, spit flying, and their teeth glistening in the morning sun, were poised to attack.

Wolf Number One, as Drake called him later, closed to within nine feet and then the communication expert heard something whiz by his left ear.

"Shit! What was that?"

The growling of the Wolf Number One stopped. A second rush of air flew by them. They saw Lt. Branley shoulder his weapon, smoke rising from the rifle that fired two direct hits at the oncoming attackers.

Aldo and Drake continued sprinting back to the lab, despite the pleas of the lieutenant for them to ease up. The military sharpshooter raised his hands high in the air and motioned for them to slow down, but neither man was convinced that their backsides were free from being consumed as part of a wolf "all-you-can-eat" buffet breakfast.

"What in the hell were you two doing out there?" shouted Lt. Branley.

"We were... ah, trying... to, ah... get a..." said Aldo, his lungs desperate for life saving oxygen. He was unable to finish his sentence.

Lieutenant Branley chided the men while they caught their breath.

"If you two thought you could meander around and enjoy the serenity of nature, you were erroneous!" His voice rose in anger as he continued to badger their extemporaneous unguided tour at the zoo.

"Apparently, you didn't get the memo. I was sent on this little journey here with you to protect you and I go to my truck for one minute and you two are gone? You better thank your lucky stars that I won the gold medal for accuracy in sharpshooter training! Mr. Drake, that wolf could practically taste the shit coming out of your ass. You're one lucky son of a bitch. And Mr. Gorrell, let's say it was fortunate that the animal got mired in a mud puddle, or you would have stitches halfway around your body."

The two men, huffing and puffing, chests heaving, walked in front of Lt. Branley. The rest of the team, who had followed Branley's explicit instructions and stayed in the laboratory while he went to find them, greeted them.

A thousand questions peppered Drake and Gorrell, but they weren't listening to any of it. All they did was commend the virtues of Lt. Branley and thanked him that he had outstanding tutelage at the Military Academy.

"He saved our butts, literally, that's for sure," Aldo said.

"I'll second that," piped Drake.

Branley raised his arms in that motion that meant everyone should shut up.

"Listen up, people. If I can't trust you to listen to me for a minute, then we're going to have more problems. If I need to use the restroom and can't trust you to stay inside, then I'll do my business right here on the floor, even in front of the ladies. If you leave the building, I must go with you. No exceptions."

Morales tried to calm the furor over that possible scenario and changed the subject. "Outside the part about getting eaten alive, how was it?"

The team broke into spontaneous laughter.

"If we can get our two happy wanderers to stay in the lab, we can finish our work here before we contact General Taft."

A group of nodding heads took their places back at their respective areas of the lab and went back to work.

"I'm afraid we don't have much to report to Gen. Taft," said Massey.

"Hey, we have forty minutes before we leave. I'm anxious to hear what Goldman comes up with. Don't give up the ship yet. We've got to keep our spirits up," said Lila to her skeptical boss.

Goldman was in the rear of the lab, experimenting with noxious odors. An advanced science degree wasn't needed to identify the horrible smell of animal feces. She worked the microscope adeptly, changing slides, adjusting the view, with Morales to assist her. Goldman peered through all the slides and samples. She doffed her pink and green hat and tossed it away.

"What is it?" Massey asked.

"You'll hear it in my report." She didn't look pleased. In fact, the downward tilt of her eyebrows gave her a surly look that made it easy for the rest of the team to avoid eye contact with her.

Lieutenant Branley's phone rang. He answered before it rang twice. He listened to the caller, and then handed the phone to Dr. Massey.

"General Taft, sir," he said.

"Hello, General. Massey here. Our report is ready for you, sir. I'll hook up the video link."

Branley assisted Drake and within a moment, a video feed was connected showing General Taft's face on the seventeen-inch monitor that sat on the largest of the three desks in the lab.

"General, can you see us?"

"Your image is fuzzy around the edges. The picture is dark, but I can hear you crystal clear."

Drake fidgeted with the controls and the image became sharper and the tints and hues fell into the proper range. "General, Dr. Goldman will go first."

"Hello, general. I've made an exhaustive search of the slides left for me here. I haven't found any abnormalities. It's similar to what we've heard from other specialists. I'm expecting new computer reports from the east coast, but I'm sure we're not looking at a disease that the animals have contracted. Every species and sub-species we've analyzed is falling within usual parameters. I'm sorry I don't have any more to report."

"That's not a surprise. Other people are making the same findings. Nothing out of the ordinary. Keep working on it." Taft sounded disappointed.

Drake went next. "General, here's a quick assessment of the situation. The animals are not showing signs of species to species communication. Remove the howler monkeys and it's deathly quiet here."

"Okay," said the General. "Next."

Morales took a turn at the microphone.

"General, I've studied the animals at the cellular level and I think that's where this baby is headed. I can't put my finger on it, but I do see a potential breakthrough in my analysis of the fine outer casing that protects the cell wall. The slightest change in the environment can lead to changes in the cellular properties of those tissues. I'm going to need to review more samples. I'd like to borrow Dr. Goldman, if that's okay with the good doctor?"

Goldman was taken by surprise and her initial reaction was a negative one, but before she could verbalize her dissent, Taft had issued a new directive placing her at Morales's disposal.

"No objections on my end. I trust Dr. Goldman will be happy to assist you."

"There are avenues I would like to explore on my own and I think that—"

Taft cut her off. "Fine. Then I trust you'll do everything in your power to help Dr. Morales in his work. We have dozens of researchers looking at multiple diseases. Our top people are doing exhaustive research on live animals and we've gone to town on the dead ones too. Necropsy results are inconclusive thus far."

Aldo muttered to Lila off camera. "Yeah, there are lots of available whales for necropsy."

Taft continued. "Dr. Goldman, do what you can to help Dr.

Morales. Jenkins, what do you have for me? I want to tell the President we're making progress."

Lila's mind drifted back to when she was sitting on the mountain with her father years ago. She couldn't have been more than eight or nine years old and she was sitting next to her father, high in the mountains, watching the white puffy clouds roll on by. They were playing her favorite game. Looking at the clouds and imagining the shapes of the clouds were animals.

Lila found a cloud that was shaped like a horse. Rex never saw the horse. He said her horse looked like a "Slippery" bird. Rex explained that Man had killed off the species by over-hunting and now they can be seen in pictures at the library. He taught Lila what the word "extinct" meant and how many different animals had lived and died in the past and more animals would disappear from the planet during her lifetime.

She went back to her room later that night and cried for two straight hours before exhaustion put her to sleep.

The booming voice of Gen. Taft snapped her back into real-time and she didn't know if she had been daydreaming for a second, or sixty. "Professor Jenkins, I haven't got all day."

Lila narrowed her focus on the small camera located at the top of the computer and was succinct with the general. "You are keenly aware of my belief in following protocol when it comes to forming opinions about the tests I run at the university. The scientific theory will win in the end. We haven't worked our way through the entire equation. Think of this as a football game, and we're in the first quarter."

"DAMMIT, Jenkins!" interrupted the General. "This is not a game. Is that clear? I have my reasons why I insisted that you be part of this team. I expect better answers from you."

He paused, took a deep breath, and tried to encourage the famed ABC Team once more.

"Look, I get it. You've given up a lot. I'm as concerned about global panic as I am global warming. Hey, you folks are the brightest minds we have. You have my complete confidence. The future of our butts doesn't look too promising if you don't stop giving me that scientific rhetoric and start producing specific reasons why every animal, insect, and organism on the planet is acting so damn strange."

"I understand. Please, I wasn't trying to avoid the answer. We haven't had much luck with our usual methodology. We're not shrinking from our task, I promise you that, general. We need more time."

Taft stared into the camera for a moment. Lila felt his gaze run right through her body.

"Professor, if I know anything in this crazy world right now, it's that you're doing everything in your power to help. I'll meet you folks back at the hotel later today. If you have anything for me, have the lieutenant call me right away. Good bye."

The lights on the camera faded to black. Lila exhaled and felt the stress flow from her body. "That was not enjoyable. I've never been dressed down like that before. What did he expect? Taft sends us here to get answers and what did we find?" she asked.

"That I could be a world class sprinter!" shouted Gorrell.

"Let's get back to work," Lila said.

"Sure, boss," replied Aldo.

The team spent the next two hours reviewing files, slides, autopsy reports, running computer simulations, and various scientific experiments. The lone sound coming from outside was the constant screaming of the howler monkeys.

When the team headed back to the hotel, Lila sat next to the driver. Her headaches were a common occurrence, but the work level prevented her from dwelling on them. She convinced herself that today's headache was due to stress and those damn monkeys. They headed back to the hotel on the abandoned highway.

Lila found herself homesick. She missed Sophie. She wondered what was happening back in Sanderell and in Canamith. She knew from her youth that they were preparing for the ultimate worldwide disaster. Was this it? Her emotions ran the entire gamut from frustration at her lack of progress at the zoo, to the guilt of leaving Sophie and J.J.

She wasn't prepared to succumb to the beliefs of others in the world that science would not rule the day and she would ultimately prove that the strange occurrences of the times were perfectly explainable. She hadn't figured it out, but she remained adamant in her beliefs.

She broke the silence on the way home with a brief speech that was brimming with confidence.

"I realize what we're seeing and reading in the news. It's easy to blame somebody for this. Man, Nature, God, your neighbor, heck, anybody can stand on the highest mountain and shout down to a scared populace, 'Hey, run for the hills! You're all doomed!' For years, whenever science is confronted with an unexplained problem, we study, test, re-test and eventually solve the problem. The scientific community has risen to the challenge to explain any unsolved phenomenon. That's what we do."

Drake didn't appear too impressed with her soliloquy. "That was a wonderful lecture. Do your students sit back and listen to that? Because you're preaching to the choir, sweetheart."

Lila cringed when she heard Drake refer to her as 'sweetheart'. She abhorred his patronizing way and would have none of it.

"Mr. Drake, I'm not your sweetheart!"

"Sorry, I didn't mean anything by it. Forgive me. I work in a different environment than you do. My tools are optical fibers and microcomputer chips. I say you are looking in the wrong places."

"What do you mean?" asked Dr. Massey.

Drake continued, "Look, there are people a whole lot smarter than me who have analyzed every animal in the world, right?"

The group nodded in agreement.

"And they've come up with nothing. Until we come up with solid scientific evidence, we leave ourselves open to other interpretations of the situation. Now, my field of expertise is communication. Somehow these animals are communicating with each other. We didn't see it in the zoo, but perhaps in the real world there are examples we should look at. We see animals communicate during fires and earthquakes."

Dr. Goldman joined the fray.

"The animals have a sense of self-preservation, Mr. Drake. The squirrel doesn't say to the rabbit, 'Hey, the forest is on fire, buddy, you better run.'"

"Ahh, exactly my point. We don't know what is happening in those moments of panic. Are you sure that Nature hasn't designed another way for creatures to communicate? Why do we believe and acknowledge that humans have non-verbal communication but we refuse to give a squirrel the same right?"

Morales didn't budge from his long-taught beliefs. "Mr. Drake, their brains are too small. If you would spend the years we spent pouring over research you'd see that—"

Drake's voice rose as he interrupted Dr. Morales. "And yet, doctor, here we are. We're on our way home from an empty zoo that should be filled with the wonderful sound of children. They were enjoying the manner in which we have kidnapped animals and placed them in a park for us to stare at them and toss peanuts at them for our amusement."

Aldo piped up next. "Hey, Mr. Drake, excuse me, sir, but there's a lot of reasons for having zoos. I started coming here when I was a kid and—"

Drake discounted the comment and was about to continue speaking when Dr. Goldman asked him a question.

"You think it's multi-species inter-communication? I think your forest fire example is a poor one. That's the sort of mob mentality that humans use. Ten people turn around and stare at the ceiling and before you know it, everyone in the room is straining their necks to see what is on the ceiling. One animal starts to run, then another, and another, and in a flash you'd be in the middle of a stampede. You are trying to interpret that as group communication. The animals are being frightened into knowing their life will end if they don't flee."

"Dr. Goldman, we have the right to disagree, but what about the insects?" asked Drake.

Before the Lila could speak, the truck lunged to the left, narrowly missing a huge hole in the ground. The driver regained control amid shouts of "What the heck was that?" and "What's going on up there?"

"Sorry, folks. I thought in our best interest I should avoid driving into a crevasse," said the driver.

Lieutenant Branley steadied the vehicle, and chipped in with his own perspective. "All you fancy folk with your advanced science degrees, have you speculated that nature is not causing the problems? What if this the work of Man? Evil men that want to kill innocent lives to gain control of the planet. There are people who would love to get the chance to run the world. Many countries in the world resent the way we have consumed so much of the world's resources."

Goldman asked the million-dollar question. "Are you suggesting that this is the work of a terrorist organization? Who could do this?"

"Why? To rebuild the world—a New World Order, if you will. A chance for the starving masses to perceive this person, or group, as a demigod who can save them from destruction," said Morales.

Lila, rearranging her backpack from the tumultuous veer to the left, couldn't wait to answer. "That may be true, but then that just reinforces what we're saying. If there is such a man, or country, and they've figured out a way to use animals against us: find them, soldier. That's your job. Let us do ours."

"General Taft is a personal friend of mine and there's no way he'd have us on a wild goose chase if they thought this was an act of terrorism," expounded Drake.

"Mr. Drake, with all due respect, if Gen. Taft is as good as soldier as he has been proclaimed, then he's following orders," said Dr. Goldman.

"Fair enough, Dr. Goldman, but I don't see him falling in line to that degree."

"We're not sure what he knows, or what he doesn't," Dr. Massey added.

"Look, you can believe what you want. I don't think there's a group out there telling swarms of bees to attack people driving their cars, or convincing dogs to stop playing fetch and start biting Timmy on the leg."

"Or little Sophie?"

"Huh?" asked Drake.

"We shall see, Mr. Drake. We shall see," Lila said.

CANAMITH COMMUNICATION DEPARTMENT

Update #303

Bees Ruin Festival; One Dead, Many Injured

A swarm of female honeybees, numbering in tens of thousands, escaped their hives today and flew in mass to the nearby town of Nordonia. The small suburban city on the east coast was celebrating Apple Festival, a local tradition honoring the 100th birthday of town founder, and apple expert Albert C. Sydenberg.

Local officials don't know how the bees escaped, but speculate they were attracted to the town by the strong smells emanating from the apple festival. Upon the bees' arrival, local children panicked, exciting the bees and they began stinging children and adults. People fled for cover and the event was cancelled. Sixty-six children were taken to the hospital, where three children remain in critical condition. Twenty-seven adults were also admitted, and sadly, a sixty-year-old man has succumbed to his numerous stings. His name is not being released until authorities can notify his next of kin.

CHAPTER 21

The hotel lobby was filled with uniformed men. Not all of them were military personnel.

Lila and Aldo spotted three men from Dead Insects Incorporated. "What's going on?" she asked.

Edgar Watkins was the oldest of the men, resplendent in white cotton scrubs and bright green nametag that identified him as Vic. He failed to respond to the question and didn't look up. He continued spraying the unique concoction of ingredients that made Dead Insects a profitable and highest-rated bug-killing franchise of the year.

"Don't breathe this stuff, lady. It'll tear your throat up. Be careful. Don't get it on your clothes neither. It'll burn a hole right through 'em. You won't notice it for a week or two, and then you'll forget you were exposed to the stuff, but there will be a hole. You might as well toss'em in the trash when you get home."

"What's in the canister?" asked Lila.

Edgar spun the purple and black cylinder clockwise so the label could be read. He removed his glasses and squinted as he tried to get the cylinder to the right distance from his glasses in order to read the microscopic printing on the two feet long container. His arms and glasses imitated a man playing the slide trombone.

"Let's see now. What's in this, you asked? Hold on, missy, you'll have to forgive me, it's my second day on the job and you're the first person that's asked that question. I bought the franchise last week and if you can keep a secret and promise not to tell. I'm not on the schedule for doing this job. The uniform says *Vic*, ya see? My name is Edgar. My brother Vic is on the schedule today, but we're busy with the infestations. He asked me if I could fill in for him. He's working at the Science Center. I'm glad I'm not there. He called and told me the place is overrun. Gross. I'm lucky that I lost weight or this uniform wouldn't even fit. It's tight, but for a day or two it'll do. He's giving me cash under the table. Hey, you don't work for the government, do you?"

Lila shook her head. "No Edgar, or Vic, or whoever you are. I work for a college on the west coast. I teach science, I'm not in the tax department. Your secret is safe with me, but I do want to know what you're spraying all over the place."

"Oh, yeah, hold on, let's see…Chronomaglio, oh, er, ah, I guess the label is worn away. There sure are a lot of these big red X's all over the tube. You don't want to see that if you're a bug. Excuse me, ma'am, I gotta finish the hallway and then I'm going outside and grab me a smoke."

"Nasty habit. It'll kill you someday," said Aldo.

Edgar was too busy soaking down the hallway to notice that Lila had walked away and headed down the opposite hallway in search of General Taft.

Wearing a jet-black overcoat, General Taft had entered the hotel through the revolving glass front doors. The doors let in a pinch of the panic that was forming in the streets. The people were glued to their television sets hoping to hear a glimmer of encouraging news from the conference. The networks suspended all regular programming. A search of the archives would find a repeat of a sporting event or a kid's TV show. Movies ran at cineplexes to empty theatres and comedy clubs shut down until further notice. Local news stations tried to fill as much of the day as they could with pre-recorded programs. "Taste of the Town", a longtime favorite cooking show, was cancelled due to the sensitivity regarding the dwindling food supply. Even the larger television markets were shutting down for the middle part of the afternoon. Advertising had all but stopped as companies slashed their budgets as business plummeted.

Companies like Mountain Retreats and One Stop Nature were doing a brisk business. These companies sold camping gear, portable gas stoves, tents, and miscellaneous products used for roughing it outdoors. The economy was sliding into the abyss. The futures market for food and grains had skyrocketed. Prices reached an all-time high and speculators couldn't go any higher on bids. The suppliers couldn't guarantee delivery of their products. Insurance companies closed. They couldn't keep up with the new claims from farmers who saw their inventory dwindle. The initial fears of a worldwide food panic grew. The government had tried to reassure people that everything was all right, but it wasn't. A quick trip to the grocery store proved whether the government was telling the truth. Many grocery stores were down to bare shelving. The run on canned goods, water, and consumables was frightening.

Taft deftly avoided the press. He ducked quickly into the first hallway near the reception desk and wiped his brow with the old, tattered handkerchief that his father had given to him on the occasion of the general's wedding day. With each washing, the beige piece of the cloth lost more and more of the original bright brilliant white color it was manufactured with. There were slight tears in the fringes of the material, but Taft used it as if was right out of the store packaging. He was meticulous in the manner in which he folded the handkerchief back into the right amount of squares, making sure it fit back into his breast pocket as neatly as it had been removed. Taft had made his mark as a soldier, but he was sentimental at heart.

Taft carried the tattered note he wrote when he first met his wife. The soon-to-be lovebirds were avoiding the lecture at the Institution on Foreign Affairs. Taft was walking the hallways, checking his watch periodically to see when he would be free from this obligation and he could continue on with the rest of the day. His mother had insisted he come to the lecture because the head of the department promised that she'd be allowed to ask a question during the audience participation section of the lecture. She wanted her son to witness it.

His future wife Elizabeth had been roped into going because her mother insisted that she be seen in places where intelligent people went for sophisticated learning, not bars and restaurants.

Elizabeth rose during the lecture and excused herself. Her mother was livid, but Elizabeth had the perfect retort. "Mother dear, how do you expect these men to notice me if I'm sitting here with you?"

Taft spotted Elizabeth from across the way. Her bright red hat and matching dress were an eyeful. He started the conversation and that led to a first date. He wrote the directions to her house, stuffed them inside his brown leather wallet, and although many years had passed, and the wallet had been swapped out several times, the note stayed tucked away. When Elizabeth would introduce the general to strangers, his note was an icebreaker to show people he was more than just a man in uniform. Many of the people that Taft met were inspired by his remarkable military achievements. There were plenty of people who never saw the romantic husband beneath the uniform until a note describing how to get to 3456 Johnnycake Lane was yanked from his pocket. The note always impressed. Taft had survived many hazardous circumstances, but the original note was in one piece. He was great at saving things that were close to his heart. Now he needed all the help he could find saving the country and perhaps the world.

As members of the media were ushered away from the front doors of the hotel, Taft reemerged.

"General, there you are." Lila called. "What's going on with the insects?"

"I see you've noticed them."

"Noticed? There are more guys killing bugs in this building than chemists and biologists."

Taft used his free hand to take a viscous swipe at bumblebees that had made their way into the hotel and had their sites fixed on attacking the general. With no regard for style, the masculine general gyrated his body in four different positions to avoid the flying black hostiles. Hands flying to and fro, a quick slide step with the right had Lila chuckling.

"Hey, quick moves for an old man," kidded Lila.

"Yikes…I hate bees. What are bumblebees doing in here?"

"I'm not an entomologist General, but I believe those were carpenter bees and they were probably looking for a snack. They're not interested in you. I heard your heart was made of steel."

"That's not a kind thing to say. I'm a softy inside, didn't you know that? I'll see you later. Thanks for telling me about the bees. I won't panic if I see them again."

"See, general? All things are indeed explainable," mustered Lila.

CHAPTER 22

Rex and Mathis sat by the pond under a clear sky. There are times when a father knows the precise words to say to a child to lift his spirits, and Rex was optimistic that this evening his words would alleviate Mathis's troubles.

"I know you are disappointed in my decision, but you must get over it. You'll face your own challenges and you'll discover a way to make it work. You're a terrific kid. I couldn't be prouder of you."

"But not as proud as you are of Buck. He's your 'chosen one' for the Village."

"Call him whatever you want, but that doesn't change my feelings for you."

"Yeah, I get it. When you're gone, what are people going to say? There are the Templeton boys. Their dad was a great man. His daughter fled the Village and his one son Mathis works doing meaningless tasks. Not much of a legacy to leave. Thank God for Buck."

"That's not fair!" said Rex. "Lila made her own choice. That's no indictment on you! You'll build your own legacy and not live off mine!"

Whatever words of wisdom Rex had hoped to impart on his son were ruined by the harsh words aimed at Rex and they struck right at his heart.

"This conversation is over. Soon we'll close the tunnel doors and you'll have to make the best of it. There are times when you will be forced to take a stand and make tough choices. I did that with you and Buck. If you want to hate me for it, then go ahead."

"You don't get it, Dad. Come on. Can't see you see that the entire village looks at me as a failure?"

"That's not true."

"In your eyes, no, but I can see it in theirs. I can't describe it, but it's there. 'Why didn't your father pick you?' 'I wonder what's wrong with him?' Dad, unless I do something extraordinary, I'm just the guy who came in second place, like Ethan White."

"Bite your tongue! You have nothing in common with him. He's petty and jealous. Those are his most charming characteristics. He's a cruel individual."

"Dad, sorry, we don't see eye to eye on this one."

Mathis stood up, gestured goodbye with his left hand, and abandoned his father for the evening.

As Mathis departed, Rex shouted to him.

"Don't forget, tomorrow morning we'll continue prepping the final activities to seal the tunnels. Don't be late!"

Mathis didn't acknowledge the question as his lanky body slipped from view.

CHAPTER 23

"Your attention, please," asked Gen. Taft. His plea fell on deaf ears. His next attempt was more animated as he raised his arms up over his head and brought them back down to his chest, palms outward, and repeated this motion seven or eight times until the distinguished scholars in the room acquiesced to his wishes and simmered down.

"Quiet please. Thank you. Let's continue. Many of you undoubtedly have heard stories of the people who live in Canamith."

Lila jumped to attention when she heard the word *Canamith*. Why would Taft, of all people, be talking about her hometown? Lila guarded her past life in Canamith with extreme secrecy.

Taft continued on. "It's rare when one of the inhabitants of Canamith leaves their city and even more unusual that one of them chooses to speak with us. I have had the pleasure of knowing one of their citizens for a number of years. In fact, he's their leader, or was the last time I met him. They call him their 'Chief Elder'. I know him as Rex Templeton. He and I used to meet every six months or so at a small restaurant not too far from their village. His daughter is in the building with us today. Professor Jenkins, your father is a great man. I've had long discussions with him in Sanderell about his beliefs. Personally, I think he's wrong about how this situation ends. He's very proud of your achievements. I'm sure he doesn't mention that to you. That doesn't seem like his style. I'm the same way…that's probably why we hit it off so well. His belief in your expertise is one of the reasons I insisted that you be part of this team."

Lila's mouth dropped to the floor. Was it true? Could General Taft have been the same man that used to meet with her father when he went on his expeditions into town? Rex never mentioned the identity of the man he used to rendezvous with. Was Taft the man who was there when her mother died and was he the man that saved her father's life?

"Lila, what's wrong? You look like you saw a ghost," Aldo said.

"In a manner of speaking, I guess you could say I have."

"Huh?"

"I can't explain it right now. Shhh."

Taft continued. "Canamith is located in the mountain region back on the west coast. I lived near there for years when I wasn't chasing hostiles. I was with my friend Rex when drug-influenced juveniles murdered his wife. That was an awful day. The reason I bring this up today is that the people in Canamith were convinced that our way of life was ruining the world. That's not so unusual to hear, but what was unusual is that Rex said his people were planning on surviving the end of the world as we know it. When I look around at what's happening today, his words of warning appear to be dead on."

Lila was too stunned by it all. She considered herself a great scientist. She was unable to understand why the world was turning inside out. She believed that all things were explainable, but she was unable to explain anything about this crisis.

Taft sighed, as if he got the cruel joke the planet was playing on him had sunk in. He brushed away even the scant thought of defeat and went on speaking.

"I have terrible news. I wanted you to hear this directly from me before there is widespread panic in the streets. The unusual heavy winter snows in the mountain ranges of the country are melting too quickly. Part of the reason for this is the excessively warm temperatures we've been experiencing for the last few years.

The record-breaking thunderstorms that have ravaged the country recently are adding to the problem. Severe flooding is predicted for many areas and the President has ordered all military personnel to report to duty for immediate relocation to the disaster zones. Our work here must continue. The President has declared a State of Emergency throughout those regions. Citizens have been told to stay in their homes unless they are experiencing a medical emergency. Funds have been reallocated from the Treasury Department to cover the emergency costs involved with this response. More thunderstorms are predicted in these areas and I don't expect the state of affairs to improve for several days. In fact, my staff tells me that meteorological experts have made rather dire predictions. They anticipate more rain in the coming weeks. That's not going to help. Wildfires are racing out of control in the western part of the country. It's not raining at all there and firefighters have been diverted from surrounding states to assist. The Army has authorized the retrofitting of military vehicles to carry water or fire-fighting material to areas in need. Thirty thousand residents were evacuated within the last twenty-four hours and we expect that number to grow. The fires are currently thirty-eight percent contained. If we can catch a break with the wind, I think our boys on the ground can contain the blaze. In addition to the aforementioned flooding and fires, seafaring traffic has come to an abrupt stop. The seaports remain open, however. Many countries, including ours, have signaled our ships to return to port, where they can dock safely until the current crisis is resolved. Money markets around the world are falling."

"I can hear the words of my old friend Rex lingering in my ears. I can't stand up here and make an official statement that says the world is coming to an end. I don't believe that the world is coming to an end and the people of this great country won't believe that either. The onus is on us to come up with answers…and soon. I trust you grasp our sense of urgency. The situation has deteriorated since I last spoke to you. I have instructed local security forces to protect this building at all costs. People are scared, and we're going to have to keep an eye on that. Scared people do dumb things. There are reports of vandalism run amok. Supermarkets have been ransacked. Shoppers are getting into fistfights and in certain cases, committing murder. It sounds apocalyptic. I have faith in you to help us see the light at the end of the tunnel. Keep up the effort and I'll be in touch soon."

With that devastating news, Gen. Taft was escorted from the building and into his heavy armored vehicle.

Massey grabbed the microphone and added his own final words for the night.

"Let's get back to our groups. I've sent new surveillance videos to each room. These images came from various parts of the country and they may help."

Lila, Aldo, Drake, Goldman, and Morales scurried back to the meeting room.

Lieutenant Branley shadowed them. Lila asked him "We have you all day?"

"Yes, ma'am. At your service. Anything I can do, just ask."

Lila was about to ask a question, but abstained. Branley could tell she had stopped short.

"Go ahead, what is it?" he asked.

"I'd love a cup of coffee. Any chance you could find me one?"

"I'm on it, professor. But you need to make me one promise first."

"Sure, name it."

"Don't go walking around any zoos while I'm gone."

"Deal," Lila smiled.

"That smile fits you well, professor." Branley returned the smile. "Perhaps someday everyone will be smiling again?"

"I hope that's true," said Lila. Her voice said the words, but Branley could tell her heart wasn't buying it.

CANAMITH COMMUNICATION DEPARTMENT

Update #388

Government Official Secretly Worries

The worldwide panic that had been feared for months has arrived. Food prices were a problem one month ago; today there is little food to be had. Government forces around the world have been hard pressed to stop once law-abiding citizens from stealing food from any source available.

Speaking under conditions of anonymity, one highly-placed member of the legislature said it this way: "This is not the world I know. We're on the precipice of the total breakdown of society. I never thought I'd see this day. It's almost as if the roles of the world have been reversed. Now it's Man that must use the phrase that we used to say about the animal kingdom: It's survival of the fittest."

CHAPTER 24

Roger Drake made things happen. His deep pockets allowed him to purchase access to files, reports, technology, and influence in high places. He detested government bureaucracy, but he was wise enough to know he required government assistance. His cash donations helped grease the palms of legislators who disregarded what was best for the country and only saw what was best for their long term financial portfolios. He had come a long way from an intern at Energy Consultants, Inc. to CEO of RDC, the world's largest and technologically advanced telecommunications giant. He was twenty-one years old at the time and fresh out of college. His first job consisted primarily of getting breakfast for his boss. It was during that time he learned how the game was played. Big financial deals were not based on what was best for the country. It was all about the money.

Eyebrows were raised when Drake was asked to join the science team in the Capital. Government officials who had been around longer than eight years remembered the trouble that Drake caused for the Piro presidency. The Department of Defense had been enraged when Drake's Company, RDE Communications, bypassed governmental regulations and installed underground cables that were not up to code. Drake considered the matter trivial and a nuisance, but in the advent of the recent war and with security at the forefront for President Piro, Drake was forced to remove many of the cables at great expense to his company. It almost cost him controlling interest in the company. The value of the stock plummeted and Drake's hold as CEO was in jeopardy. He managed to stay in charge by promising to avoid collecting any salary until the stockholders had regained their money. That choice, combined with the development of new products released two years later, elevated the company to new heights, and when President Griggs was elected, he called on his old college fraternity buddy Drake to install an entirely new communication system throughout all government offices. The system worked to perfection, and came in under budget. Drake used this exposure to elevate his own ego and pocketbook to new uncharted levels. Nobody would suspect Roger Drake had seen this worldwide disaster scenario coming and built his own "safety bunker". He couldn't have predicted the current state of affairs, but he had sensed a change in the world, and he thought he may be forced to "hide out", as he called it, for a while.

His fortress in the desert included several years' worth of supplies for him and his new wife. It was a hi-tech version of what the Canamithians had built in the tunnels. Rex and his ancestors took 2,000 years to complete the tunnels. Drake built his retreat in twenty-eight months. The cost of building a living environment for the citizens of Canamith was incalculable. The cost of building Drake's little hideaway: forty-three million dollars. Drake built similar bunkers in strategic places around the world. He was three steps ahead of the curve on this one. He sensed the calamity coming, prepared safe dwellings in case they were needed, and hoarded boatloads of cash figuring that in the post-crisis world, cash would be king. He hoped his mega-million-dollar hideaways were unnecessary, but insisted on preparedness.

General Taft had outlined the plight of the world in a medium-sized hotel in the middle of the capital. Drake secretly uploaded all the data collected at the capital to his own computers in the desert.

The government had a special announcement on the Emergency

Broadcasting Network. The message hadn't changed in days. The masculine voice sounded stern, but not angry or panicked.

"Please listen carefully. There is no reason for alarm. Local and national authorities are doing everything they can to keep you safe. Please stay in your homes if you are frightened of the outdoors. Stay tuned to this channel for further updates."

When word filtered out that scientists were making little progress, the thin fibers holding the country together disintegrated like cotton candy in water.

Drake would never be accused as the person responsible for the leak, but he had the ability, motivation, and technology to do precisely that.

Massey was completing his last sentence to his group of experts when the lights in the hotel flickered for a moment, then went out. The lights blinked again and then went black. Emergency generators responded and the lights returned at half their normal illumination.

Massey's phone rang and he answered it quickly. He didn't speak for a moment as he listened intently to the caller before replying.

"I understand, sir. Will do. Thank you, sir."

"Who was that?" asked Lila.

"That was President Griggs. The entire east coast suffered a major hit to the electrical grid. It knocked out power to millions of people. People are desperate to maintain a level of confidence in their government and this is not going to help. Hot, hungry and broke don't make for happy campers," said Massey.

"What happened?" asked Lila.

"He wasn't exactly sure, but it seems that animals are digging at underground cables and chewing at the ones on ground level. There are scores of reports of dead birds seen around the power stations."

"You don't think that the birds were trying to—".

Massey wouldn't let her finish her sentence. "I don't get paid to think."

"This is one case where people would say you do indeed 'get paid to think.'"

"I'm not going there, professor. Let's get back to work."

The men and women assigned to fix the power grid couldn't do much until the damage was identified. Emergency crews were sent to key power transfer stations and within an hour they isolated the cause of the power failure. Thousands of birds had infiltrated the exhaust fans and clogged them to the point where the fail-safe systems within the plants automatically shut the system down. Twelve different plants were affected, which forced the Department of Energy to shut the system down throughout the Eastern part of the country to avoid any more domino-effect closing of power stations in the Midwest.

Energy Director Nathan Barron predicted that it would take close to a week to fix the damage caused by the invading flocks. Coupled with rising food costs, and shortages throughout much of the country, people would soon be dealing with the crisis without the comforts of air-conditioning or an ice-cold glass of water to quench their thirst.

The trickle-down effect of the crisis was beginning to show up in unexpected places.

Tankers hesitated to enter harbors to unload their goods. The freighter named *Scruthers* was a flash point for ships entering the country. As she was safely tucked away in her designated dock, the *Scruthers'* load sat unloaded for four days because workers failed to show up for work. The entire ship, filled with fresh fruit, now was a total loss. Dockworkers had been attacked by millions of flying, biting insects the previous week and many of the men were incapacitated from their injuries. Port Authority administrators had tried in vain to find temporary workers instead of the union workers, but the union leaders filed a restraining order at the local courthouse and that appeal to prevent the Port Authority to replace the ill men was upheld, forcing the Port Authority into a no-win solution. They couldn't hire scabs, but the union men were too ill to unload the boat. The ship and its well-traveled riches were left to rot.

Not all ships entering the country were infected by flying, biting insects, but union workers were staying home in droves to stand united with their fellow brothers. This led to other workers failing to report to their jobs too, starting a spiraling chain of people too fearful of attack or too loyal to the union to go to work. Either way, the shipping business was grounded. Roving gangs searched out the wealthy and ransacked homes, stealing everything that could be readily consumed or bartered for other useable goods on the growing black market.

These new reports were detailed on the monitors at the conference.

"We must give people a reason not to panic. That's the biggest problem we face," said Dr. Morales.

"Lila replied, "people are a hairsbreadth away from panic all the time. They never think about it because there is always food and water and shelter. Take any one of those out of the picture for a week, and boom: stand back and watch the explosions. But this is different. I believe people have accurately identified that their leaders are clueless to help them. When the terrorists attacked us on own soil, that radically changed the way we lived. It changed how we traveled and the way passengers were inspected. Now the government can listen to any conversation they wish to hear, under the auspices of 'Protecting the People'. This is different. How can the government stop birds from flying into a power plant? Can the government explain the crop failures? Did you know that our insecticides have become useless against sixty-three percent of those little buggers that ruin our food? I could go on and on. Do you think I'm nuts? Dr. Goldman does. I've spent my entire life believing that science has an answer for every problem and I accepted that challenge. What if this time we're not up to it?"

"Do you have a better plan?" asked Morales.

Lila began to think about Canamith. Lila had questioned the

entire "two-thousand-year-old promise to the ancestors" thing. That was a large factor in her decision to leave Canamith in the first place. Now, what Rex had been saying didn't seem so farfetched.

Lila grabbed her ever-present notebook and scribbled a sentence that she would ponder until she left the capital.

Theory: science can't explain it because it's too unbelievable for the rational mind to allow the idea that the planet can identify man as a threat.

She turned back to Dr. Morales. "Yeah, I do have a better plan. I'm calling it Plan B."

CANAMITH COMMUNICATION DEPARTMENT

Update #432

Electricity Grid in Danger

Jacob Burke, a spokesman for the International Energy Regulatory Commission commented yesterday. "While I'm not at liberty to discuss the reasons for it, continued disruptions at power plants and sub-stations around the world are becoming a problem. If we can't provide a safe work environment for our employees, we'll be unable to continue to sustain the high volume of energy that our customers demand through the electric grid on a daily basis."

Burke was responding to concerns that the unusually high number of sick days that employees have used during the most recent fiscal quarter. Two months ago Burke had been asked if employees were afraid to come to work, to which he stated: "What in the world do they have to be afraid of?"

CHAPTER 25

Mathis stared back at the mountaintop where his people were now safely nestled in their tunnels, waiting for the world to collapse. He trusted the note he left for his father and brother would give a satisfactory explanation for his sudden departure and violation of village rules. His plan was tight on time. The tunnels would already be sealed if he returned home too late.

Rex hadn't mentally recovered from Lila leaving the village. He wouldn't be happy knowing his son had bolted the confines of the Canamith too.

Lila had left for new adventures and challenges. Mathis left to bring her home.

Mathis took one last look back at Canamith and thought to himself, *Well, dad, you said someday I'd be needed for something important...I hope this is what you had in mind. What could be better than bringing your father his daughter, son-in-law, and granddaughter? I've got to make Lila believe me. If she wants to live, she'll come with me.*

He had been traveling an hour or two when his first near disaster struck.

Heading down the mountain, he stepped clumsily and tweaked his right ankle. He momentarily feared the damage was worse, but within a few steps the pain dissipated and he returned to his quick gate. He hadn't planned an exact timeline, but he knew that if he left the village too soon, Rex would have sent out a search party to bring him back home. If he waited too long, he'd never have a chance to make it back before the tunnels were sealed. If his timing was right, Rex wouldn't even notice his departure until it was too late to go and find him. Mathis risked it all for that chance.

Mathis had now ventured farther from Canamith than he had ever been. He had no desire to see the rest of the world the same way Lila craved. But the variety of birds, trees, grasses, and other natural wonders he saw along the way that were not present in Canamith surpassed his expectations in beauty.

Four hours into his journey, Mathis's confidence grew. He knew where to find the college where Lila taught. It was one full day's walk and part of the next. He had studied the maps from the library and had them safely stuffed into his backpack. He set his sights for a small campsite near the main road.

He brought enough supplies for three days. Two days for the trip to find her, and one for the return to Canamith. His pack included a blanket, rope, flashlights, various natural insect repellents, a first-aid kit, rations, and lots of water. The water was weighing him down, but he couldn't rely on the water outside Canamith being safe for him to drink.

Mathis was surprised his trip had been free of danger, but then realized his situation was changing. A small pack of dogs were following him. He couldn't see them at first, but he had been blessed with a keen sense of smell, and had kidded with his mother years ago that her dinners had to pass "The Mathis Smell Test" before he would even try the delicious food on the table. He would grab the plate with both hands, slowly bring the food to his nose, and breathe in deeply. More often than not, he would wink at his mother and devour the meal, but there were occasions when no matter how hard Sara tried to convince Mathis to "just taste it", he wouldn't budge from his convictions and skipped dinner altogether.

This moment was beginning to smell like a rotten dinner.

He quickened his gait. Beads of sweat burned as they dripped into his left eye. It had been a long day, and the warm temperatures, heavy load and the distance traveled took a toll on him. He knew he was no match for a pack of wild dogs. If they were hungry, and they found him, his right leg would be a late afternoon snack.

The two weapons Mathis brought with him were a six-inch hunting knife and a four-foot-long stick. The wooden stick would be handy to ward off a single creature, but one man with a knife and a stick versus an unknown number of wild dogs was not a proposition that interested him.

Mathis checked his map and noticed that a small creek ran parallel with his route to Sanderell and he could use the water for two purposes.

He entered the creek on the eastern side. The water was colder than he imagined. He held his pack high to keep it dry. The middle of the creek surprised Mathis. It became shallower and he stumbled. His knee buckled, but he planted his lower leg into the soft muddy bottom of the creek and it took hold. His regained footing, and crossed the water safely. Mathis covered his arms with mud from the embankment. He hoped it would eliminate his scent and the dogs would lose his trail.

Minutes later, six hungry and mangy-looking dogs gathered on the far side of the creek. They lapped up water to quench their thirst. The alpha dog raised his nose and searched for Mathis, but couldn't find his scent, and walked away. The rest of the pack followed close behind. Mathis waited another fifteen minutes before moving. He brushed the dirt from his clothes, wrung out his shirt, and headed back on the trail to Sanderell. Daylight was fading and now he was behind schedule. His original overnight plans were out of the picture.

"Looks like this a good time to implement my own Plan B," he said to himself. "Now, if I just had one, I'd be in good shape. I'll be prepared for the next one. Thanks, Dad."

Mathis found an abandoned barn to stay for the night. The doors were locked. He shattered a small window with the stick, reached in, and unlocked the door. He entered the building making as little noise as possible. His feet trampled scattered bits of trash on the floor, but nothing else tripped his senses. Once inside, he locked the door and blocked the window as best he could with a piece of cardboard he found on the floor. He spotted some old aluminum cans, tied them together and placed them next to the door. If anyone or anything decided to push through the glass, the falling cans would be his alarm.

Mathis set his watch to wake him at dawn, laid his exhausted head down, and was asleep in minutes.

When the horn of a passing train blared, Mathis jumped to his feet, heart racing. He got his bearings, found his bag and assessed his immediate surroundings. He appeared to have survived the night. He planned on returning to Canamith before he slept again.

The rest of the journey to the college was uneventful. His new route was free from populated cities or towns. The world he found hardly appeared headed for destruction. Birds sang. There weren't any raging fires or explosions. Mathis had no doubt that the end was coming, but from his early morning stroll towards Sanderell, the world seemed a fine place to live.

Mathis saw the main gate of the college by mid-afternoon. His mapping program worked and he stayed on the outside edge of the campus as he made his way closer to the science building, where he hoped to convince his sister to return to Canamith. The hardest part was figuring out how to get past the security checkpoint in front of the building. He contemplated how he would approach the guard and realized that his body and clothes must have smelled from his dip the river. That would not be a good first impression. The small towel he carried wasn't going to suffice to provide the type of the cleaning required getting into that building. He thought about telling the guard the truth. He had practiced the lines repeatedly during the trip to the college.

"Hello, I'm Mathis Templeton. I'm here to see my sister, Lila Jenkins."

"Hi, I'm Lila Jenkins little brother. May I come in and see her?"
"Hi, I'm here to save my sister's life. Can I come in?"
None of these options sounded great. But first, he had to clean up. He spotted a kiosk and found the Recreation Center on the map. He stashed his bag, knife, walking stick and anything that the college would consider contraband under some brush near the Science building. Confident that he hadn't been seen, he made a direct path for the recreation center. He would find a shower facility inside the building where he could clean up.

Students came and went from various buildings and the strange looks he received were expected. He stunk, he was dirty, and he looked more like a local townie coming off a three-day bender than a member of the student body.

One co-ed passed him and said in a voice loud enough for him to hear, "Rough night, buddy?"

Mathis couldn't have known that campus had been in shut-down mode and half the student body had returned home over safety concerns. To Mathis, this was the largest group of buildings he had ever seen.

He didn't respond to the question but when the next group of students, four of them, all well-built males, stopped in the middle of the path, essentially blocking his way, he wished he had either the knife or the stick. He wouldn't have harmed them, but could have used the weapons for self-defense. As he approached the group, they laughed and the shortest kid of the group said, "Hey, pal, you stink like shit."

This was not the welcome he had anticipated, but under the circumstances it wasn't much of a disappointment. When he reached the recreation center, a student stood by the turnstile, checking for proper identification. Mathis quickly came up with his own Plan B.

"Can I help you? Whew! Whoa, I gotcha man! You need a shower!" The student grabbed his nose and gestured to Mathis to stop in his tracks with his other hand.

"Uh, yeah. Hey, I'm having trouble getting my ID card out of my pocket. It's kind of full of mud and I thought you could—"

The one hundred and twenty-five pound guardian of the building interrupted his plea.

"Seriously, man, go ahead. You know where the showers are, right? Dude, you stink. Whad'ya do, sleep in a barn?"

Without missing a beat, Mathis answered, "Yeah, you could say that. Thanks."

He combed the building, trying to avoid more security and find the shower facilities. He came across a large gymnasium. He saw a group of men playing basketball and working up a sweat. It seemed logical that the showers would be located near the place where people were sweating. He saw two entrances at the far side of both ends of the court. He couldn't distinguish from that distance, but one of them had to be the door to the men's locker room. He waited for movement from the openings. Minutes later a woman came out of the opening that was closest to him. He made his move for the other room and ducked inside before any else could call him out.

Mathis spent the next few minutes showering, washing his skin and his clothes. He stood in front of the automatic hand dryers and the machine instantly turned on when he placed his hands below the opening. He had never seen these before, but the metal boxes gave him an idea. He put on his clean, but soaking wet clothes and stood in front of the dryer. He held small portions of his shirt in front the hot air machine, which dried his shirt slowly. He wisely turned a second dryer to blow hot air on his left pant leg, and he positioned the machine on his right to blow air on his right leg. It was a decent idea. His pant legs were drying, but his crotch was soaking wet. Any student would have described him as a man who had urinated in his own pants. He disregarded the sign that read "Please place used towels in the basket" and used one towel to hide his wet pants.

He exited the building without talking to anyone and returned to the brush where he'd hidden his belongings and was relieved to see that they were still there. He used the towel to brush off as much dirt from the bag as he could. He was moments away from seeing his sister for the first time in years.

Confidence rising, he arrived at the small brick security area where the guard was responsible for securing the Department of Science parking lot. The science department was accessible by using the walk-through next to the parking lot. A school ID machine was there for the students to swipe their card into the magnetic reader and allow them entrance into the area. Mathis was clean, but he lacked the ID card. He was going to have to gain entry by talking to the security guard.

Mathis felt prepared to give his speech that he memorized back in Canamith. He felt more confident that ever that he would get his sister back to Canamith. He wasn't sure how Lila would receive his message, but that didn't matter. He had to try. This effort would give him the respect he longed for from his father.

Mathis was spotted near the entrance to the science building. The security guard, Finch, the same man who spent many a night protecting the woman Mathis was coming to see, stopped him.

"Hello," Mathis said.

"The building is closed. Nobody is allowed in or out."

"That's not going to work for me. I need help right now," begged Mathis.

"We all need help 'bout now. There ain't no help today. If truth be told, I'd just as soon go home, but my boss said that nobody comes into this building. That sounds pretty clear to me, what about you, son?" said Finch.

"I'm Mathis Templeton. Lila Jenkins is my sister. I must speak to her right away. It's urgent. Can you tell me where I can find her?"

"Her brother? She doesn't have a brother," declared the guard.

"I'm afraid I misspoke a moment ago. She has two brothers. Can you please tell me where she lives? I've made a long journey and I need to speak to her right away."

"You're not making this up, are you? I see the resemblance, a bit in the nose… yeah, I see it now. I'll be damned, she's been holding out on me all these years. That girl. I'm gonna get her for this one. Two brothers you say? This is a joke, right?" questioned Finch.

"This is most assuredly not a joke."

"I'm sorry, even if I believed you, and I'm inclined to do that, she's not here. She went to the capital with the ABC group. Didn't you hear about the big conference? It's been all over the newspapers and TV lately. Do you live in a cave?"

"Not yet, but soon. Can you help me reach her?"

"I could. I'll call her mobile phone. It's been hit or miss lately with the signals. Problems with the cell towers."

"Yeah, I believe that," said Mathis. "Could I borrow your phone? I have the number. She has a landline that should be working. I've got it tucked in my bag here."

"You and your sister close?"

"Uh, not exactly, but I'm here to change that."

Finch sized him up. "Are you as smart as she is?"

"I doubt it. She was the smartest one in the family. I don't mean to rush you, but I'm in a hurry…"

"Oh, yeah, the phone. Hold on a sec, let me try from the gatehouse. What was your name again? Mathias?"

"Mathis…Mathis Templeton."

Finch tried the reach Lila's number several times. "Sorry. The call won't go through. It's against my better judgment, but I'll try to reach her husband. Maybe I can get him on the line?"

"That would be great. Thanks."

The Security Guard turned his back on Mathis and whispered into the telephone. Mathis couldn't make out the words. Two minutes later, Finch handed the phone to the young man.

"Here you go. I thought it was a prank, but her husband wants to talk to you."

Mathis wiped the sweat from his hands on his damp pants and grabbed the phone.

"Hello."

"Is that you Mathis?"

"Yeah, it's me. I'm trying to get a hold of Lila. Do you think you can help me?"

"The phone lines to the capital are for shit. You'll never get through. What are you doing there? What about the tunnels and the 'we are doomed' talk?"

"Please, J.J., I'm not looking for an argument. Can you help me or not?"

There was a long pause on the other end of the telephone. "Stay there. I'm coming to get you. I don't know why I'm doing this. I guess it's because I love your sister. Wait in the gatehouse. It should be safe there. Don't walk around. You'll get funny looks. Or worse."

"I already got those. I'll stay put."

"I'm leaving soon. Don't move. Put the security guard back on the phone."

"Okay, got it," said Mathis.

Mathis handed the phone back to Finch who talked with J.J. for a moment and then ushered the young man into the gatehouse to wait for J.J. to arrive.

Two hours later, J.J. pulled up next to the gatehouse and stuck his arm out of the window and shook hands with the man that had kept a watchful eye on his wife during the late nights she had stayed at the college.

"Hey, old timer. I heard you met an interesting trespasser today."

"You could say that."

Mathis stuck his head out of the guardhouse and scampered to the car.

"Get in," J.J. scowled. "Thanks, Finch. Be careful."

"Say hello to the missus when you talk to her."

"Deal."

Mathis started to speak. "J.J., I wanted to thank you for—"

J.J. interrupted.

"Skip it. I don't want to hear anything you have to say, but I'm sure Lila does, so I'm gonna make sure you're alive and in one piece. Do me a favor? Don't speak to me right now. Keep your eyes open and let me know if you see anything that looks like trouble, all right?"

Mathis was disappointed with the answer. "I can do that."

This wasn't the way the plan was supposed to unfold.

CHAPTER 26

Three days in the capital came and went without any new revelations. The terrorism plot theory had been eliminated from the discussion, but events throughout the world continued to escalate. The scientists huddled in the capital spent hours poking, prodding, examining, and drawing blood from every type of living creature on the planet. Drake insisted the species were communicating with each other. Morales thought that their biological code must have mutated or changed, and Goldman didn't have anything to add that she was confident enough to bring to Massey. Aldo was in his glory, soaking up knowledge from this wise, but overworked and tired, collection of experts.

Roger Drake used his communications skills to tap into the computers of the ABC team and found the thread of articles linking him and Rothschild. Nothing good could come from that association becoming public, so Drake sought a way to remove the two eager detectives from the building. His plan was part genius, part chivalry.

On the fourth day of meetings, Drake asked Aldo to make up a reason to dine alone with Lila. The group usually worked together while they ate. This enabled the rest to meet without Lila.

Aldo went on to great lengths about a girl that he had met in the makeshift library at the hotel and wondered if Lila knew anything about her. While his conversation dragged on, the rest of the group met to discuss Lila's fate.

Drake opened the impromptu meeting.

"It's come to my attention that Lila has a young daughter back home in Sanderell. I assume everyone is aware of that?"

Hearing no dissenting voices, he continued. "I believe a mother's place is with her children. There's no question that Professor Jenkins is a smart woman, but I feel she'd be better served spending this time with her child. Wasn't her child one of the kids hurt a few weeks ago? Something like a rabbit bite?

"Billy goat bit her daughter's leg," corrected Dr. Goldman.

"Either way, rabbit or billy goat. I think she should be with her child during this crisis. She hasn't come up with the magic answer yet, and perhaps she never will. In the meantime, something terrible may befall her daughter and I'd feel partially responsible for that if I thought I was part of the reason she was sitting in this hotel with us and not spending every waking minute possible with her baby girl. Dr. Goldman, you had small child at one time, didn't you?"

"It wasn't that long ago, thank you, and yes, I see your point. You don't know Professor Jenkins too well. As much as she loves the little girl, that would be viewed as giving up, and one thing I can assure you, Mr. Drake, there's no quit in that woman."

"I agree! I can see that for myself. That's why I think we should present this idea as a united front...as a group...to insist that she leave this place at once and return to her child. We can send her assistant with her too. He can keep tabs on her, and let's face it; the poor boy almost got me killed at the zoo. His loss will be easier to overcome. There are plenty of brilliant minds in this room to figure out what's going on. What say the group?"

Doctors Massey and Morales looked to Goldman to take their cue.

"I suppose it would be better for the child if she was with her mother..."

"Good! Then it's decided. I'll get Aldo and we'll tell Professor Jenkins at lunch. I've already prepped General Taft about the idea and I have a driver and a car ready to transport both of them back home."

When the team entered the lunchroom, Lila was already seated with Aldo, eating their salads with fresh chopped chicken. Everyone else kept standing, looking restive.

"What's up with you people? Did I miss something?" she asked.

Drake, in his first stoic moment of his life, sensed that nobody else was ready to talk, so he did. "Lila, we've been talking, and—"

The slender professor stood up with a jolt. She wasn't pleased. "Who's been talking?"

"Please, Lila, hear me out. Things are getting worse out there and we were talking and we want you to go home."

"What are talking about?" Lila steamed at the suggestion she leave the capital.

"Just listen for a minute. You have a small child. The rest of us have grown children or, are…unattached," said Drake, and Lila noticed Aldo cringe.

"What is your point?" Lila demanded.

Goldman stepped in. "My kids are in their mid-thirties now. They are scattered all over the place. Same with Dr. Morales. Your daughter needs you. You've got to get out of here while you can. Mr. Drake said he's made transportation arrangements with Gen. Taft for you. I'm afraid the wheels, as they say, are already in motion."

Lila despised other people making decisions for her. It harkened her back to her youth when her father insisted she stay in Canamith. *I am an accomplished scientist in my field, a published author, a guest speaker and professor at a major university, and now I'm being told to go home.*

Lila eyed Massey with disbelief. He turned away, ashamed that he had not reached out to her first.

"Lila, the way things are going…I feel…we all feel…I couldn't live with myself if something happened to Sophie and you weren't there for her."

"Please, Dr. Massey..." Lila began.

He turned back to his colleague and muttered, "I'm sorry, Lila, I mean it, but you should be with Sophie. This decision is irrevocable."

Lila plopped back down in the chair and hit the cushion with a thud. She tried to invoke the brilliant sentence that would persuade her peers to acquiesce to her way of thinking, but the words didn't come. As the right side of her brain searched for the reasons to stay, the left side conjured images of Sophie. She saw Sophie crying in the hospital, her leg bitten by an unassuming billy goat. The wound was healing, but the world had been turned upside down and thrown sideways since that day at Sanderell Hospital.

Lila kept her head facing the old tattered carpeting, a combination of blue and green paisley wool that was designed to hide stains. Now it found a new purpose that the manufacturer hadn't thought of. It was absorbing Lila's tears.

She didn't cry often and certainly wouldn't have thought she would find herself breaking down in front of this group. She'd cried in front of Massey once. That was when Sophie was born. Massey brought an appropriate gift to the hospital, but the Junior Scientist Kit came seven or eight years too early for her to enjoy.

"Look at me, I'm a mess," whispered Lila.

Dr. Goldman handed her a tissue, and Lila dabbed at the salty remnants of tears on her face.

Drake, the pragmatist of the group, changed the tone, tried to rush her out the door.

"Well, so much for mushy good-byes. Professor, you'll have to excuse us. You have a daughter to hug and kiss, and we're going to try and save the world for the two of you. If you don't mind...." He motioned her to leave with his the gestures of his right hand.

"That's it?" questioned Lila. "Dr. Massey, can I speak with you in private for a moment?" They moved to the side of the lunchroom, far from Drake and the rest of the people. "I don't trust him," said Lila.

"Who?"

"Who do you think? Drake. I'm telling you. Keep an eye on him. This is all happening too fast. This doesn't feel right. Can't you sense something odd about him?"

"He certainly doesn't fit the type of academia we associate with, I'll give you that."

Lila grunted.

"Sometimes you drive me crazy! I'm telling you, I can't pinpoint it. Please, be careful around that guy. Can you at least promise me that?"

"Promise. Now, go and get your stuff together. We'll be laughing about all this in two weeks back at the college."

Lila shook her head, disgusted with Massey's lack of foresight, and walked away.

Massey walked back towards the rest of the group. "Mr. Gorrell?

No response. Aldo stared into space, lost in thought.

"Mr. Gorrell?" This second request was louder and got the young man's attention.

"Yes, Dr. Massey?"

"I want you to go with Professor Jenkins. She thinks she can handle anything thrown her way, but I want you to keep an eye on her for me. I'll need her back at the school when this calms down and I want you to escort her back safely. What do you say?"

"No problem. Are you sure?" chirped the eager assistant.

"We can handle it here without you."

"Dr. Massey, are we flying back home?"

"You won't need vomit bags today, Aldo. You'll be driving. Air travel has been curtailed to the military. I'll see back at the university soon. Please be careful, both of you."

A couple of swift good-byes and hug from Dr. Morales and Lila and Aldo headed out of the lunchroom. Lila turned at the door and offered one last bit of encouragement. "Remember…all things are explainable. I'll be thinking of you guys. I'll try to call you if I think of anything. Goodbye."

Lila rushed back to her room and gathered her belongings. She tried for an hour to reach J.J., but the telephone lines were busy. On her fourteenth attempt to reach her husband, the line connected to Kate's house.

"J.J.? Is that you? The phone reception is terrible. It's no use, honey, I'm leaving here."

"Sophie and I have been worried sick. We were going to get in the car and try to find you. I didn't know what to do. What's going on there? You wouldn't believe what's happening here, it's crazy. I'm trying to keep Sophie calm, but she can tell that everyone is upset."

"Is Sophie all right? Tell me the truth," Lila demanded.

"She misses you and she's doesn't understand why the schools are closed and why we're eating out-of-date food from the pantry. What have you guys come up with?"

"I don't know what to tell you, but I'm leaving here in an hour. They're not letting me fly home. I'm going to have to drive. Three more planes fell out of the sky yesterday and passenger planes have been grounded. Massey was able to commandeer one of the heavy metal-plated military vehicles and if we can find enough gasoline, I'll be home. It'll take at least nine hours, maybe longer, I'm not sure. I don't know when I'll be able to reach you again." Lila paused, then added, "Have everything ready to go when I get home."

"Go? Go where? All the emergency shelters are full. While you've been trying to save our sorry asses, the majority of the coast is in shelters and bunkers. We're like the last ones last inside a house. There's people going up and down the streets looking for food and I've heard horror stories about what they're doing to people who don't give up their food," said J.J.

"Those shelters won't last for long, if I'm correct in my assumptions. I'll tell you about it when I get there. Can I talk to Sophie?"

"Yeah, hold on."

A minute passed as Lila waited for Sophie to pick up the telephone. The little blue-eyed blonde love of J.J. and Lila's life spoke softly.

"Mommy, when are you coming home? I miss you."

"Oh, baby, I miss you too. I want to give you a great big hug and a kiss. I'm coming home real soon, sweetie." Lila wasn't able to control her emotions and began crying while Sophie spoke on the other end.

"Mommy, are we gonna die?"

"Goodness, no, Sophie. Don't say such a silly thing. Daddy and I are going to keep you safe."

"Mom…my, I…I…want you to come hooome nowwww."

"Oh, my angel, I'll be home as soon as I can. Daddy will take care of you until then. Put daddy back on the phone, my love."

"Okay."

"Lila, it's me. Hurry home, but be careful. Call me if you can. Sophie is scared to death. I don't mind saying that I'm scared too."

"J.J., being scared is okay. Keep it together for Sophie. I expect we'll make it home soon."

"There's one more minor item I should mention."

"What?"

"Your brother Mathis is here."

And with those words, the call dropped. Lila tried the number again, but it was no use, and before she made a third attempt, Aldo was waving his arm frantically for her to follow him to the garage, where the military vehicle was gassed up and ready to leave the capital.

171

CHAPTER 27

Aldo waited in the truck when Lila tossed her duffel bag in the back seat. Lila saw that the driver was equipped with several rifles and the front seat was filled with boxes of ammunition.

"How did Dr. Massey pull off this nice ride?" asked Lila.

"Thank General Anderson when you get back home. Do you remember him? He's the man I wanted to neutralize not too long ago. We can thank him for the vehicle and our driver. His name is Jay Kenyon. He lives out by us and he's made this trip a dozen times."

Lila was relieved that neither of them was going to have to drive this over-sized truck all the way back to the coast themselves.

Lila flashed the driver a big grin. As much as she was disappointed to leave the capital, she couldn't wait to see Sophie. The driver smiled back and gave Lila and Aldo a chilling, but welcome greeting.

"Hi, I'm going to do my best get you both back home safely. Don't worry. I have this truck, these brains in the top of my head, and my friends sitting next to me."

Kenyon pointed to the assorted weapons easily within his reach in case of an emergency.

"Ready?" he said.

Lila and Aldo nodded and away they went. They drove through the underground parking lot and then on to the street where a hint of sunlight temporarily gave them a false sense of security that everything would be all right.

When they emerged from the lot all three occupants of the truck realized that the world had changed in the last few days while they were kept within the confines of the hotel.

"Aldo, look!" shouted Lila.

"What is it?

"It's that guy from that Dead Bugs company."

Kenyon slowed as if to stop, but everyone let out a startled gasp when they got closer. Edgar had been killed. A pool of dried blood formed on the sidewalk next to his head. A half smoked cigarette and the rest his of smokes lay strewn all over the street.

"I told him smoking was gonna kill him," said Aldo.

"That's not funny," Lila whispered.

"I meant he should have gone back inside his truck, not hang around the parking lot smoking those damn things."

"Don't look at him," said Kenyon.

Lila buried her head in Aldo's shoulder and covered her head with both hands.

Her younger assistant touched her gently on the back. "It's going to be all right. You're going home. Close your eyes. I'll let you know if there's anything going on."

Without any verbal acknowledgment, Lila let of the weight of the last few days out of mind and fell into a deep sleep while Kenyon sped the truck out of the city and on to the road heading west.

They had traveled several miles when the first signs of trouble began. Kenyon had taken his eyes off the road for an instant to view the remains of a smoldering cargo truck and missed the red light signal and plowed through the intersection. The southbound tail end of another vehicle missed their truck by inches. The force of the sudden stop sent luggage and laptops flying, startling Lila awake. One of the smaller computers struck Aldo a glancing blow to the side of the head. Dark crimson blood began to ooze and dripped on the leather seat, giving the bench a disturbing mix of leather and blood.

"Damn it," yelled Aldo. As he wiped his forehead, he wasn't surprised to see his right arm and sleeve soaked in blood.

"Sorry back there!" shouted Kenyon. "Is everyone all right?"

Lila grabbed a pair of sweat pants that were sticking out of her suitcase and handed them to Aldo, who used them to at first wipe, then press and hold on his wound.

"Yeah, just a flesh wound, as you guys would say." Aldo shouted to the driver. He turned to Lila and said softly, "Maybe the Army didn't want Kenyon driving any of their troops. They probably thought we were expendable."

"I don't believe that. Look out there: people are going nuts. I wouldn't want to drive to my neighborhood grocery store and Kenyon is driving us all the way back home."

The next hour was uneventful but their easy drive west on Highway 29 turned ugly forty-five miles from the spot where Aldo received his first injury of the day. His second came when Kenyon stopped on the side of the road to relieve himself. He was gone less than a minute, but he failed to protect the guns in the front of the seat. When he left the car, he forgot to lock the door. Two young men in their mid-twenties ran up to the opposite side of the car where Kenyon couldn't see them. They crept down low against the driver's door. As Kenyon was whistling the Army fight song, one of the youths opened the door, reached inside the truck and grabbed one of the guns sitting on the passenger seat with his right hand. His left hand grabbed a round of ammunition and he was out of the vehicle again, running across traffic on the highway to a waiting car that sped away before Kenyon had finished zipping up his pants.

Gorrell opened the rear gate and tried to jump out to catch the criminal, but he landed awkwardly on his left ankle and stayed down on the dusty road for a moment.

"Are you trying to get yourself killed?" yelled Lila.

"Damn it, Kenyon. You forgot to the lock the door! How stupid is that?" Aldo yelled to the returning soldier.

"Shit," said Kenyon, "the gun they stole doesn't work. I'm angry they lifted the ammo, we might need that."

"Kenyon, why are you carrying guns that don't work?" asked Lila.

"That was your gun, if we needed it. The general authorized me to bring along one working weapon. I requisitioned another one without him knowing it, and then I asked him if I could take the busted revolver, you know, to give to you in case we ran into trouble. At least it would make you feel better. He agreed. It's best he didn't see the stash of ammo I pilfered on the way out the door," said Kenyon.

"What makes you think I'm incapable of using a gun?" Lila asked defiantly.

"Well, can you?"

"That's not the point, and for the record, no, I've haven't shot a gun in years, but I hope that you will not discount my abilities. Can we get moving before somebody steals the steering wheel from under your nose?"

Aldo rose and tested out his twisted ankle. "Don't worry about me, guys, I'm fine. I was just trying to save the fair maiden from the bad guys."

"Sorry; is your ankle okay?" asked Lila.

"Yeah, it's okay. Do you have any ice up there?"

"That's a negative," said Kenyon. "Do you think that in the future you can stay in the vehicle and leave the heroics to me?"

"You're already injured and we've barely left the capital," Lila chuckled to Aldo.

"Let's hope I can withstand the rest of the journey without needing my insurance card," Aldo replied.

"Good luck finding a hospital with an empty room today. Let's see what Kenyon can do now that his bladder is empty," said Lila.

"Whatever you do, don't offer him anything else to drink. I think my cat has more holding power than our driver."

"Shhh! Not so loud. If he decides to dump us out of the car, we're dead meat. Maybe we're making him nervous. Try talking to him about something he likes."

"What do you suggest? Hey, buddy, do you prefer to shoot bad guys in the head or in the leg?"

"I was thinking of a less violent and hostile option. Listen to this. Oh, Kenyon?"

"Yes, Professor Jenkins," replied the driver.

"What is your favorite facet of the Army?"

"Let me see…" said the driver. He removed his hat, rubbed his hair, short as it was, and replaced the cap. "I guess if I had to pick one thing it would be shooting bad guys in the head."

Lila and Aldo look at each other with astonishment.

"You should remember the truck has a built in communication transmitter located above you. I can hear everything you say, and don't worry, I've got your asses covered if there's trouble. Aldo, I can hold it a long time if I have to."

Kenyon laughed out loud at his own joke and all Lila and Gorrell could do was sit back and keep quiet until the next problem arose.

They didn't have to wait too long.

Darkness began to cascade on the horizon and Kenyon brought the vehicle to a complete stop at mile marker seventy-five.

"Hey, professor, it's getting too dark to keep driving much longer. I think we'd better find a place to shut it down for the night," Kenyon said.

"Are you nuts?" snapped Aldo. "We shouldn't stop out here, in the middle of nowhere."

"That's precisely why, smart guy. I'm not comfortable putting us around a lot of people right now. I don't know who we can trust. I'd say hotels are out the question. Now, if you have relatives out this way, I could be convinced to drive there, but I'm suspecting you don't know anybody in the middle of this wasteland we're driving through either."

"Damn, I wanted to get home to see Sophie. Is there any way we go a few more miles?"

"We could, but it won't help much. We're hours from our

destination. We lost time because the highway is closed. If anything happens in the middle of the night and we're too far out in the wilderness, I don't want to take any unnecessary risks. I am responsible for the two of you. I think both of you should catch up on your sleep."

"I'd rather keep going," said Lila.

"That's why I'm in charge." Kenyon put the keys back in the ignition and drove another half a mile before he found a spot to park the vehicle in a wooded area. He left the car briefly and flung large branches on the hood for camouflage.

He jammed the keys deep into his front pants pocket and gave his final command for the night. "Goodnight. I'd suggest keeping the talking to a minimum. The animals out here are nocturnal and have excellent hearing, but you two scientists already know that. Any little noise may intrigue them, and we don't want that."

CANAMITH COMMUNICATION DEPARTMENT

Update #565

President Griggs Made a Brief Speech to the Country Today

"Today I'm faced with realization that our society has collapsed into chaos. I urge all citizens that care about this great country of ours to stop the violence. Return to your homes. The government will take care of you as we work our way through this crisis. We've recalled all of our troops from around the globe and are making efforts to get them safely home as quickly as possible. I've activated the reservists and they should be arriving at their designated locations within two days. As you know, transportation has been a problem. If you are on the road, please cooperate with our troops and allow them access through the highway system.

"Our citizens living abroad are urged to stay put. Traveling home is too risky at this time. Official staffers have been ordered to keep the gates of our embassies closed.

"Please listen for more updates from the government on the Emergency Broadcast Network. Communication has been spotty, but we're working hard to protect our communication towers and substations to keep you abreast of the situation. I don't know when we'll be able to coordinate our next message.

"Please stay calm. Turning against each other will accomplish nothing. I know you're scared and you want to protect your children and get them food and medicine. We've established emergency transportation trucks to begin providing emergency food rations. Potable water trucks are on their way to every large city. You folks in the rural areas, we're trying our best to get to you, but it may take some time to provide assistance to your locale. I understand your frustrations. Now is the time that we need to show our resolve and prove to the world why this is the greatest country in the world. The terrorist attacks could not defeat us and we will overcome this crisis too and be a stronger nation because of it. Goodnight."

CHAPTER 28

General Taft never made promises to his wife that he couldn't keep. His bride of many years was used to the late night phone calls and early morning departures that placed her husband in harm's way. He had returned home in one piece after every battle. It wasn't unusual for Taft to enter the house with an additional medal sewn on his uniform that served notice to all that he had achieved another accommodation of valor or bravery. The battle he was waging now was a challenging foe. It couldn't be seen, or talked to, or bombed into submission. This made for restless nights and long talks with his wife. Much of the material was classified and he was unable to discuss the details with her, but he had become frustrated that even the famed ABC team of scientists wasn't having success. Failure on his part would not be welcome news by the higher-ups in the government. If he were replaced as the lead man on the crisis, he would face a demotion and a cut in pay.

That wouldn't sit well with Elizabeth, who had become used to purchasing items more costly than Taft could afford at his current salary. That harmful habit started years ago with the beautiful rugs from Canamith and had grown in scope and value over the years.

Taft played by the book. A military man all the way. Follow orders, do what you were told and don't ask questions. This served him well as he moved up the ranks. Now his pay grade was maxed out. His efforts to protect the country didn't compensate him appropriately compared to men he knew that owned small or large businesses.

One of those men was Roger Drake. They first met years ago at a conference and while their relationship couldn't be classified as friends, they did reach an understanding that each of them might be able to help the other with information that could be mutually beneficial.

Drake contacted Taft directly after media reports of the nuclear waste problem became public.

Taft was sleeping on his sofa when Drake called. "General, Roger Drake here. I trust I'm not disturbing you?"

Lying, Taft answered, "Nope, just resting."

"I wanted to discuss that Rothschild guy from the border facility. Know him?"

"You mean, 'knew him?'"

"What?" asked Drake.

"Knew him. He's dead. Left a bunch of memos about how he was able to pocket millions of dollars in profit due to unscrupulous misallocation of government property, namely hazardous waste material. Apparently he decided to kill himself rather than testify before any sub-committees that could rip him a new asshole. What was he thinking?"

Drake was silent on the other end of the phone. Taft knew Rothschild had been a key player in Roger Drake receiving no-bid contracts that paid Drake millions of dollars in fees for setting up the communications network at the border facility. The work had been done years ago, but routine maintenance contracts were given to Drake at astronomical prices and Drake in turn had given Rothschild generous amounts of hush money. If those facts were to come out in public, it wouldn't bode well for the much-respected Drake. Drake knew Rothschild was dead. His people on the inside told him Rothschild was dead before the ambulance arrived to take his stiff body to the morgue.

"General," said Drake. "Does the military pay their heroes satisfactorily? You men make the ultimate sacrifice for our country.

You are ones that give up traditional family lives so that people like me can go out and make a lot of money, date a lot of beautiful women, and set our futures with boatloads of cash for our retirement."

"What are you getting at Drake?"

"General, I have an idea that can set you and the missus and that lovely daughter of yours up for the rest of your life. All it would take is for you to help me out with this entire border plant incident."

"Are you suggesting that I bury the report?"

While Taft was trying to determine what Drake wanted, Elizabeth interrupted her husband by showing him a stack of overdue bills. Elizabeth's free spending had put Taft in a difficult position financially. He was thousands and thousands of the dollars in debt. The stress was beginning to show and it bore into their relationship daily. The once tough but sweet man had turned sour and frustrated at the low wages given to those that served the country with pride. In a moment of weakness, staring at the stack of bills, wondering what difference the report would matter with the world in turmoil and without thinking how foolish it all sounded, he took Drake's baited hook.

"Are you saying it's in my best interest to help you out? That is, financially?"

"Are you okay with that?" asked Drake.

"We're still talking, aren't we?"

"We are. What I'm suggesting is if you can find a way to get rid of any connection in regards to the flow of money from my company to a certain person who might not be alive any longer. There could be a windfall bonanza of benefits to you."

"Such as?"

"How does ten million dollars sound for a start?"

"That's a big bonanza."

"That's the kind of money you should have been making all your life. You're a smart guy, too smart to live the life of a pauper. This is your chance to give your family financial security. This is why you put in all those hours. Think of the missing birthday parties and anniversary dinners. In addition, I have a 'safe-house' for lack of a better term, in case this situation with Mother Nature gets worse. I can arrange transportation to the safe house for you and your family. You can stay there until things settle down. Once that happens, it's essential to have strong leadership at the top of the ticket."

"You're talking public office."

"Absolutely. With my financial backing, you'd have as good a shot as anybody. People are drawn to you. The uniform and the stripes, you know, not everyone is against protecting the country. They trust you. What's the point of putting Rothschild's family under the microscope any further? He's deader than shit. I went to high school with his wife. Nice girl back in the day. She didn't have a clue about any of this. Here's what I have in mind. If things get critical, you'll know I'm outta there, and if I leave, that's not a good sign. You'd be wise to follow suit. You should pack your bags in advance. I can have your luggage waiting for you at the safe house, just in case. If things go south, call your wife and I'll have a ride ready for you and bring you to my location."

"Where's it at?"

"That doesn't matter now. What do you think? Do we have a deal?"

CANAMITH COMMUNICATION DEPARTMENT

Update #589

School Bus Gangs

The sight of a yellow school bus traveling down the street used to be a sure sign of autumn and the opening of the school year. However, as society stands on the precipice of collapse, yellow school buses have been appropriated by gangs of adults, using the fleet as a sign of power and danger to anyone that stands in their way.

Norman Dell, a 75-year-old resident of Taylorville, recently had an ugly experience with three such buses last week. "I heard these buses stop in front of the house. I live alone and my children haven't ridden the bus for over thirty years. When I opened the door, three men pushed me down and raided my pantry. They grabbed every perishable I had in stock. Then they searched for medicine and they took that too! I begged them to leave my diabetes medicine, but they took it anyway. When they left, the last man helped me up off the ground. He had the saddest look on his face. It was like he was stealing from his own grandfather."

CHAPTER 29

"Wait here," demanded J.J.

Mathis listened to his brother-in-law and stayed in the car.

"This is going to take my best work. My sister will not be happy to see you. I'll be back in a few minutes. It'll be to either invite you in or to give you a sleeping bag and a pillow."

"J.J., I'm willing to— "

"Quiet. Stay in the damn car and don't move."

J.J. returned from the house within two minutes. "Mathis, come in. Can I get you something to eat?"

Mathis grabbed his bag and entered the three-bedroom ranch style home. Kate had taken Sophie and gone to the far back bedroom.

"I'll pass. I don't have much of an appetite and your food may not sit well with me. The pesticides and chemical additives might make me sick. I'd love to see Sophie."

"I think it would be best to see her in the morning. Kate is not too pleased with the way the evening has unfolded."

"If you want me to leave…"

"That's not necessary. I wouldn't have driven all the way to the school and back if I was going to throw you out now."

"That's reassuring."

J.J. looked around the family room. Two couches made an "L" shape and J.J. grabbed one end of the couch and pushed it next to the other one.

"There. It reminds me of a big crib, but it will be more comfortable than the floor."

"Thank you, that'll be perfectly fine. When do you think Lila will be back?"

"It's hard to say. She said things were terrible at the capital, and the ride here could be hazardous."

"I'll see you in the morning, or sooner, if Lila arrives," said Mathis.

J.J. started to walk away. He turned back to Mathis.

"Why did come looking for Lila?"

"You'll think I'm crazy. I had to try. I came here at great risk to tell, I mean to ask, no, I came here to use all of my verbal skills to convince her to come back home with me. I was hoping for your support in the matter when she returns."

"Uh, don't think that's going to happen."

"Then goodnight."

"Goodnight it is."

CHAPTER 30

The night spent on the side of the road was uneventful, other than Aldo's constant snoring. Lila rammed her foot into the side of Aldo's leg repeatedly, causing him to switch positions and bring quiet back to the vehicle.

When the morning came, Lila greeted her fellow passengers with a groggy hello. "I'm going to try sleeping, and if anyone wakes me up, it better be to tell me we're home."

Kenyon and Aldo didn't respond. Lila had made it clear that this was not the day to mess with a sleep deprived, heartsick mother.Lila pulled the blanket over her head to block the sun and road noise coming from the tires bouncing in the ruts of the freeway.

Kenyon and his academic passengers were twelve miles from Taylorville when trouble came calling again. It wasn't a bathroom break that forced them to stop the vehicle this time.

A large gathering of people had assembled on the freeway and made the road impassable. Kenyon slowed to the truck to a crawl, and stuck his head out of the window.

A heavyset man waved his arms back and forth, indicating he wanted the truck to stop.

"What's the problem here, neighbor?" Kenyon asked.

"You ain't my neighbor. What's your business here?"

Kenyon turned around to his passengers. "Fasten those seat belts and cover your heads."

Lila and Aldo followed orders without hesitating.

The man blocking the road was almost as wide as the westbound lane. He wasn't moving out of the way as Kenyon accelerated.

"What is your business here? Shut off that truck and let me see some identification."

Kenyon wasn't going to stop the truck. He wasn't the brightest man in the Army, but he knew a trap when he saw it. He turned the truck sharply to the left, sending Lila plowing into the rear door.

Kenyon heard the large man say, "Fire!" and within seconds, the truck was under attack. Eight men fired semi-automatic weapons at the truck. The truck was equipped with heavy armored side panels and bullet resistant tires. The bullets bounced harmlessly away from the truck. Kenyon drove the truck off the road and into the far eastern edge of the Sanderell mountain range.

The angry mob shouted obscenities at them as they drove away. Kenyon sliced and diced his way through muddy paths and steered the truck through several downed trees and one large roaming buffalo. Kenyon was confident the truck was out of harm's way when he noticed an animal rushing towards the side of the truck. Kenyon sent three forty-five millimeter bullets into the behemoth's side. The animal let out a loud grunt and collapsed.

Lila yelled, "What was that noise, Kenyon?"

He didn't respond. He concentrated on the road and disregarded a second and third request from his passenger. The fourth attempt, this one louder and assisted by Aldo drew the secret out from the driver.

"We had a situation, and I fixed it! We're almost there. Sit tight and shut up," said Kenyon.

Lila's frantic voice rose with each passing minute. "He shot something, didn't he? I knew it, Aldo… Kenyon, tell me what is going on! Did you kill someone? What's going on out there?"

"Professor, please settle down. We're not on a picnic ride."

"I demand to know what's going on!"

"Look out your back window! I hope you're happy," snapped Kenyon.

He lowered the armored window and saw the carcass of the buffalo fading in the distance. Lila felt a sharp pain in her head and fell backwards. Gorrell caught her and she regained her composure quickly.

"What was that?" the young man asked.

"Headache, and that was a bad one."

"You don't look so good, Professor."

"I used to think it was nothing, and now the pain is more frequent, and wow, sometimes it sends me for a loop."

"You better get to a specialist when we get back. I'll have you see my friend Dr. Hayden. He's the head of the Neurology Department. You call her right away and tell her you're a friend of mine. She'll see you."

"Aldo, look around. I think we're past the point of worrying about a headache."

"When you get back home, you should take a few days off."

"That's funny. Days off? Now? I can just picture it… I'll get a call tomorrow from the General and I'll tell him I'm under the weather and need to stay in bed. I don't think that'll fly."

Kenyon interrupted with positive news.

"Hey, guys, we'll be back on the road in a minute, and it looks clear ahead. Professor Jenkins, I'll have you in Taylorville soon."

"Taylorville?" asked Aldo. "Doesn't your sister-in-law live in Taylorville? Lila, what's going on?"

"I'm not sure how to tell you this, Aldo, but I told J.J. to leave Sanderell and go to his sister's house in Taylorville."

Aldo was surprised. He sat there dumbfounded for a second or two before he implored Lila to reconsider her choice. "Lila, are you serious? Taylorville? Why did you do that? You know the barrels have been removed. The whales are dead. There's no less danger in Taylorville than in Sanderell."

"Maybe, maybe not. It's hard to explain. I wanted Sophie with family while I was gone. His sister Kate hates me, but she'll help take

191

care of Sophie in case anything happened to me. I never realized how much I missed that girl until I got to the capital. I'll never leave her again."

"I understand that. Perhaps if I had a wife or family it would be different. The closest thing to a family I have is the university and, well, you."

"Aldo, you have people that love you."

"I have people? I've got nobody."

"I thought you and that Alisha girl were an item?"

"I wish. I've buried myself in my job and Alisha told me that I was putting her second in my life. I'm not the first person guilty of that."

"You're not the first or the last. I haven't exactly told you everything. I haven't even told J.J. yet, but I'm thinking about taking my family back to Canamith. There's so much to tell you…"

"How about telling me how you came to Sanderell. Your records are a bit sketchy on that part of your life."

"Why were you looking at my records?"

"Hey, don't shoot the messenger. That came from the top of the department the first week I started. I didn't even know you then."

Kenyon jerked the truck to the right and Aldo hit his head on the side of the truck in the same spot that was injured earlier.

Aldo shouted, "Can you watch it, please?"

An hour later, Lila had finished telling Aldo all he needed to know about Canamith and Lila's departure from the village. Kenyon pulled into Kate's suburban development. It was quiet. Too quiet. They passed by the local elementary school. The school was closed and the parking lot was empty. The local grocery store was empty and broken glass littered the sidewalk and parking lot. Kenyon used his GPS device and when the female voice said to him, "Your destination is on the right," Lila was seconds away from a reunion with her family.

Kenyon opened the door for his weary traveler and grabbed her luggage and laptop, put them on the driveway and before he could say anything, Lila raised her right hand to her mouth in a gesture to silence the man who saved her life.

"Kenyon, don't speak. I want to thank you a million times for everything. I started out this trip questioning you, but you came through with flying colors and it's given me all the more reason to love and respect you and your fellow soldiers. You are the bravest, toughest men and women I've met and I wanted to say thanks." Lila tried to wrap her arms around the soldier, but his girth made it impossible for her hands to reach around him. She managed to get a big squeeze on his shoulders, and that was enough to make Kenyon blush.

"Oh, it's nothing, Professor Jenkins. I'm just doing my job. You take care now."

"Yeah, not a care in the world."

Lila realized it was time to say goodbye to Aldo. They had worked together for many years and now the uncertainty of the situation made their reunion in the foreseeable future tenuous. Lila's hunch was that she wouldn't see Aldo for months and that pained her.

"Shhh," Aldo said. "There's nothing for you to say. You know where I'll be. I'm not done fighting this thing. You've made your decision and it's not my place to stop you. I didn't drag you out of the capital, and I'm not going to stop you from marching back into the mountains. Lila, trust what your heart tells you."

"I have to make a decision that gives Sophie the best chance to live. Where will she be safe? Can you promise that the University is safe? Where does this end? I don't even have a one-week supply of food and water in the house. Who knows what Kate has, or wants to share? It's the last thing you'd expect from me, but I can't put my rational thoughts ahead of my emotions. Not this time."

"I never thought I'd hear you say that, professor."

"Yeah, me either. I think from now on you should call me Lila. I think we can dispense with the formality under these circumstances. Why don't you come with us?"

"I'm not the adventurous type. I throw up on planes, remember? You should see me in a tent. Where would I even go to the bathroom?" Aldo said grinning.

"Aldo, always the jokester. Are you sure you won't come with me?"

"Yeah, thanks for asking, but I'm going back to the University and see what I can do there."

"Goodbye, Aldo. Be careful. I'll call you, or see you, or who knows what."

They hugged for a minute. Gorrell kissed her on the top of her head and said, "Go on, get going...Lila. You are the mother of a girl who is waiting for you. Hurry up. Grab your gear. I hate long goodbyes."

With that, Lila grabbed her backpack and laptop computer, and strode to the front door of the house.

Lila would never see Aldo Gorrell again.

CHAPTER 31

"Mommy!!!!!"

Sophie leapt into Lila's arms. Lila gave her kisses over her head and face. Sophie smiled and tears of joy ran down Lila's face.

"What's wrong, mommy? Why are you sad?"

"I'm not sad, Sophie, I'm happy. These are happy tears, sweetheart. See, I told you mommy would be back."

"That doesn't make any sense, mommy. What are happy tears?"

"You'll understand someday when you have children."

Lila hugged J.J., who was equally glad to see his wife return home safely. Even stoic Kate offered a smidgen of affection and gave Lila a welcoming hug. The four of them stood by the doorway talking. Sophie tugged on her mother's shirt, asking for Lila to pick her up.

J.J., Kate, and Lila were talking simultaneously when a new voice joined in.

"Hey, sis, remember me?"

Lila turned and rushed Mathis. He stumbled backwards when the force of her hug was stronger than anticipated.

"It's great to see you," she sobbed. "I've missed everyone. The last few days have been, well…I'm emotionally drained. I missed you and Buck so much. What is happening to our world?"

"We've missed you too."

"What are you doing here? Is dad okay?"

"He's fine. That's not why I'm here. Can we speak in private for a few minutes?"

J.J. shot a look at Lila making his aggravation clear, but understood that Mathis and Lila were going to speak in private whether he wanted them to or not. He steered Sophie down the hallway to her bedroom.

"Come on, Sophie. Daddy's going to read you a story. Mommy will be there in a minute." J.J. looked at Lila again and made sure she knew Sophie was eager for her to join them in the bedroom.

"I love your stories," Sophie bubbled. "I want to sleep in your bed tonight."

"We'll see, sweetie, we'll see," J.J. answered.

"I'll be right there, Sophie. Listen to daddy," Lila added.

Father and daughter skipped down the hallway. Kate retreated toward her bedroom, and before she closed her door she issued a warning to them.

"Don't venture off the porch. Stay close to the house, and make it snappy. I don't want a bunch of wild animals picking up your scent."

"Yeah, I've had enough of that myself," said Mathis.

Lila and Mathis stepped outside and sat side by side on the porch swing, with a faded flower pattern on the cushions and a metal chain link that squeaked as brother and sister gently pushed the swing to and fro.

"This brings back a lot of memories, huh?" asked Mathis.

Lila smiled a little and said, "Yeah, it takes me back a few years."

"Everything about your life was different then."

"I'm the same person you knew. I've just drastically altered my mailing address." She laughed, then continued. "Here we are."

"So much for small talk."

"We don't have time for small talk. If dad is okay, then why did you come?"

Mathis sat back in the swing and planted his feet firmly on the ground, preventing the swing from moving.

"Lila, for the people of Canamith, this moment is a culmination of 2,000 years of hard work and courage. How can you explain what's happening out there?"

"I can't," Lila stated with a sigh. "There's a reason out there and I thought I could find it, but the people I was working with thought I should come back home and spend every possible minute with J.J. and Sophie. Your archaic belief that this has been planned or orchestrated by nature is crazy. Those types of things don't happen. You've been raised to believe it, but science doesn't work that way."

"I never said, nor did the Elders ever say, that the readers of the ancient scrolls ever said that this is orchestrated by nature. Those are *your* words. I *do* believe the planet somehow is responding to the threats that Man has brought against it. The ancients in Canamith predicted that this day would come. How did they know? Perhaps I'll find out someday, but for now, believing is enough for me. I don't need to see the lab results, the testing of theories, the research papers. I don't need that stuff to see what I can plainly in front of me. Lila, look around. You've destroyed the world beyond your ability to fix it. Dad always says, 'have a plan B'. What's your Plan B, Lila? What's your Plan B?"

Her younger brother's words repeated in her head. Lila had heard those same words when she was a young woman talking to her father before she left the village. She remembered that night like it happened yesterday.

"I'm worried about your safety out there. I insist you stay here. This is where you belong. How would it look if my only daughter left the village?"

"Father, I'm going to report to the Dean of Admissions. I'm confident with the education I have I'll be welcomed with open arms."

Then she heard those words from her father in her head.

"Lila, what is your back-up plan? What is your Plan B if the dean doesn't accept you?"

And Lila remembered the last thing she told her father that night before heading out away from Canamith that night.

"Oh, Dad, I've had it with your damned Plan B...Goodbye."

It would be five more years before Lila and her father would talk again.

Lila returned to the conversation at hand.

"I don't have a Plan B, Mathis. I guess I'm sticking with the original one for now. I understand your comments, and believe it or not, I was defending your position earlier in the week to people at the capital. I'm torn between my love for you and Dad and Buck, and my chosen field of expertise that flies right in the face of what you're saying. I don't know what to do, Mathis. I don't know what to do."

"That's unfortunate, sis. Everyone would love to meet that daughter of yours. You know where I'm headed in the morning. I've got a tight time frame to get to Canamith before they seal the tunnel doors. I hope you join me."

"You think Dad is waiting for me and my family with open arms?"

"Don't write him off that easily. Dad loves you. He wants you back. More than you could know. What are your choices? Do you think it's safe to stay here? You've seen the reports of death and despair. J.J. filled me in on the way here. People are dying. What makes you think it will get better?

"Please come back home," Mathis said with more than a tinge of pleading in his voice.

"I don't know. That's asking a lot."

"What's a lot? To choose to live? People are locking themselves in their homes. How long do you think it will be until the food supply is dried up? The trans-ocean underwater cables have been damaged. Care to speculate who is responsible for that? The lines are deep under the ocean, and it will take months to fix them. Can J.J. protect your house? You're going to require protection if you manage to find any food because roaming packs of criminals will be there to steal it. I wouldn't take my young girl out in that kind of environment."

"You're painting a bleak picture. I believe we'll figure this out any day and life will get back to the status quo. People need to calm down."

"That's a dream, sis. All you have left are dreams. The current state of the planet is going to get worse."

"That is your unscientific opinion?" asked Lila.

"Those are the facts, not opinions!"

"There are a lot of smart people working on the problem as we speak. In fact, I should still be at the capital with my colleagues."

He had been practicing this message and he wasn't going to stop until he had used all his skills. "The world that *you* know is going to end. It's too late to go back in time. The warning signs have been around you for years and you failed to heed them. Perhaps not you, but enough of you have ignored the signs that disaster was imminent. You shouldn't be shocked and surprised by this. You're the scientist. I said your world is going to end, but I should have used a word you scientists are familiar with… extinction. That is the strongest word I can use for what I believe will happen."

"I'm exhausted and I want to see my husband and daughter, if you don't mind. Do you have anything else to say?"

"You have poisoned the air. You couldn't even imagine the air back in Canamith. It's clean. Do you remember clean air? You indiscriminately spew pollution into the air, as if the atmosphere was a harvesting site designed for your filthy habits. You filled the oceans with garbage and hazardous waste. Listen to me, Lila, I'm not making this up. Is this a world you want Sophie to live in? You've destroyed everything you touch.

"Our village has maintained a healthy population based on the crops that we can grow. Your population increases by millions every year. How are you going to feed these people? And now, with mass food shortages and random gangs killing people for cans of food or water? I can't think of one good reason why you'd stay here.

"You've tried to make a difference. I believe your intentions were true, but it's wasn't enough.

"The people of Canamith have been preparing for this day for 2,000 years. My message for you today is clear: The planet has found that 'someone else' to clean up Man's wanton actions. It is the planet and the creatures on the planet that have begun reclaiming what once was theirs. As foretold by the ancient scrolls in Canamith… Man's reign over this planet is near an end.

"The planet has reached the breaking point, Lila. There's nobody to negotiate with. All you had to do was to take care of the planet as you would have taken care of your own children. The people of Canamith will survive. Come with me. Please, I'm begging you. You have no chance to survive out here. Bring J.J. and Sophie. You can return to the outside world when it's safe. Think of Sophie. What is in the best interest of your daughter?"

"Are you done?" Lila asked.

"Yes."

"Where's the boy I left in Canamith all those years ago?"

"He grew up."

"Let me ask you again. Did Dad send you here?"

"He doesn't even know I left the Village. I don't know which is worse, staying out here in your world, or dealing with the wrath of Dad when I get back home to Canamith. Will you at least think about what I've said before you say no?"

"I'll think about it."

"I'll see you in the morning either way. It's too dangerous to try and leave tonight. I'm pushing my time frame to the max. I must leave at first light in the morning. The tunnel doors are closing tomorrow night and I'm going to be there before they do. 'Night, sis."

Lila stood with Mathis and the two shared a long embrace.

Lila spent that night at Kate's cuddled close to J.J.

"What's happened at the capital?" J.J. asked in a soft tone, careful not to wake the sleeping child between them on the bed.

"It's awful. They showed us video of a power plant releasing nuclear fuel into the air. They were evacuating people for miles and miles around the contamination site. Somehow, rodents penetrated the core and thousands of rats died, but not before they did considerable damage. They disrupted the power, or the backup system, I can't recall... anyway, the plant operators couldn't provide water to keep the rods cool and radioactive waste is spilling out into the atmosphere at the Johnson Nuclear Facility."

"I hadn't heard anything about it," said a shocked J.J.

"That's because President Griggs has shut down the media. I'm not authorized to discuss it with anyone. Cell towers have been blocked in certain parts of the country to prevent people from sending messages via their mobile devices. I wasn't supposed to know of it, but Aldo intercepted the direct feed from the President to Drake's private line. At least 3,000 people are dead there and the damage to the community will last hundreds of years. They're going to have to move everyone out of there. Can you imagine? You grow up somewhere, your memories, your high school, the local stores... all those things. It's terrible."

"Why does Drake have a private line with the President?"

"He's heavily involved with many projects. It's not a big surprise to me."

"I'm frustrated that I can't do anything to make it better. I wasn't raised in Canamith. I grew up in the city. I'm out of my element."

"J.J., you've been great. You've dropped what you've been doing while I'm running around from the school, to the capital, wild car chases through the countryside. My colleagues were almost eaten by wolves. I've had more excitement recently than in the last two years."

"Wolves? Car chases? We definitely need to catch up."

"We will, I promise, but first let's talk about tomorrow."

"Can't it wait until the morning?"

"This can't wait another hour."

"Alright, go ahead."

"J.J., we must leave here."

"Wait, you were insistent that I get here and now you want us to leave? I understand you and my sister don't see eye to eye, but—"

"No, no, it's not her. She must think I'm nuts. Don't answer that. I've been giving this a lot of thought. All three of us need to go to Canamith. It's the one place that'll be safe."

J.J. sat up in the bed, dumbfounded by the words he just heard.

"Lila, what's going on with you? What did your brother say? I should have left him at the College to fend for himself. I don't even know who you are anymore. Canamith? The place you couldn't get away fast enough from. You're buying that load of crap from your brother?"

"It's not crap. Please don't say that."

"Pardon me, but you've been the one calling it crap for years! You call me in a panic and tell me I've got to get Sophie and come here, then you get here and a few hours later you're chasing us out of here too. What's the rush?"

"It's not that easy to explain, but what matters is we must survive. It doesn't matter who is right or wrong. We can't eat the fish. It's too full of poison and heavy metals."

"We won't eat fish. Who cares?"

"It's not only the fish, J.J. You were at the grocery store with me. Is that how you want to live? We're going to have to buy a gun. Have you ever fired a gun in your life? The way I see it, we've got to get somewhere safe. Somewhere with shelter, food, and water. The only place that exists like that right now is in Canamith."

"Lila, you promised that you'd never go back there."

"I guess that's one promise I can't keep."

"If you can't keep that one, why should I believe any of your promises?"

"That's a cheap shot, and it's not fair. What do you think is going to happen around here?"

"I don't know. Kate has food stashed away. She said that it'll last awhile."

"A while? What if we can't get food for a month? Or two months? What then? What if Sophie's leg has a problem?"

"Stop it! Her leg is fine," J.J.'s voice grew louder.

"Shhh, you'll wake her. She needs her rest. We're leaving first thing tomorrow."

"That's it? You decided our fate?" he asked.

"I decided long before I walked in the door. Mathis gave me the strength to say it to you that we're leaving."

"Wait a second. We don't give each other ultimatums."

"I'm sorry, J.J., but you'll have to trust me on this one. It's going to get a lot worse before it gets better, and I don't want to witness any of it. This is hard for me to accept. You know how much I want to fix everything. Right now I'm playing the role of mother, not scientist. And mother wants to keep her baby safe and the best way to do that is to go to Canamith."

"That's it? We're leaving? How do you suggest we get there?"

"Your sister can drive us to the outskirts of city, or as far as she's comfortable going, and we'll have to walk the rest of the way. We have to leave early in the morning."

"Glad we discussed this together as a couple." J.J. mocked.

Lila was not amused. She turned away from him and faced the window, catching a glimpse of the rising moon. "I love you, J.J. I was sure I could fix this. I wanted to show myself, you, Dr. Massey."

"Your father?" asked J.J.

"Yes. Him too. Him more than anybody. I wanted him to see that there was another way to live."

"You did live another way. Now you're going back."

"I don't want him to feel ashamed of me, or think less of me."

"Is that what kind of man he is?"

"No, but—"

"Then don't think like that. Lila, I have one question for you."

"And?"

"Are you absolutely sure?"

"I've reviewed the scientific data. I'm totally sure of it. With every bit of my heart."

"Your heart? When did you ever make a scientific decision based on your heart?"

"I guess it's better now than too late."

"I'll go ask Kate. This ought to be interesting. I'll be right back. If you hear her throwing lamps at me, don't be surprised. I can't imagine she'd be on board with packing up and following you anywhere."

"Then she can stay put if she wants. I can't believe I'm suggesting this, but tell her I think she could come with us."

"There's a better chance of Sophie going back to a petting zoo first."

Lila was sound asleep before J.J. returned to the room. Her exhausted body needed rest to recharge for the emotional and physical journey her family was about to take.

CANAMITH COMMUNICATION DEPARTMENT

Update #718

Mass Suicide

Unspeakable. Tragic. Heartbreaking. Those were the words used to describe the human carnage found in the sanctuary of the New Heart Church.

Church members heard discussions about a "historic" event planned by Minister Aloyouius Renalt from online chat rooms and Internet banter, but nobody believed the rumors.

Church janitor Charles Whitson was the first to find the dead bodies, totaling 419 men, women and children.

"It was unimaginable. I drove into the parking lot, and wondered if I'd missed something. I mean we've never had a full parking lot at four in the morning. My mind started playing tricks on me. I was thinking, *Charles, what in the world is going on?*

"Well, when I saw the sanctuary filled with those people...them good people in there. Minister Renalt, Kathy Reynolds, the Simmons boys, Nick and Steve... fine kids and good athletes too. They were all dead. I know I screamed, but nobody moved. I ran out of there before somebody struck me down too and I called the police."

RICHARD FRIEDMAN

Details are still coming into the newsroom, but insiders at the scene have told detectives close to the case that a note was found on the pulpit, allegedly a hand-written note by Minister Renalt describing the decision to commit suicide was in response to the current world crisis and the choice to die in Church was better than to die in the streets fighting over a piece of bread.

CHAPTER 32

The bell rang three times. The people of Canamith came to the conference hall for the Closing of the Tunnel ceremony.

Several hours earlier, instructed by Ethan, and having seen the documents with their own eyes, Four Elders grabbed the large wooden doors located on the right hand side of the tunnel opening. They disengaged the latch that kept the doors open. Free from the confines of their mechanical bindings, the doors began their slow, deliberate path to the other side. The doors slid along their rails silently as they made their way along the path, hesitating briefly at the half way point, where another set of gears engaged and helped pull the doors the rest of the way. The doors would be closed within three hours.

Rex was nervous, constantly looking at his watch, anticipating that Mathis wouldn't miss the ceremony. He hadn't slept in the two days since Mathis went missing. He called on a few advisors to go and find his son. The band of men had gone out within a few miles of Canamith on a limited search, but they failed to find him or any clues to his whereabouts.

"Dad, he's around somewhere, but we can't wait. The Book is clear about these things," said Buck.

"You're not in charge of this village, young man. I know what the Book says. What are these people doing here so early? And don't you start telling me about our sacred texts! You've had access to them for a matter of weeks and I've been looking at them for years! Let's give the men a few more hours to find him. Once the door is closed..." his voice trailed away.

"I understand, dad, but we're running out of time. He knew the timeframe. Is he hiding somewhere?"

"That doesn't sound like your brother. I can't imagine where he's off to."

Two hours passed and no sighting of Mathis. The crowd began grumbling, questioning the reason for the delay. Only a handful of people knew that Mathis was missing. Most people were too busy with their own affairs to worry if Mathis had departed. He didn't have a formal part in the ceremony. The event could go on without him. Nobody would be suspicious of his absence.

The search party returned and reported to Rex.

"I'm sorry, Rex, there's no sign of him anywhere. We searched up to the village limits. We didn't dare go any further. It's already a firestorm of danger out there. And with the doors closing so soon... I'm so sorry," said Victor, the man who led the group.

"Thank you for your efforts. You can't imagine how grateful I am. I'm sorry if I placed you in any danger."

The search party disbanded and went their separate ways to find their own families.

Rex walked to the tunnel entrance and stared out into the vast distance that separated Canamith from the rest of the world. He noticed a foul smell in the air. It came from a burning building in nearby Sanderell. He could see flocks of birds heading east. He shaded his eyes and scanned the long path that led up the mountain from the flatlands below. No human forms could be seen. He grabbed his handheld telescope from his back pocket and focused on the areas where Mathis might be headed back home. Mathis was nowhere to be seen. Dejected, he tossed the spyglass on the ground and turned to his trusty old friend Braham.

"Let's get started. We've got to close the doors by sunset," said Rex.

"Sunset? Rex, the doors are closing in an hour."

"One hour! Who ordered that?"

"You did. Ethan showed me the paperwork earlier today. That's why the crowd is growing. You must have been distracted by the search for Mathis…I've got the papers right here."

"Never mind the papers…stop the process. Why didn't you ask me about that? Ethan must have tricked me or forged my name on the documents. Damn him. Find him! No, I can't see him right now; I'd kill him for his treachery. Stop the doors from closing. Do you hear me? I'm still the man in charge around here. I ordered the doors to be closed at sundown!"

"Rex, I'm sorry, but you know better than any of us that once the process starts we are helpless to stop it. Think for a second. You helped developed the system yourself."

"Let me see that!"

Rex grabbed the papers out of Braham's hand. Canamith protocol insisted that every document be signed and witnessed by at least one of the elders. On page three, clear as day, Rex's signature was written on the paper that started the engineering phenomenon to begin closing the tunnels doors two hours earlier than Rex had recalled from previous meetings. The signature was his, as was the witnesses.

"Rex, I'm sorry but there's no time to stop the closing. Our only hope is that Mathis has found a place to hide inside our hallowed grounds."

"That appears unlikely, my friend. How could I have miscalculated the timing of the doors so badly?"

"You have had quite a bit on your plate. It's only natural that something had to get out of order in that head of yours."

"Yes, I understand, maybe something…but not something this important."

It tore at Rex's heart to follow the meticulous procedures written for this special day. Entrenched in the detailed life of Canamith, Rex couldn't break ranks. What was done was done. This moment had taken hundreds of thousands of hours to create. His wife, his daughter, and now his son were going to miss it. He had to concentrate. He could discipline Mathis at a later date, if in fact he was there at all, but this was not the day.

The Elders promenaded to the pulpit and formed a semi-circle encompassing their leader.

Rex stared into the gathered crowd. They waited patiently for him to speak. Two minutes passed. Elder Braham inched closer and placed his right arm around Rex's shoulders.

"Rex, my friend. We can't wait any longer."

Rex acknowledged his old ally with a reassuring voice. "You're right. I'm afraid you've seen me at my lowest. You've been a wonderful friend, advisor, and confidant. I want to thank you."

"This isn't the time for sentimentality. A few more years of me and you'll be sick of looking at this old face."

"I don't think that'll happen. If this situation doesn't change, I won't be charming company these next eight years."

"It will all work out Rex. Think positively is what I say."

Rex tapped Braham on the back a few times and began the short walk back to his place with the other Elders. Rex stepped up to the podium and faced the village. He opened one of the sacred books. Before he read from it, he made a short opening announcement.

"Friends, I speak to you now with a heavy heart. My responsibilities leave me with the unenviable task of fulfilling our legacy. It is both a privilege and a tragedy. Nobody within these revered halls knew that it would be in our lifetime we would close ourselves off from the world. As you are aware, part of my task as your Chief Elder is to prepare my replacement. I have chosen Buck to lead us into the New World. We will open the tunnel doors and go back out into the world when the time is right. He has the attributes you deserve and require. We have followed the words of the ancients carefully and those before us knew that a commitment unlike anything ever seen in this world was required for us that culminate today."

Rex turned the page and read the instructions for closing the door. "Millions of people outside these walls will die soon.

"Citizens of Canamith: I have gathered you here today for the ending of one era, and the start of another. We will begin anew someday free of these walls that protect us. These walls protect us from the planet's retribution and they protect us from our fellow man. You have waited your entire lifetime to learn why this was necessary. Closing these doors today, we reaffirm that mankind can be evil and we are not. We choose to forge a new path. That path will allow freedom for all inhabitants of the world. I know that each of you spent the first part of the today taking a final glimpse of the world you will temporarily leave behind. The wonderful memories you hold dear, the sky, the mountain air, nature, you will see it again when you leave the tunnels. As you can see, the doors have already begun their final path."

As the sunlight faded from the room, small lights began to shine inside the hall, compensating for the loss of natural light from the outside. The layers of the rock doors were sliding into place, just as designed. Seven interlocking pieces came together at precise angles and formed a perfect seal. If an outsider happened to come upon the entrance to the tunnels, the multiple layers of rocks that protected the people of Canamith wouldn't even appear to be an entrance, just a wall of solid rock. Only the trained eye of a villager could find the seam.

When the doors reached their final destination, a loud thud brought an end to 2,000 years of work.

Rex Templeton stepped back to the podium. He choked back his grief as he addressed the crowd once more. "That concludes the closing ceremonies. Thank you for your hard work." Rex reached out to Buck, who gave his father a big, lingering hug.

"Dad, I don't know what to say."

"There's nothing left to say. It is what it is. Today we fulfilled our obligations. Tomorrow will be another day. Come, walk with me."

Rex heard a distant yell from afar. He prayed it was Mathis.

It wasn't. It was Elder Braham, holding a sealed envelope.

Panting, out of breath, the Elder caught up with Rex and Buck. "Here, it's a note from Mathis."

CHAPTER 33

Roger Drake excused himself and left the room.
"Where's he going in such a hurry?" asked Morales.

Dr. Goldman shook her head. "Probably went to the bathroom. He's been chugging down coffee like it's going out of style."

"It may in fact be out of style," said Morales. "We've heard reports that the coffee crop has been devastated by a potent form of a disease that we've been unable to identify. Nature better not mess with people's coffee or we've got big problems."

Drake did go the restroom, and once he entered the stall closest to the window, he reached up under the toilet roll dispenser and fiddled with the controls until he heard a snap. A small piece of plastic fell between the seat and the door. A roll of single-ply toilet paper dropped to the floor. He reached inside the dispenser again and removed a small black box. He slid his fingers along the top of the box, pushed it open and removed a key. He turned his pockets inside out, inspected them for any holes, and finding none, pocketed the key. He then replaced the roll of paper, leaving the next guest no reason for suspicion.

Drake stepped out of the bathroom and turned left, instead of right, leading him further away from his colleagues. He thought he heard someone shout his name as he reached the end of the hallway. He ignored a possible second request and pushed open a door that had been guarded by two heavily armed men.

"It helps having the money to buy what you need," Drake mumbled to himself as he opened the door and strode another hallway toward a set of double doors. Drake had arranged for these doors to remain unlocked. He heaved a sigh of relief when the second set of doors opened too.

Drake arrived at the helicopter pad. Sitting on the pad was the prettiest black helicopter Roger Drake had ever seen.

He removed the key from his pocket and opened the cockpit door. It swung open wildly, slamming back into the body of the flying machine. Drake worried that it damaged the door. He climbed in and closed the door without a problem.

"Careful there, buddy. Stay cool, now, stay cool," Drake said to himself.

He turned sideways and slid his right leg over the control panel that was mounted to the front seats. As he turned, he heard a "ping".

"Dammit!" The key had fallen out of his hand and on the floor… the black floor that was the same color as the key.

Drake searched the panel in front of him and flicked on the interior lights. He craned his neck to search the area under the seats, hunting for the small key using the tips of his fingers.

"Gotcha!" Drake found his treasured key.

He flipped on the ignition switch on the instrument cluster and the engine started to churn. He locked the door with his left elbow. He had more trouble with the passenger lock. It was stuck in the "unlocked" position. He'd fastened himself in the cockpit seat and secured the safety harness. In order to get enough force placed on the passenger lock, he had to unfasten all he had done and scoot over and use his right hand to thrust down on the lock. It clicked into place and Drake secured himself back in place.

"Dammit. Wasted twenty seconds." His blood pressure rose with each delay. He grabbed the small caliber weapon hidden inside his right pant leg, but sensed gunfire wasn't required at this point and left the weapon holstered.

The extra seconds of engine noise gave the rooftop security guards time to notice something was awry.

"Stop! Stop!" yelled the guard that was rushing towards the helicopter.

Drake pretended not to see or hear them and focused on his next job. He connected a small electronic device to the radio controls, blocking the GPS signals of the copter. He took another small object of out his back pocket and attached it to the top of the cabin.

"Good luck tracking me now, boys," he said. The guards couldn't hear him, and now with the anti-radar detection unit in place, no one would see him. He could fly without being monitored by any electronic device. No one would know his location, or destination. Once airborne, the guards would not shoot him down. General Taft issued orders directly to them in a pre-conference briefing two days ago. "We don't want to start a panic by firing bullets into the air. I want you to use extreme caution and you are not to discharge your weapons unless you are fired upon."

The guard repeated his request for Drake to stop and the young looking man removed his weapon from his holster, but a slightly older looking man with a three-day-old growth of beard grabbed the gun and forced it to the ground.

General Taft's phone rang once and he picked it up. He hated listening to the phone ringing. He didn't have many pet peeves, but a telephone not answered on the first ring was his biggest.

"Taft here."

"Thank you, General. I'm on my way to our new home. I'll see you shortly?"

"I'll be there as soon as I can."

Drake chuckled, "You don't have much time. You know where I'll be."

CHAPTER 34

Drake had smooth flying as he headed back to his fortified bunker. Two of his staffers saw the chopper coming and prepped the landing pad.

They guided Drake to the landing position with large yellow and red flashlights. The powerful LEDs were modifications of his own design. He spared no expense in designing any piece of electronics that he wanted. The world of electronics was his domain and Roger Drake loved his toys.

Drake waited for the blades to slow down before leaving the seat. He checked a few settings on the panel and put the key back in his pocket. He exited the pilot side door.

The assistant grabbed the fuel line. "Gas her up, boss?

"Don't bother, Frank. We're not going anywhere for a while." Drake jogged up the walkway to the thick double doors that separated the world from the safety of Drake's fortress. A long staircase led to the back door.

Drake's new home appeared impervious to the dangers facing the world. Each package that entered the storage facility had been hand searched for purity. Each package had been chemically washed to remove any foreign substance. Each piece of wood had been chemically treated to remove the slightest possibility of contamination. There wasn't any system that could prevent human error, and this was Drake's biggest fear in allowing others the responsibility to build his safe house. Drake had to relinquish control during the building of the safe houses. He would wake from a sound sleep and call one of the contractors to ask a trivial construction question. He berated one foreman because the nails used in the upstairs closet doors were too small. One time he threatened to decapitate the man who incorrectly measured the kitchen cabinets. He fired him instead.

"It's great to be home!" he bellowed to no one in particular as he skipped down a flight of stairs two at a time, pleased with himself that at his age he was able to traverse the distance without falling or twisting an ankle.

"I'd better be careful. It may be difficult getting a doctor to make house calls for a while," he joked to one of the guards.

He plopped down in the leather recliner for a moment as his gaze met the seventy-one inch monitor located on the south wall of the room. He searched for the remote control and then remembered that this set had been converted to "voice command" mode.

"Sonya, darling, are you here? Can you hear me? Sonya?"

His wife hadn't seen the news. Not today, not yesterday. She'd been organizing the supply of beauty products. Her storage area was fifteen feet wide, ten feet high and ten feet deep. She had been ordering cases of products that Drake told her she would want to hoard while things on the outside were unstable. The room was filled with soaps, ointments, body washes, perfumes, hair sprays, skin treatments, anti-aging gels, dental floss, dental picks, toothbrushes, toothpaste, and at least nine different products for her long hair. Drake had no idea his new woman was this high maintenance before they wed. He did fancy his women that way. If this was the price to pay, Drake was happy to comply. In a small stack in the same storage room, Drake had found a place for his items. It included hair gel, deodorant, and three cases of razors complete with a substantial pile of new blades.

He went to the over-sized refrigerator and popped open a cold beer. He chugged down half of the frosty ale without stopping.

He let out a contented sigh, then called, "Sonya, do you want a beer?"

She didn't reply. Drake opened another in case she did, and walked past the stainless steel table in the dining area that seated ten guests. Four more could be seated if the extra leaves were slid into place. Sonya had saved the table from falling into the hands of another when her mother's best friend was about to give the table away. At the last minute, Sonya had called a company to pick up the table and Drake had it delivered to his shelter. Drake and Sonya argued over the cost of the chairs for the table. Drake had enough money to make the chairs of out gold, but thought the chairs found at the local furniture store were adequate. Sonya wanted imported chairs. The shipping costs alone were more than Drake's middle-class parents had ever spent on any single piece of furniture in their entire lives.

Drake accidentally clanked the bottles of beer together as he passed in front of the outrageously expensive chairs. A few drops fell on Sonya's seat cushion. Drake couldn't help but mutter, "Serves the bitch right. It's just a fucking chair."

Drake's bunker was built to withstand anything that nature could do to man. Perhaps the animal world could chew through a cable, or disrupt communications from a television tower, even ruin underground wiring, but the real fear that Drake prepared for was other men. If the fear spread as Drake anticipated, law and order would become a footnote for history books to recall.

When the crisis subsided, there would be a country to reunite and Roger Drake planned on becoming a power broker in that new government.

CANAMITH COMMUNICATION DEPARTMENT

Update #790

Parental discretion is advised.
Some of the material included
may not be suitable for children.

Killing Caught on Video

The video showed a large group of people fighting in the street. There was no audio to go along with the video. The factions were split evenly between the races. Dark-skinned people fighting white-skinned people. The camera zoomed in and caught a hand-to-hand fight between two men. The white man pulled out a small knife from his front pocket. He lunged at the black man, who deftly moved out of the line of attack, and responded by landing a forceful blow to the white man's head, knocking him to the ground, where he doubled over in pain and dropped the knife.

The dark-skinned man retrieved the knife from the ground, and then in a stunningly quick move, inserted the knife into his attacker's mid-section. The white man fell forward, blood exiting the wound and the man with the knife turned to see if anyone was watching. His eyes fixed on the cameraman. The black man yelled something, and the video ended.

CHAPTER 35

When word filtered through the hotel that Roger Drake had commandeered a helicopter and fled, nobody on the scientific team was surprised.

"Cowardly, that's what I think," said Dr. Goldman. "It shouldn't have caught us off guard. The bigger question is why he was here in the first place?"

Morales nodded in agreement. "You're correct, and I'm pointing my finger at General Taft."

Goldman disagreed. "Drake couldn't handle not being the smartest one in the room."

Massey chipped in with his own opinion. "Our so-called friend Mr. Drake is trouble. I wish I could prove it. All his departure really means is we're down another opinion. There will be time to judge Mr. Drake at a later date. I suggest we go back to our own problems."

Goldman, Morales, and Massey returned to their books, videos, slides, and notes.

They were interrupted by the sound of the public address announcer.

"Attention. Attention, please. There has been a water main break down the street from the hotel and we've lost water pressure. We have plenty of bottled water available at guest services in all food stations. Do not drink the water out of the fountains or the sinks throughout the hotel. This concludes this announcement."

"How come I just got real thirsty?" asked Morales, to nobody in particular.

In another part of the hotel, General Taft had secretly made arrangements to leave the hotel. He was too important a figure to make a mad dash for the bathroom and slip into a helicopter like Drake. He was in charge of the greatest collection of scientists the country had ever gathered in one building. He would have to leave under the cover of darkness. A few hours of sunlight remained before Taft would abandon his responsibilities.

As the clock struck eight in the evening, Taft picked up his phone and dialed the number that he had committed to memory seven days earlier. He entered a message with the keypad and hung up the phone. He walked to the bathroom of the presidential suite and gathered his belongings. Outside the hotel basement door, free of reporters and camera crews, Taft's driver waited with the truck running. In the back of the vehicle, Taft's wife Elizabeth and their daughter Allesandra sat quietly. They were instructed to keep a low profile in the rear of the vehicle and avoid being spotted.

Taft dismissed his aide from his room, and made two more calls. The first call was to the President.

"Mr. President, I'm sorry to bother you this late in the day. No, no progress. We're working on it. I have an idea but it's going to require me to leave the building for a several minutes. We're going to have limited communication coverage and you may not be able to reach me right away. I'll check back with you when I return. Yes, sir, I'll be careful. Thank you. Goodbye, sir."

Taft collected his bags and hid them behind the drapes.

He pushed the buzzer and his personal aide, Avrum Kinowitz, charged into the room.

"Yes, sir?"

"Please go down to the hotel kitchen and get me a sandwich and a bowl of fresh fruit."

"Yes, sir. Right away, sir. I don't believe there is any fruit in the building, but I'll give it shot. Will you be safe here without me?"

"Avrum, I think I can stay out of trouble for a few moments, don't you?"

"Sir. I didn't mean to imply that you couldn't, sir. I was given specific orders. Your safety is paramount, sir, and I—"

"Nonsense, Avrum, go get us some food. Find yourself something, too."

"Yes, sir, thank you, sir, right away."

The sound of Avrum walking down the hall coincided with the sound of Taft pushing away the drapes and grabbing the suitcases from their hiding place. The general scribbled a note and tossed it on the bed and left the room.

When Avrum returned to the room and read the note, his heart sank to his shoes. He had been given one task to perform and he had failed. The President himself had said to the young soldier, "Son, your job is to keep an eye on General Taft. If he goes to the toilet, I want you to listen. If he showers, make sure you hand him his towel."

Avrum read the note out loud, this time to make sure his ears matched what he saw.

"'Dear Avrum, gone fishing. You can eat my sandwich too! Good luck. G.T.' Gone fishing? Now?"

Taft headed down the three flights of stairs to the lobby. He pulled his hat down over his eyes and headed to the basement exit of the building.

Taft slipped into the passenger seat and kissed his wife and daughter hello. The car zipped away from the hotel grounds and jigged and jagged through the city streets on the way to their destination.

After a while, Taft told his driver to pull over to the side of road.

"Sir, I don't understand."

"Pull over at the next light," barked the general.

The driver complied and Taft unlocked the doors and intoned, "Get out. I'll be driving from here."

"But, general, do you think that's a wise idea?"

"Get out, soldier. I've got plenty of protection." Taft flicked open his coat pocket and exposed his semi-automatic handgun.

The driver exited the truck and Taft and his family sped away.

There was no turning back now for the highly-esteemed general. He had left his post at the hotel, a sin that would leave him disgraced and dishonored if proven. He had risked it for the chance of keeping his family alive, and ten million dollars. There was no guarantee that Drake's palatial compound would deliver what he'd promised, but Taft was convinced that Drake was speaking the truth. He believed that Drake was the single living soul on the planet that could help keep his little girl alive and that was worth risking everything. Years of putting the country ahead of his desires vanished in a blink.

Taft used his driving skills to avoid shards of metal scattered on the road. One false move could cause a flat tire and that could lead to an unhealthy risk of spending additional time on the roadway. He felt confident once they turned on the side street that led to Drake's hideaway.

Taft picked up his mobile phone and a moment later Roger Drake's voice was on the other end of the call.

"Hello, General. Perfect, it's you. Have you arrived?"

"In a minute or two. I believe my career with the Army is in jeopardy."

"You get yourself here as soon as you can. Sonya and I are looking forward to your arrival. Everything will be fine."

"I'm in possession of my satellite phone, but I'm afraid the satellites are offline. I've removed the positioning device. I didn't want to be tracked to your location in case they re-establish communication. I'm able to get reports from around the world. I'm getting them on channel B-four-X. That sat-feed has remained clear. It's frightening, even for a man like me. I think Rex underscored the danger to man.

He was talking about the dangers man faced from nature, but man should have been worried about the dangers he faced from other men."

"How do you know he didn't know that all along? What did you expect him to say to you? You were a rising star in the world's largest army. He didn't have to tell you his secrets."

"My training has covered every conceivable kind of disaster, even terrorist attacks that have poisoned the water supply, or gas attacks, but this is everything at once. Our military people are scattered over the world. Our troops are busy helping people where they're at. We're stuck with the troops and the reserves we have on hand. The problem is that a lot of them are not reporting to duty."

"You mean like you, general?"

"That's enough, Roger." Taft's mood soured as Drake's words struck too close to home.

The steel doors of Drake's mansion didn't open when General Taft honked the horn. Two minutes went by and the door remained closed.

"What's wrong?" asked Elizabeth. "Why doesn't he open the door?"

The general's better half didn't wait much longer for her answer.

The armed guards motioned the general to pull his truck forward another six feet until it was positioned above a small red "X" spray painted on the dusty reddish ground beneath them.

"Close the windows tight!" the first man said.

Taft checked the windows and held down the button that prevented the windows from accidentally opening by mistake.

A blast of pinkish-red soapy material blasted the vehicle. Instinctively, the women ducked. When they recognized they weren't in any danger, they lifted their heads and watched as the specially designed chemicals disinfected the vehicle before it entered the compound. The treatment lasted a full six minutes and when it ended, another ferocious blast came at the truck, this time a clear rinse covered the metallic silver paint. Taft thought it was water, but it left a thin coating.

"Don't worry, honey. It's probably a sealant to protect the truck."

Elizabeth and Allesandra seemed pleased with the answer, even though the general had no idea what the substance was.

The doors of the gate opened. The armed guard motioned for the Tafts to enter the covered garage. They pulled ahead, parked the car, and exited the vehicle.

Drake stood waiting for them as they arrived. The outer doors closed behind them.

"Welcome to your new home, General," yelled Drake.

Elizabeth hesitated.

"Welcome. Please, come in. Don't be nervous. You're with friends now," Drake grinned.

"Thank you, Roger. Let me introduce my family. This is Elizabeth, my wife, and you've heard me talk of my daughter, Allesandra. Now you get to meet her, albeit under strange circumstances."

"How do you do, sir. Thank you for letting us stay here," Allesandra said.

"You're welcome, my dear, and let me say, the general was far too conservative when he said how beautiful you were."

The teen blushed; the words of such a handsome man sounded mature and sensual to her. Out of the corner of her eye, she found Drake's girlfriend Sonya wasn't pleased.

"I'll show the girl to her room, Roger," cracked Sonya, emphasizing the word "girl" as she picked up two of the suitcases. "Come on with me, hon. You can freshen up with a quick shower. Roger has restricted each shower to just three minutes. How's a girl supposed to get her hair clean that fast?"

The general nodded the approval to his daughter and that left the three adults standing there with an awkward moment of silence to share.

Elizabeth knew in within seconds that Drake was a cad. She

theorized that her home in the plush suburbs of the capital was overrun with wild animals, contained no edible food and probably no running water at this point, and their chances of survival were dim. Given that assumption, she put on her best face and vowed to never give Drake a reason to end their relationship.

Drake raised his glass in a gesture for a toast. "Come, general, let us celebrate our success. Together we have forged a new beginning for the country."

They downed the first drink.

"Quite a fortress you've built here, Drake. You are the first person to convince me to live in a home without ever seeing the floor plan or a security layout. You can imagine how Elizabeth feels. She hasn't seen the closets," he chuckled and continued laughing when he saw his wife enjoyed the humor of the joke, too.

The general raised his glass to offer another toast.

"To Rex Templeton, and his wife Sara, may she rest in peace."

"Who are they?" asked Drake.

"Just some old friends."

Glasses knocked as the first bottle of wine from the private collection of Roger Drake's expansive wine vault was finished.

"General, my lady Elizabeth, pardon my flair for the dramatic, but I give you…."

Drake stood near the bookcase that lined the library. A dark sheet of cotton was covering a plaque. Drake swept away the material and underneath was a golden plaque with the words *The Elizabethan Hotel.* "I named it in honor of your lovely wife. This is the name I have given our humble abode."

Neither Taft knew quite what to say.

"What do you think of it? It's sounds noble. 'The Elizabethan'. It sounds expensive. I love it," boasted Drake.

Elizabeth broke the silence and was her gracious self. "Mr. Drake, I'm flattered."

"I thought it was a modest gesture to show you how pleased I am that you decided to join us. I'm going to check on Sonya and Allesandra. I'll be back shortly. I'm sure they'll be fast friends. You know my little sex kitten isn't much older than your daughter."

"I'm aware of that, Roger. You haven't brought in any single men to *The Elizabethan* have you?"

"The security men have their own dwelling down the road. It's located one mile from here. There's an underground tunnel that connects those two buildings, but they can't get in unless I let them and I have sole possession of the key. There will be no funny business in this house, not on my watch. I don't have kids, but oh boy, she's a looker general. You're going to have your hands full when this is over."

"Let's wait until that day arrives before we even think about that."

"You can think about that day anytime you wish, general. This house was built with every conceivable sanitary safeguard option. Nothing's coming in and we're not going out."

Sonya, coming into the conversation from the other room, couldn't help her interest in joining."Hey, what are you guys talking about? By the way, Mrs. Taft, your daughter is great. We're going to get along famously."

Drake was disgusted that he had to re-do part of the conversation. He hated that. But, not wanting to be the selfish creep that Sonya was already suspecting, he answered anyway.

"We were just saying how this building will protect us while the world reworks the master plan."

"What's the master plan, hon?" she asked.

"That's where the general here becomes president of the country. He'll emerge from our dwelling here and step into the presidency. I've built twelve of these impenetrable buildings around the world. Each is connected to a series of self-contained power grids that are impervious to whatever is going on out there. Come on, let's take a walk and I'll show all of you hi-tech gizmos I've put into these places. Allow me to boast about what I've accomplished the last two years. Sonya, you may have thought I was cheating on you and I was. But not with another woman. It was these twelve safe houses I was building."

"Roger," began Taft, "how sure are you the design functions and the ability of these twelve fortresses, or shelters, or whatever you call them will be able to withstand outside interference?"

"General, as we discussed in our meetings, these buildings are sealed tight. If anything did happen in one of the other facilities, I'd be shocked."

Allesandra re-entered the room, fresh from her quick shower.

Her hair was tied back in a bow and her full figure gave her the appearance of being older than she was. Drake would have to wait several years before she was fair game. Perhaps her transition from girl to woman would occur within these walls.

"Great! We're all here now. I promised you a tour. Follow me."

Allesandra shrugged, but her parents whole-heartedly agreed that they should check out their new surroundings. Every room that they passed was pristine and covered with white paint.

Drake was proud of his new domain. "It looks more sanitary in white, don't you think?

"I think it's too stark," said Elizabeth. "You should have added color elements for contrast."

"How rude of me! We named the place after you and we didn't have the decency to ask you how to adorn it," chuckled Drake. "It was done this way by design. If we have any security breaches, whether by man, or in this instance, by nature, the slightest dark spot on a white wall will be easily seen. Or perhaps water damage, staining, etc…it's done for our protection. This dwelling is a temporary location for us. When we leave here, you can find that magnificent home with any color walls you wish."

"You certainly don't lack confidence, do you, Mr. Drake?"

"Please, Elizabeth, call me Roger. I'm a self-assured man by nature. I'm lucky that way."

RICHARD FRIEDMAN

"You've never been disappointed?" asked the general's wife.

"My first marriage didn't work out the way I planned," Drake smirked. "In business however, I would say they all have worked out, but like I said, I've been lucky. Let's move on to the hub of the building. I want you to see the communications center. Please, follow me."

Drake, Sonya, and the Taft family headed down a long hallway until it came to a dead end. There were doors to either side of the dead end. The door on the left led to the control room where the communications center was housed. The door on the right had a huge red letter X painted above it. In the middle of the door, a sign read: "EMERGENCY EXIT ONLY".

Drake stopped two feet from the door. He raised his hand and a loud siren above the door blasted their ears. The general, his wife and daughter cupped their hands tightly over their ears. Drake shouted through the sirens.

"This is a one-way exit out of the building! If you get within three feet of the door, an alarm will alert security! The worst part about this door is you can't get back inside once you leave! Don't *ever* open this door. As a general rule, you ladies shouldn't be even heading down this hallway, but if you do, don't go near this door." Drake waved his hand to his employee and the room fell silent.

More white walls greeted them as they passed by a room that had eleven video monitors hanging on the walls. Each monitor was paired with the city where a safety bunker was located.

"If you look at the monitors, you will see people living at my other bunkers," said Drake. "We have two-way communication with them, at least at this point. We're counting on the integrity of our satellites to maintain orbit, which could be tricky depending on how much power we can get to them. Each of the twelve bunkers has backup generators that have enough juice to last up to six years. If it's necessary to stay in here longer than that, I'm guessing we'd be going a little bonkers by then anyway, but if we absolutely had

230

to, then we could divert power from the systems to keep our life support running for another two years. I don't even want to think about staying in here that long. Let's keep the tour moving."

Red diodes and small speakers affixed on the video monitors were designed to light up and sound an alarm in the event that one of the safety bunkers had a security breach. As the group passed by monitor eight, located on the East Coast, the frantic look of the man on the other side of the screen spoke volumes. Fear didn't need an explanation.

The man in the white lab coat was shouting at the monitor, but his words couldn't be heard.

Drake forgot his guests and went into crisis management mode without hesitation. "Problem in Building Eight, cross checking voice parameter settings in the system, Code Three, people, Code Three. Let's go! Get me answers!"

Drake barked more orders to the men running the lab. The men were indistinguishable to the Taft family. They both were tall, muscular, and covered from head to toe in white coats.

"Did you see the look on that man's face on the monitor? He's terrified," said Elizabeth.

"I saw that too, but we don't know anything. Take Allesandra and keep her away from the monitors."

"Dad," said the girl, "you can't lock me away forever. If there's something going on, I have the right to see it. You always treat me like a baby."

"I do no such—"

His daughter wouldn't let him continue. "Please, daddy, I hear it in your voice, the things you say. You may not realize it, but I hear it. I'm not going anywhere. Mom? A little help here?"

Elizabeth stood side by side with her young daughter. "You military types don't get it, do you? You need to treat her more like your daughter and less like one of your new recruits."

While the argument ended, the red light over monitor eight

began spinning and sounding an alarm that made Drake reach for the volume button and silenced the audio portion of the alarm. That didn't stop the emergency situation in Sector Eight, but there was no reason to listen to the sound of the alarm any longer. Its purpose had succeeded.

A crackling sound came from the speaker attached to the monitor. The words were hard to decipher, but Drake knew what the man had said. Drake snatched a clipboard off the desk and slammed it to the ground. It shattered into hundreds of pieces, dozens of them flying at Elizabeth.

"What did the man say?" asked Elizabeth.

"Cotramtion and fold radge lantaner, cameer rant incestion found," said the General.

"That doesn't make any sense," said Elizabeth.

Allesandra repeated the words to her mother and father.

"Mom, Dad, I can read lips. I had a speech class last semester with Professor Dachner. I'm pretty sure the man said 'Contamination in food storage container. Severe rat infestation found.'"

"Oh, dear," her mother said.

"I'm afraid your daughter is right," said Drake. "We can expect Building Eight to go offline within a month. If those little critters found there way in, then they're bound to have other problems soon. That's troubling because the facilities were built with the same specs and same design. We were the prototype that the others were built upon."

"Or in this case, the same design flaws?" asked the general.

"Don't rush to judgment, general. You're not going anywhere. Let's wait and see before we panic. I have complete confidence in my staff."

"I bet you Rex Templeton isn't worried about a rat infestation right now."

Drake was perplexed. "Who is this Rex Templeton you keep referring to and why should I care?"

"Tell me, Roger," continued the general, "are you surprised that

Building Eight has been compromised?"

Drake didn't like the tone of the question. He didn't answer it either.

"One last question, Mr. Drake…

"What is it?" replied a disgruntled Drake.

"Can you please tell me more about the emergency exit?

CHAPTER 36

The men from Dead Bugs were long gone (in one case, gone for eternity), but the bugs were not. The chemicals in the cylinders temporarily defeated the infestation. These bugs were a resilient group and the reserve troops overwhelmed the stream of poison that killed the thirty thousand of their brethren.

Massey first noticed the tiny sharp pains in his feet. The bugs found their way to the soft tissue of Massey's toes by climbing up his comforter, which had fallen to the edge of the bed.

Massey leapt from his bed and landed on a carpet of insects, each of them squishing beneath his bare feet, which were now covered with tiny red sores from the stinging attacks. He knocked over the knee-high sofa table on his way to the bathroom, and immediately jumped into the shower, peeling his clothes away from his body as fast as he could.

Water blasted his torso for a minute and then slowed to a dribble as Massey recalled the message about the water line break. The bugs fought to stay out of the drain, clinging to anything they could. Massey turned the faucet head downward.

"Get off me, you damn bugs!" He waved his arms furiously in a feeble attempt to remove the insects from his hairy arms.

"AHHHHYYYYYYY!" he screamed. The bugs were not scared off by his cries. They buried themselves closer to his skin. Massey clawed at his arms, killing dozens of the pests and small specks of their blood collected under his fingernails.

"Damn this place!" he yelled.

The water came to a complete stop. It was hard to distinguish where the skin had turned red from the frigid cold water or from the hundreds of bites. Massey flicked away a few stragglers clinging to his chest hair and sent them to a watery grave.

Massey slid his body against the wall of the bathroom and moved across the room until he reached the sofa. He was naked, covered in bites, fresh out of water, and hundreds of miles from home. The man with all answers to many of the world's toughest scientific questions was out of solutions, petrified, disgusted, and ready to leave the building.

Certain the worst was over, he edged his way to the closet and found a clean shirt and pants. He dressed and tried to call Dr. Goldman's room. She didn't answer. Instead a voice on the line said, "All operators are busy now. Please try your call again in a few minutes, thank you."

He slammed the phone down, found his keys and wallet, and headed next door to Dr. Goldman's room. She met him in the hallway.

Tiny red bites dotted her face.

"Dr. Massey, I'm scared to death. You wouldn't believe what's happening in my room. I turned on the television and the entire screen was black. Bugs covered the entire area. Then they seemed to jump off the screen towards me. Some of them bit my leg. It hurt like hell! I screamed so loud I hurt my throat. I got out of there just in time. There must be a million of them in my room right now. The sound of them crunching underneath my feet almost made me throw up."

She stopped talking long enough to see Massey's red face and terrified expression.

"Where's Professor Jenkins when you need her? This would be the right moment she would tell us that there was a scientific explanation for all of this. She's not here and I haven't a clue what to tell General Taft. I'm going to his room and see if he can help us."

"I'm right behind you," Massey said. Sweat poured from his blotchy face.

The two scientists, one clad in a nightgown, the other in a thrown together mismatched shirt and pants, arrived at the hallway where they were confronted by two sentries.

"Sorry, folks, no access allowed in this hallway," said the taller of two men. In a crisp shirt, sharp edges on his hat, he could have been in a fashion magazine, not the military.

"We want to speak to General Taft right now!" demanded Dr. Goldman.

"I'm afraid that's not possible, ma'am. The general's not here."

"What do you mean he's not here? What is going on around this place? First Drake, now the general. Young man, insects infiltrated our rooms and attacked us. Do you see these grotesque bite marks on my face? What are you going to do to protect us?"

The Guard looked away from her face and failed to respond to her question.

"Is there anywhere in this building that's safe to go?" Massey asked.

The guard hesitated. "I don't think I can answer that question in the affirmative, sir."

"Ahhh, of course you can't. Dr. Goldman, let's get out of here. Morales. We have to get him."

When they reached Roberto Morales he was on the phone, talking so fast in his native tongue that neither Goldman nor Massey could understand a single word. When he finished his call, tears filled his eyes.

"I just hung up with my wife. Our neighbors attacked our home and stole our food. Our own neighbors! What is happening to our society? I must get back home. I'm afraid for my wife's safety. I never should have left her. None of this would have happened if I was there."

"You don't know that, Bob. How many people came to your house?" asked Goldman.

"I don't know for sure. My wife said eighteen or twenty people. She was scared and there was nothing I could do to help her."

Morales put his arms around Dr. Goldman and continued to cry. Massey tried to help.

"Look, there was nothing you could have done... just the two of you against all those people."

"We're here figuring out what's wrong with nature? We should be figuring out what's wrong with Mankind," Dr. Goldman sighed.

"I have caused my wife irreparable harm! What kind of man leaves his woman alone in this situation? What was I thinking?"

"Come on, Bob, don't be that hard on yourself. You had no idea that would happen. Your neighbors should be the ones you can count on during an emergency. This is the place you wanted to be a few days ago. What happened was terrible, but when we're done here, I promise one more thing to you—"

Morales cut him off. "Done here? I *am* done. I'm not staying in this place another minute! I'm going home where I belong. I suggest you do the same before something happens to your family. We never asked if Drake's family was in trouble. We're getting a crash course in what man is capable of doing to his fellow man. My wife said that when the crowd left our house they went next door to Mr. Wheeler's house and broke down the door when he didn't answer the doorbell. He's 91 years old and deaf in both ears. My wife said she heard screaming. She heard a man wailing and then nothing but the sound of things being tossed and toppled in the house. She thinks Mr. Wheeler is dead."

Massey was quiet. Thinking. "Bob's right, Emily," he said at last. "Maybe we should go home. I can't go back to my room. I refuse to talk about what happened to me in there."

Morales and Goldman looked at their boss, waiting.

"We need to figure out a way to get to our homes without getting ourselves killed. We might be safer in the long run staying here," said Massey.

Morales shook his head.

"I think our survival is in the hands of the military. I'm going to tell General Taft that I want an escort back to my house. That's the least he can do when I tell him what happened."

The guard broke the news to the trio. "Apparently General Taft has left the building and nobody is telling us where he went. I think we're all on our own."

"That's just typical. They drag our sorry asses here and when it gets tough, they disappear."

"Let's try to find a ride or appropriate a car. We'll meet in the lobby in five minutes."

Massey nodded, "That's a good idea. I'll go with you, Emily. I've got my bags. Bob, five minutes. Not a minute longer. Are you going to be all right?"

Morales gathered his composure. "Yeah, I'll be there."

Four minutes later, Doctors Goldman, Massey and Morales met in the hotel lobby.

Each of them had one small suitcase and their computer case. With Taft's exit, the meeting had broken down into chaos. It was every man for himself as scientists rushed through the lobby grabbing military people by the arm and demanding safe passage back to their respective cities- without success. The camaraderie that Taft worked so hard to forge had dissolved with his departure. The food supply may not have been scarce in the hotel, but morale was scarce and the three doctors formed a new, smaller circle of trust.

"My cousin owns a farmhouse no more than fifty miles from here," offered Goldman.

"Fifty miles? It might as well be five hundred miles!" exclaimed Dr. Morales.

"If you have a better idea I'm listening," Goldman replied.

"Hopefully we can find a ride along the way," Massey added.

"I'm leaving right now!" Goldman declared. "There's bound to be food and water at the farmhouse. It's off the beaten track and tucked away from the road. It's difficult to find unless you know where to look. I think we'd be safe staying there."

Morales fell to his knees. "I've got to get to my home!"

Massey looked at Goldman and then at Morales.

"I'm going to the farmhouse with Dr. Goldman. Robert, I think it makes sense for now. We'll do everything in our power to get you home as soon as we can. Isn't that right, Emily?"

"Of course we will."

"I'll come with you, Morales said. "I suppose we're safer together than alone."

Sirens wailed as the trio left the hotel and headed west toward Goldman's farmhouse. The famed ABC team was now defeated and in full retreat.

CANAMITH COMMUNICATION DEPARTMENT

Update #850

Like the image that first showed up on the big screen long ago, Rex Templeton returned to the big screen.

"Dear Friends,

As the video feeds from around the world begin to fail, we will be unable to see all that is happening to the world.

"We expect information to trickle in for the next six months. After that, without proper maintenance, the satellites won't be able to transmit data, and we'll be blind to the current conditions.

"As you can see from the images on the screen right now, it's a sad state of affairs for mankind. The Sanderell that I know is gone. The restaurant near the spot where my dear Sara was killed years ago is on fire. It's hard to see the charred remains now because smoke has filled most of the sky.

"There will be people fleeing the city and some of them may try to find sanctuary with us. Of course, they won't be able to get in. Nobody will.

I have instructed our operators to turn off the cameras that surround Canamith. There's no point in witnessing people die in a violent way. I've seen it once, and that was more than enough."

CHAPTER 37

The sunshine came through the windows of Kate's guest bedroom and woke Lila from her sleep.

She knew that a prompt start to the day would be prudent. She lay on her side, staring at the child she and J.J. cherished and wondered how a few key decisions in her life had brought Sophie into this world.

What if she had stayed in Canamith and married within the village? She turned over and fell back into a state of semi-consciousness, thinking about her life back in Canamith. It was easy to second-guess the choices she made back then. It's simple to look back and wonder how one choice leads to another, and then another. Lila refused to allow herself to play to the "what if" game.

Her alarm clock buzzed, startling her from thought. Lila gave J.J. a strong push in the middle of his back. "J.J., wake up. Let's go. Get out of bed. We've got to leave as soon as possible. Is Kate coming with us?"

"You know the answer to that."

"I guess so, but will she drive us anyway?"

"She will be happy to drive you anywhere as long as you don't talk to her and promise not to return."

"That's harsh. But I understand. Please wake up Sophie and get packed."

Eighteen minutes later Kate pulled the old six-cylinder beater out of the garage. The car was seldom used these days. Kate was out of work and only used the car at night for her part-time job at the community center where she checked ID cards. People weren't venturing out much and the director of the center told her that her services weren't needed at the moment. It was a long fall for the former director of sales for a large pharmaceutical company.

Mathis and J.J. stood and watched the women organize how the luggage would best fit in the trunk of the car. To the surprise of nobody, they argued about the best location for each piece.

"Stubborn, huh?" asked Mathis.

"Which one?"

"Both."

They laughed.

"That's one thing we have in common...stubborn sisters," said Mathis.

Kate honked the horn, which sounded like a dying bird, an ironic sound for the times, and the men got in the car and they eased down the driveway.

When the vehicle reached the city limits, Kate abruptly stopped the car.

"Ride's over. Everybody out." Her bitter tone betrayed her feelings—which she'd done little to mask. She had been distrusting of Lila right from the beginning of her relationship with J.J. years ago and this entire episode wasn't helping. This whole "walking into the mountains" didn't work for her and the sixty-five minute trip to get to this point was filled with awkward silence.

Kate got out of the car and gave Sophie a big hug and a kiss.

"Won't you reconsider?" asked J.J.

"Not a chance little brother. You take good care of that little girl, okay?"

"Deal."

J.J. wrapped Kate in his arms and whispered to her, "Be careful, sis. I love you."

"Kate, thanks for the—"

Kate raised her right hand and gave Lila the palm of her hand to look at.

She jumped back in the car, and headed back towards home.

Mathis stated the obvious. "I guess she's not too happy with us."

"That woman doesn't like me," said Lila.

"I like you, mommy," said Sophie, her voice filled with the excitement of starting a new day.

"Let's get going. We've got no time to spare," said Mathis.

CHAPTER 38

Fresh dents accented the guardrails as a monument to the new dangers that drivers faced as they raced down the road. Several lost control due to excessive speed, others to the hooligans that enjoyed shooting cars as they whizzed by. Others, like Jesse Presser, claimed that he was attacked by a swarm of bees that came in through an open window. His arms flailing to keep the flying attackers away, he lost control of the car and crashed his vehicle 600 feet from where J.J., Lila, Mathis and Sophie now stood.

Jesse survived his eighty-mile per hour contest with the metal rail. Michael Knapp wasn't as lucky. There was no evidence why his car traveled off the road and crashed headfirst into the rails, but when police found his body, they noticed he'd been stung hundreds of times all over his face, neck, and hands. Police assumed that he had been a victim of a swarm of bees and lost control of the vehicle.

The first hour of their walk to Canamith was eerily quiet. An occasional bird flew by, but no other humans were taking this trip.

Lila winced once or twice as the pain in her head returned. Rubbing the base of her neck, she hurried to catch up to J.J. and Sophie, who were holding hands as they walked ahead. Mathis patrolled fifteen feet ahead, checking for possible danger.

"What's wrong?" asked Mathis, staring at his sister.

"Oh, nothing, I'll be fine."

"It's her daily headache," said J.J. "I've been trying to get her to the doctor, but your sister is stubborn."

"I certainly remember that."

"Wait up, guys, I'll be right there." Lila quickened her pace to make up the distance. As she closed the gap, the unmistakable sound of a gunshot rang out. J.J. scooped up his daughter and covered her with his hands and body, protecting her as best he could. Sophie started to scream, forcing J.J. to cover the young girl's cries and muffle the sound as best he could.

"Hit the ground!" Mathis shouted at Lila, but she was already there, huddled next to her husband.

A loud motorcycle tore down the road and six more shots rang out. The lone rider was firing shots indiscriminately into the air. The sound of his bike faded as he sped down the road. J.J. released Sophie. "It's okay baby, he's gone." Sophie jumped into Lila's arms and cried.

"This was a great idea, yeah, just great. Crazy people driving down the road shooting at us. It must be our camouflage that's helping so much," J.J. snarled.

"Keep moving. The sooner we get there, the better. He wasn't shooting at us." Mathis ignored J.J.'s sarcasm.

They encountered no other dangers as they reached the outskirts of Canamith. It was like the animals in the area were giving this desperate group a slight head start before pouncing on them. A small sign indicating they were crossing the county line wasn't the only clue they needed. The foreboding mountains near Canamith stood ever closer.

Sophie started favoring her injured leg, developing a slight limp. J.J. whisked her up and plopped her on his shoulders as he headed uphill, destination known, but unsure of much else.

"It'll take us an hour from here. J.J., do you want to rest?" asked Mathis.

"I'm afraid if I rest, my legs won't recover." Sweat ran down his forehead and stained the front of his shirt.

A small narrow path led from the entrance of Canamith and ran all the way up the hilly terrain until they reached the town. Lila paused at the base of the path and took J.J.'s arm. "This is strange for me, you have no idea. I hiked this entire area as a kid. It's been a long time since I've been here."

"Remember, this was your idea, not mine."

J.J. trudged up the last part of the hill until the ground mercifully flattened out and he placed Sophie back on her own two feet. He twisted his shoulders from side to side, an attempt to relax the muscles that had worked overtime keeping Sophie firmly in place. They kept walking until they reached the outskirts of the Village.

"Where are the people?" asked J.J.

"This isn't good," Mathis grumbled.

J.J. shot him a glare. "What's wrong?"

Mathis hesitated, but Lila said it out loud.

"We're too late. They've closed the tunnel doors."

"What are you saying? Where's the door? Use your phone!" said J.J.

"Phones won't penetrate rock. Not a chance." Mathis replied. "The silence doesn't prove we're too late."

"Are you serious?"

J.J. fumed while they continued following Mathis.

The group reached the center of town. It was deserted. Small cottages that once were filled with the sound of laughing children and fathers telling stories about the huge fish that they caught years ago were silent. The village market was closed. Everything was sealed tight.

Three large carts were parked in front of the general store. Stacks of hand-made rugs reached six feet toward the sky. The only sounds coming from the store was the light pinging of the sign, hitting the window that still read, *Open*.

"It sure doesn't look open to me. It's empty," J.J. said, exasperated. "Where is everybody? Helloooooo."

"J.J., be quiet! We don't want to scare anyone. They have no idea who we are and they might start shooting at us," said Lila.

"Lila, it's empty. Who's gonna shoot us? There's nobody here."

A flock of chickens walked by, searching for food at every step.

"Those are Bill Johnson's. I recognize the cockerels. He wouldn't have left them loose like that unless...follow me to the tunnel's entrance," Mathis said stoically.

He stopped a short time later in front of a large flat section of the mountain.

"We're here," he announced, glumly.

J.J. looked around and didn't see anything.

"What do you mean 'We're here'? We're nowhere! Is this your idea of a joke?"

"I wish it was. Look closely. Stand right where you're at," said Mathis.

The door wasn't visible to the untrained eye. Mathis knew this location from years of training. The entrance appeared to be nothing more than a huge stone that was part of the mountainside.

A series of fossilized imprints on the rock was a possible clue that this rock was different from the other huge stone boulders that made up the outer walls of the mountain that protected the citizens of Canamith.

"Open the door, Mathis. Come on, open it," pleaded J.J.

"It won't work, you see—"

"Just try it!" shouted J.J.

"J.J., I knew the drill. Make it back to the village in time, or else. The residents of the Canamith had thought of every safety option. The mechanism self-destructed after the doors were sealed from within."

J.J. went right up to the door, saw the finger tipped imprints on the stone and pressed it firmly before Mathis could stop him.

"Don't bother."

"What? I just stuck my fingers in there. Maybe someone will let us in? It's a doorbell, right? Did I forget to say the magic word? What are you so afraid of anyway?" J.J. sensed success, "See, I told you, we had to try. I hear noises."

"It won't help," Mathis sighed.

The buzzing continued for sixty seconds. A small mist of steam was jettisoned from the stone that J.J. touched. When the buzzing stopped and the steam cleared away, J.J. viewed the door with astonishment.

"What the—"

"You people have absolutely no patience," Mathis stated.

"What do you mean 'you people?'"

"Look at the door."

J.J. eyed the spot he had touched a moment or two ago and it was gone. Left in its place was a sticky, brown substance that J.J. was afraid to touch. Heat emanated from the door and Lila barked orders at her husband.

"Don't touch it, it's hot."

"Gee, thanks. I couldn't have figured that out on my own."

"You did touch the door," she countered.

J.J. filled with rage. He turned away from them and walked alongside the door until it met the side of the mountain that the door had been built into. He clenched his fist and raised his hand as if he was going to strike the stone with his hand, at the last possible second J.J. heard Sophie shout.

"No, Daddy, no!"

He stopped short of smashing his hand into the stone and saving himself the embarrassment and pain of breaking his fingers, wrist, or both.

CHAPTER 39

Mathis knew what lay in front of them if the door was locked. "Forget the door, guys. It's locked and it's staying locked. The door wasn't supposed to be locked this early. My timing was planned to the hour. Something must have gone wrong. I don't understand. I was so careful. We should have had two more hours! We've been preparing that door for years. Nobody is getting into the village this way," he declared.

Lila concurred with her younger brother. It had taken a long time, but they finally found common ground. "It's true, J.J. Everyone knew once that door was sealed nobody was getting in. Tons of explosives wouldn't get through the rock that protects the integrity of the door. It wasn't built for the neighborhood children to sneak in," said Lila.

"That's great. What are we going to do now? Walk back down the mountain and call Kate. 'Hi, Kate, it's J.J. Yeah, I know you just dropped us off at the city limits at great personal risk, but do you think you could come back and pick us up? I guess the welcome mat has been pulled out from beneath our feet. My brother-in-law miscalculated the time. Kinda like showing up at a party after it's over."

"J.J., stop it. You're scaring Sophie." Lila snapped.

"Look around. What do you want me to do?"

Mathis interjected. "Let's stay calm and think for a minute." A shiny, small object garnered his attention. He reached down, picked it up and recognized the carved bottom. "Lila, look…Dad's telescope."

"Why is it out here?" Lila asked.

"It's either a sign that he was standing out here looking for me, or he threw it away in anger that I disobeyed him and left the village."

Lila sensed her brother's anguish.

"If you hadn't come back for us, you'd be inside those walls and safe."

"That was my own choice to make. I'd do it again if given the chance."

"We should have left last night," said Lila.

"It would have been far too dangerous to travel at night. Something must have forced dad's hand to close the tunnels earlier than I thought."

A lone bird sat perched on a branch and stared down at him. The bird tilted his head from side to side, sizing him up.

"What are you looking at?" Mathis asked the bird. The bird took the hint and flew away up the mountain.

"I wonder how long the doors have been closed?" J.J. asked.

"Does it matter? Five minutes or five hours, the door is sealed," snapped Lila.

"We're better off not knowing," said Mathis. All he knew at that moment was that their best chance of survival was literally sealed in stone and the immediate future didn't look too bright.

J.J. offered a suggestion to Mathis. "Couldn't we stay in your house in the village? There's a chance we could find extra food and at least there's shelter."

"It's too dangerous. People are going to be heading out of Sanderell, looking for a place to stay. We can't take that chance. Can you give me a minute to clear my head? Will you please do that?" begged Mathis.

His mind raced with ideas, but each twisted thought ran into the next and soon attempts at rational thought were a waste of time. *I'm going to die right here? Is that what my fate is?* he thought to himself. Had he brought his family here to die a few feet from salvation? Gale force winds assaulted the trees, forcing them to bend slightly towards Mathis, as if they were bowing to him for his gallant efforts.

Mathis regained his composure. "We need to go higher. I have a thought."

J.J. bellowed with sarcasm, "I hope it has a better ending than the hike we just finished."

They traveled upwards to the wondrous views from atop the mountain in the same place where his father had taken him and Buck many times before and one last time two weeks ago when they had argued.

The bird returned and squawked at the young man preparing to go higher up the mountain.

"You again? Have you come to mock me too?" he asked the bird. "You better be careful, don't get too much closer or you'll be my dinner tonight."

Mathis gathered his belongings and encouraged the rest to do the same.

J.J. didn't move. His legs were sprawled out and Sophie was lying on his lap, her legs on top of her weary father.

"You listen for once," J.J. said, his voice dangerously even, as if forcing himself to stay calm. "I thought this whole thing was crazy, but I have a wife and a daughter. I wasn't going to stay in Sanderell and let you destroy my life, but this is too much."

Mathis tried to reduce the tension. "I understand your apprehension about coming here, I do. I wish we had arrived a bit sooner. Come on, follow me a little longer," said Mathis.

J.J. stared in disbelief. "Doesn't going higher limit our options? I mean, what's up there?"

"Peace and quiet," said Lila.

"That's where our father went when he needed to think," said Mathis.

J.J. looked up at the hill. "How much higher do you want to go? It's going to get colder up there."

Mathis looked at Lila, who seemed to know what he was considering. She nodded.

"I think we should go higher to dad's favorite spot. It'll be safer in the interim," said Mathis.

Lila started walking before J.J. could offer any other objections.

CHAPTER 40

Mathis held Lila's hand while they walked.

"Tell me, big sister, why the change of heart? You said it was for Sophie's sake, but the scientist I know would have fought forever to prove she was correct in assuming this could be explained by science."

Lila paused for a moment of reflection. "I've seen things in the last month that I never would have imagined. I can't describe them within earshot of Sophie. I left Canamith for the path I chose. At least it was the correct path for me then. Look around the world now. I'm not the smartest person on the planet but I'm at a loss to offer any viable reason for this horrific loss of life. My peers don't think there will be enough food for people to eat within sixty days. What's the point of being right if Sophie is dead? I'm convinced that this can be explained in scientific terms, but while I do that, what is the risk to my family? I saw an orange tree picked clean by people in a minute. I saw an apple tree near Kate's house covered with rotten apples. Worm holes everywhere. If I can't explain how to save the food supply, then even if it is 'Explainable', as I've come to say, it doesn't matter if I can't be part of the solution to fix it. People are saying nature is killing us, but it's the early stages of this crisis. Man began to panic and I'd say the bigger problem right now is Man versus Man, not Man versus Nature."

"That means, big sister, that perhaps not everything can be explained by science. You found another rationale to keep your daughter alive," said Mathis.

"What rationale are you referring to?"

"Faith."

"Faith? You must be kidding."

"What else could it have been but the belief, or faith, that coming here was the proper thing to do? You may not want to admit it, but in the end, when all appeared lost, where did you turn? Was it your science books? No. You found a possible answer to your problem in faith. I wish Dad were here to see this. The big shot scientist comes full circle and heads home because she has faith that this mountain could have saved her. He would have loved that. You have had an epiphany. You have enough smarts in that head of yours to know when to try and take a new approach to a problem." Mathis grinned. "I think coming here was the right approach."

"You make some interesting points, little brother. Dad raised you well. He'd be proud of you. Perhaps when I'm not completely exhausted and frustrated by our situation, we'll have a nice debate about those ideas of yours."

They walked until they reached the mesa were Rex had taken his sons to the old path that his grandfather had helped built many years ago. Mathis would have blown right passed it, but he remembered the wildflowers and the big leaves on the tree that marked the spot.

J.J. didn't look or sound too pleased. "Mathis, exactly how much higher are you planning on going?

"It's too high, Mommy! I don't like being this high," said Sophie.

Lila and J.J. paid no attention to Sophie's comments. This was not the time or place to deal with her acrophobia.

Mathis hesitated at the path in front of him. He looked left, paused, then turned to the right. "Here, this way," he said, and led the way down the narrow path.

Lila had no recollection of this path, but kept quiet and grasped J.J.'s hand in a reassuring gesture that he should play along for the moment.

They came to the clearing where Mathis had stopped with Rex in his previous visit.

"Let's stop here to rest."

"What's special about here?" asked Lila.

"I'm not sure, but Dad liked it." Mathis unloaded his heavy pack and it landed on the ground with a thud. J.J. did the same with his duffel bag, and the four of them sat there. Mathis was resting his head on the same rock that Rex had leaned on many times before.

Miles away and barely visible, small fires burned in Sanderell. J.J. turned Sophie in the opposite direction to keep her from asking questions about the smoke and the fires.

Occasionally, explosions could be heard from the city in the distance. The sounds were a grim reminder of why Lila had brought her family to this point.

"Let's set up camp here tonight. I'll get a few things from my house and we'll see what the morning brings," said Mathis.

"It better bring a plan to get us to safety," declared J.J.

CHAPTER 41

Mathis rose first the next morning and put out the burning embers of the firepot. He surveyed Lila with a wry smile and asked her one simple question. "Lila, you up?"

Lila nodded, but didn't speak.

Mathis's voice was filled with excitement for the first time since he had seen Lila at Kate's house. "What was the one thing that Dad said over and over again?"

"Are you kidding?" Lila replied, her voice struggling to find its morning tone. She cleared her throat and thought of Dr. Massey and how he used to start sentences by clearing his throat. It was a sound and a habit that greatly annoyed her. She missed it. She did not know if he was even alive.

"I don't think I'm in the mood to talk about Dad right now."

"Lila, I'm serious. What did he say?"

"'Always have a Plan B.' This is not new information, dear brother."

J.J. looked at her with disdain. "Do you mind filling me in on your little family sayings? How does that help us now?"

Mathis approached J.J. and said, "I think I found our Plan B."

"What?" Lila jumped up.

"Look where my head was resting. What do you see?" Mathis asked.

Lila moved closer to the spot. She turned to her brother and said in a low tone, "I don't see anything. Can you please tell us what's going on?"

"I had a thought. We know one thing about dad. He always had a Plan B. We know that. He brought us here all the time. Why? To have us listen to the birds or see the trees? I don't think so. I'm guessing there was a profound reason. You were gone, but one of the last times I was here with Buck, dad told us about the original entrance to the tunnels."

"An original entrance? He never told me about that," said Lila.

Mathis explained.

"I'm sitting against that rock, right? The same one dad used to sit at when he was telling Buck and me about his 'Plan B'. Over and over again. J.J., you can't imagine how sick and tired we were of hearing that phrase."

"Yeah, but what does that have to do with—"

"Listen for a second, will you? I'm sitting there and I look straight ahead and what do I see?"

J.J. contributed another stream of sarcasm. "Aha! You see four magical coats that will let us walk through stone! Hurrah, we're saved!"

"J.J., stop it," Lila snapped.

Mathis walked back to the rock. "Lila, come over here. Sit here."

"Mathis, I don't understand. What's the purpose of that?"

"Just do it! Please!" He gestured with his hands for Lila to sit in a specific location.

Lila reluctantly agreed.

"Perfect. Now look straight ahead. Tell me what you see?"

"I see a rock," Lila said with exhaustion in her voice.

J.J. had his own reply for Mathis. "Hey, genius, there's ten trillion tons of rocks around here. What's so special about that one?"

Mathis ignored J.J.'s attitude and replied, "That one, J.J., is where Dad told me and Buck that the villagers had started working on a the main entrance to the tunnels years and years ago, but stopped and eventually built that entrance that you saw last night. I bet he never imagined that we'd be in this position, but think about how ironic it is, us sitting here in the same spot that Dad used to take me and Buck to and talk about another entrance."

"Ironic…or fate?" asked Lila.

"Either, I don't care right now. I want to get out of the elements before it's too late."

"Uh, Mathis, I'm not sure what you see," said J.J., "but all I see is a big rock. Maybe it's me, maybe if we get closer we'll see a big red panic button that reads 'press the button and the door will open!'"

"It won't be that obvious. Remember, this is Canamith. Things were built to make it impossible for outsiders to know what's going on."

Mathis approached the rock with caution. Barely visible on the rock were five small imprints nearly worn away from the passage of time. He wiped away dirt from the grooves and raised his left index finger and placed it firmly into the first groove. He followed that by placing various fingers in different patterns. He must have tried thirty different configurations before he heard a magical sound.

Click.

They all heard it. Mathis backed away. As if on cue from the stage director, the front of the massive rock slid upwards into the top of the huge boulder.

"YES! YES! That's your Plan B, Lila! Right here, baby, YES! That's a serious Plan B if there ever was one!" shouted Mathis.

"Where does it go?" asked J.J.

Mathis grinned, and turned on his flashlight. "Why don't we find out?"

CHAPTER 42

Inside the tunnels, the mood was somber. The village of 453 was ready to face the ultimate challenge of survival. There had been talk and preparations for this day for a millennium. Generations had come and gone and this was the particular group of people that fate had chosen to live within these walls for the next eight years. Status reports from all departments were on schedule and operating above minimum compliance standards.

Buck found Rex poring over status reports in the dining hall. Mathis's note was stuffed in his shirt pocket.

"Dad, I'm sure he convinced Lila to come back. He's persuasive. I know he can do it. What if they are waiting outside the tunnels right now trying to get in?"

Rex didn't look up from his papers.

"What if a thousand military men are there instead? Are you willing to risk everything for that possibility?"

"No," said Buck.

"You're speculating on 'what ifs'. You won't have the luxury of 'what if' as Chief Elder. You'll have years of tough decisions. You must choose the safety of everyone over the needs of one person. Even if that person is me."

"I know that."

"I've learned it the hard way. There's a chance that Mathis will survive. It's a long shot. There's no way for me to contact him, but perhaps he'll figure it out."

"Figure out what?"

"It's pointless to explain. Let's get back to work." He had proven his worth as Chief Elder many times over. Now his problem was plowing ahead with living in the tunnels and dealing with the probable death of his daughter, her husband and child, and his youngest son, Mathis.

Rex put Mathis out of his head and gathered the population of the Village in the main hall. This large, rectangular room ran one hundred yards from end to end. At the far north entrance of the room there was an elevated platform that the Elders used to address the crowd. The people were anxious and shell-shocked by the reality of their situation. They wanted their leader to tell them everything was going to work out all right.

Long tables filled the room. The tedious work of carving the tables and chairs out of the stone was finished hundreds of years ago. That same design was featured in the individual family suites. Village rules had kept the population constant throughout the years, and this enabled the architects to build the exact amount of rooms, chairs, tables, and dressers necessary to accommodate the citizens.

Rex gazed at the crowd of 453 people. Buck stood by him, soaking in every piece of advice he could.

"I've got to make sure these people stay calm," said Rex. "We've talked about this forever, but actually living in here is not going to be easy. The people are going to take their cues from us. We've given everyone a few tasks to keep them busy for a day or two, but after that, the reality of our situation will be clear. No matter the difficulties we face, you and I must remain positive at all times. Is that clear?"

"Absolutely. Give them what they want," said Buck.

Rex stood on the podium for a moment. He scanned the crowd and smiled as he saw the faces of his friends. His heart ached not knowing where Mathis was. He wondered about Lila too. He put his personal crisis aside. "I want to first thank you all for remaining resolute in your work. Your outstanding efforts and those of your ancestors made today possible. We owe a great deal of gratitude to those who came before us. Let's take a moment of silence to honor them." Rex bowed his head and thought of the people in his family that had sacrificed to make this day possible.

"Today begins a tragic time for mankind, but for us it is a culmination of the effort that preserved our heritage. What world will await us when we re-open the doors? Even the ancient scrolls do not predict the answer. During the eight years we remain in the safety of our shelter, we will study our books. We will learn, we will grow, our beautiful children will turn into young adolescents, and they in turn will become men and woman. Some of us may die here. There were times in my youth when I questioned if all this work was necessary. As I grew older, it was obvious that trouble lay ahead. Now, all these years later, I am proud to see us together. We remain grateful to the past, united in the present, and hopeful of the future." Spontaneous applause greeted Rex. He had never been the recipient of such adoration during his reign as Chief Elder.

"Thank you, thank you for your support. It means a great deal to me and especially now, with Mathis out there somewhere..." He couldn't continue. The grief had temporarily overtaken him and he turned his back to the crowd to regain his composure. Buck joined him on the pulpit and placed his arms around his heartsick father.

Buck whispered softly in his father's ear, "I know that Mathis is going to make it. I don't know how, but you've got to believe. Have some faith."

Rex nodded and answered back in a hushed tone, "I know all about faith. I'll never give up on Mathis...ever."

Chants of "Rex, Rex" filled the room. As he departed from the podium, Buck and Rex strode through the crowd and received words of encouragement.

"Way to go, Rex!" shouted one of the Elders.

"Thank you for everything!" hollered a girl no more than thirteen years old.

A voice from the back of the room yelled, "We're eternally grateful for your service."

Rex nodded with approval and hid his personal torture.

Buck uttered, "Dad, you're doing great, they're reveling in your confidence."

Rex changed his expression to a smile as he and Buck made it through the final group waiting to congratulate him on his speech. They headed down the long hallway to their living quarters. "You see, Buck, I can turn my emotions on and off like a light switch. When my people need me to be strong, I can be the leader they require. You will need to remember these lessons. Now please leave me alone, I need some time to myself."

CHAPTER 43

In another part of the tunnels, Mathis, Lila, J.J., and Sophie closed the door to their new-found entrance. Two large levers controlled the panel that brought the boulders back in place. Mathis checked the locking mechanism. The instructions were faded, but the hand-carved drawings inside the mountain showed Mathis how to lock the door. He did, and the levers shattered into a thousand slivers of stone.

"I guess nobody is getting in now," said Mathis.

"Or out," J.J. countered.

The four new arrivals made a slow, methodical trek along the old stone path, hoping to find the rest of the villagers. An hour into their journey, Sophie asked the typical kid question. "Mom, are we there yet?"

"It's hard to say. It's impossible not to lose my bearings with all the twists and turns we've made. I can't answer your question right now."

"Shhhhhh," said J.J. "Hear that sound?"

They listened, but they did not hear any voices. Instead, they heard running water.

"Dammit," said J.J. "I thought we were on to something."

"We might be, might not. But hearing water is a positive sign. That means that the system is working. We worked feverishly to make sure the water intake lines worked perfectly. Without water and food, and air, we'd be history in a matter of days. Hearing the sound of the water is a good thing."

"Mommy, I'm getting cold," said Sophie in a concerned voice.

"We'll stop in a few minutes and I'll warm you up, sweetheart," J.J. answered before Lila could reply. The path had narrowed and the air significantly cooler than when they first entered the tunnel. Mathis noticed Sophie hung in there without much of a fuss. Her tiny feet allowed her to maneuver down the narrow path without trouble, but she was bound to tire sooner than the adults. It would be too risky for anyone to carry her.

The lights on Mathis's headlamp illuminated the next 20 feet. Lila had a small flashlight tucked away in her backpack for an emergency.

"My GPS unit is useless inside, but I'd guess we've already descended close to 150 feet since we entered the tunnel," said Mathis.

"How much longer do we need to go? asked J.J.

"That's hard to say. I know the main entrance to the tunnels was a thousand feet above sea level, and the entrance we stumbled upon was approximately four to five hundred feet higher than that. I think we're going great. Don't look back."

Up ahead of them, lay a damaged section of the path.

"This must be the section that I heard about from Dad," said Mathis. "See? This path ends in another fifty feet. Stay here. Let me check it out."

"I'm coming with you in case you get in trouble." said J.J.

"Absolutely not! Stay with the girls. If anything happens to me, you'll have to decide what to do. Stay here and I'll be back in two minutes."

"Be careful," said Lila.

"Wait here for my instructions. Is that clear?"

J.J. nodded.

He reviewed the content of his backpack and glanced back at Lila with a half-smile. Her response left him lacking. Lila's eyes gave it all away. They said to him, *"If Dad were here, he'd figure out a way, but you're just my little brother and we're going to die."*

"Lila…I got this…relax." His words were meant for his own doubts as they were for hers.

Mathis proceeded down the path three or four inches at a time. Small pebbles crunched underneath his feet and loose dirt pushed off the edge of the path and tumbled hundreds of feet to a new resting place, past a series of edges and jagged rocks into darkness. Mathis couldn't see the bottom. He inched closer to the last few feet. He stopped and reviewed the choices that lay directly ahead.

A three- or four-foot-wide section of the trail was missing.

J.J. shouted to him. "Whad'ya see?"

Mathis didn't respond.

"Hey, what's happening?" J.J. asked, this time with more concern.

"Wait a second, will ya!" shot back Mathis.

Mathis used his walking stick to measure the space between the paths. The stick was four feet long. He grabbed a small rock and made four quick slashing marks on the stick, each scratch in the stick was approximately twelve inches apart.

He approached the end of the path and laid the end of the stick a few inches away from the edge. He went down to one knee to get better leverage with the stick and found the footing more to his liking. With one hand on the end of the stick, he delicately placed the rest of the stick over the crevasse and rested the other end of the stick on the far side of the path. He spun the stick in a clockwise direction. The spinning of the stick drew concern from his fellow travelers.

"It's okay. I'm trying to get the exact distance we need to clear in order to get to the other side," he called.

Six spins later, Mathis was convinced the stick had been scuffed enough on the other side to retrieve it. He brought the stick back and subtracted the distance from the edge of the stick to the scratches on the stick that indicted the front of the other side of the path.

He returned to the anxious trio and gave his report.

"We need to clear three feet, seven inches to make it across one side of the path to the other. This won't be too difficult for us," he pointed to Lila and J.J., "but it'll be hard for Sophie. Here's what we have to do. We'll get to the edge of our side and then take one large step with our left foot and plant it on the left-hand side of the path on the other side. Our shoulders will be close to the large outgrowth of rocks on that side. The rocks could knock us off balance, and that could be dangerous. Really bad. Step over them with great caution. Dip your left shoulder down, and place your right hand on the ground in front of you to gain better balance. Then it looks like if we crawl for three more feet, we should we okay."

"And Sophie?" asked J.J.

"I don't think we can carry her. It'll be too risky with her weight shifting when you come over."

"I can jump mommy. We jump in gym class."

The three adults reviewed their options and couldn't find a better solution.

Lila took Sophie by the hand and knelt down beside her.

"Honey, we can figure out another way."

"Mommy, I want to get out of this place right now."

Lila grabbed the girl tight and hugged her close.

"I've got an idea. Baby, you know mommy has a Plan B, too!"

Mathis groaned as he heard that dreaded phrase.

Lila perked up with her new plan. "Here's what we'll do. Mathis and J.J., you guys go over to the other side first and I'll stay here with Sophie—"

J.J. interrupted, "I don't like this plan."

"It'll be fine. You two go to the other side. Mathis, you'll get behind J.J. and grab his waist. You can use that stick of yours to notch out little grooves in the dirt and stick the edges of your shoes in there for better traction. J.J., you'll be close to the edge. You'll have to use caution. I'll be holding Sophie around the waist from this side, and she'll lean over towards you. Plus, the rope is keeping us together."

J.J. said what nobody wanted to hear. "If either of you start to fall, that rope won't save either of you."

Lila ignored his plea and now directed her attention to the child. "Sophie, it might be a little scary, but I want you to close your eyes and I'm going to have you lean forward towards Daddy and then you will reach those cute arms of yours to him. He'll grab you and Daddy and Uncle Mathis…hmmm, that sounds funny, 'Uncle Mathis'…but Uncle Mathis will be holding Daddy, and Daddy will be holding you. We'll make a train."

Mathis and J.J. couldn't find the fatal flaw in that plan. They were getting more tired by the minute. They agreed to go with Lila's plan, agreeing it sounded safer than having Sophie jump across to the other side.

Mathis was the first to step over to the other side. His athleticism made the transition from one side to the other easy. J.J. didn't carry any extra weight, but his muscles didn't respond in the same manner as his younger brother-in-law. Mathis helped J.J. transfer enough of his weight on the far side of the path. As his back foot crossed over, it banged into the path and knocked off another few inches of the further side of the path.

Lila, watching from her side of the path, her mouth in anguish as pieces of the path crumbled away, shrinking the margin for error by a few more inches.

"I think we can still do it," said Lila.

"Not much choice now, is there?" said Mathis.

Lila removed her bandana from the bag and covered Sophie's eyes.

"Here you go, baby, no reason for you to be scared. I've got you tight on this end and daddy will grab you on the other."

Sophie nodded to J.J. that she was ready.

Lila inched the child closer to the edge. Sophie sat on her knees, arms up in the air, as if she was reaching for an angel to guide her across. Lila had the child tight around the waist, and kept nudging the girl little by little to the end of the path. A few small pebbles fell away and Lila gasped, but the footing was sure and when it was time for Sophie to reach across with her arms, she did so without a sound.

"That's it, Sophie, just another few inches," said J.J. He wiped his hands on his pants to remove perspiration. "Come on. Reach out for me, honey."

The girl responded and J.J. locked his arms in hers.

"Now, Mathis! Pull! I've got her."

Mathis used his strength to ease J.J. and Sophie back away from the edge. They tumbled backwards and Mathis had nothing to break his fall. The back of his head sustained two blows. The first when his head landed on a small, but sharp rock and the second when his head rebounded but struck J.J.'s head on the rebound.

"Ahhhhh!" cried Mathis. The pain was real, but he had a firm grip on J.J., who had an equally strong grip on the child.

"We did it! Mathis, are you all right?" asked the relieved father.

"Yeah, I'll live. You have a hard head."

"Lila tells me that all the time."

Mathis grinned as he used the palm of his hand to search for the blood that was trickling out of the back of his head. "Yep, I'm bleeding. Sophie, you all right?" asked Mathis.

"I'm fine." Sophie used to the back of her shoes to inch away from the edge. J.J. was holding her and as they backed away from the ledge, the path opened enough for them to switch places.

"Let me help mommy, honey. Stay right here."

"I've got her, not to worry," said Mathis.

"It's a little weird on this side all by myself," Lila called.

"Then hurry up and get over here," her husband answered.

"Let me check everything on this side first."

"Easy honey, easy. I won't let you fall," encouraged J.J.

Mathis whispered into J.J.'s ear, "Say it like you mean it this time."

"C'mon, Lila, I know you can do this."

She took a large step with her right foot, not the left as she had been instructed, before Mathis could speak, she attempted to plant her right foot on the ground. The recent damage to the edge of the path required her to take a longer stride, which brought her right knee further away from her body. Her left leg strained to hold on to the near side of the path. J.J. hesitated, unsure whether or not to try and grab her. Lila's right foot started to slide off the path, loose stones fell away and over the cliff.

Lila's right leg slid, her head was too far upright, and her left shoulder headed for the side of the inner mountain path. Her left hand had nothing to grab on to, and her right hand reached out in desperation for the lunging J.J. His long fingers latched on to his wife's forearm. Mathis watched as J.J. found the strength of three men to pull her towards him. She bumped her nose on the side of the wall. It made a nasty sound. Blood poured out of her nostrils.

She started to fall near the edge but J.J.'s grip was sure and he pulled her down on top of himself. Blood dripped onto his shirt, as they lay face-to-face. She was wounded, but safe on the other side.

"Do you newlyweds need a room?" said Mathis.

"That would be great. Can you help us find one?" said Lila.

"The new path was wider than the previous side. All three adults were able to walk without fear of falling over the side.

Lila stuffed packing material up her nose to help restrict the flow of blood. She touched her nose. "Ow! Mathis, do you have a surgeon in the village? I'm going to need a nose job."

"Yeah, I know a guy. But I don't think you've reached your deductible. It could be rather costly."

Exhaustion caught up with Sophie, and at this point there was no choice but to carry her down the path. Lila and J.J. took turns, each lugging the forty-five pound child for a few minutes at a time until their arms and legs burned with pain. This slowed their pace to barely more than a crawl, but every step along the way brought them closer to the end of the trail. Lila's nose throbbed with pain, but the bleeding had stopped.

They found an area large enough for them to rest.

J.J. rubbed the muscles in his legs, and then his shoulders, and his arms. He sat behind Lila and rubbed her shoulders. Sophie started to cry. Lila consoled her as best she could, but the child needed more reassurances than what the circumstances allowed.

"Mommy, do you know where we are? It's dark. My leg hurts. You said everything would be okay. I don't like this place."

"Uncle Mathis is here to lead the way. We have nothing to worry about."

"That's right, Sophie. I know these walls like I know the seventh and eight generations of Templetons that helped carve out the dining room."

"Huh?" said Sophie.

"I'll show what I mean as soon as I can."

CHAPTER 44

Several minutes of sitting and stretching had given their aching muscles a rest before continuing their quest.

Two slow, tedious hours later, Lila's strength fading, and she could no longer assist J.J. in carrying Sophie. He carried the girl without objection. Mathis stole Lila's shift. The girl's weight slowed him down and made each step more perilous.

Sophie slept tossed over her father's shoulder.

"What kind of reception is waiting for us Mathis?" Lila wondered.

Sweat dripped off Mathis's forehead. He wiped his brow, took a deep breath and answered her question.

"Can we worry about that when we get there?"

"Do you think everyone will be happy about us coming back? There's bound to be some concern about how we got in, three more mouths to feed, J.J. and Sophie don't know that customs of the village."

Mathis turned to J.J. "Does she always ask so many questions?"

"You have no idea."

Mathis stopped dead in his tracks. "Lila, please, if other people aren't happy about it, too bad. Dad's still in charge for now, and then Buck will work it out."

"Buck?"

"You've missed a lot."

Each step brought them step closer to the answers to her questions.

Mathis returned to the front of the line and as they moved ahead another couple of hundred feet down the treacherous path, he stopped and said, "Quiet. Nobody move."

He motioned to the others to stay quiet with his right hand and flicked off the light on his headlamp with his left hand.

"Hold up a second. Look!" said Mathis.

"I can't see anything," said J.J. "What do you see?"

"Look!" said Mathis. "Up ahead."

Lila and J.J. strained their eyes to look down the road.

"I see light," said J.J.

"Yeah, me too," Lila agreed.

"I'm not crazy, then. But keep quiet. I don't want to startle anybody," Mathis cautioned.

They followed the light, with a bit more pep in their step, but cautious of the conditions. There were several last twists in the path, but Mathis reached the end of the old tunnel entrance. He could see the ceiling of the main room. The rocks formed a four-foot railing that prevented an accidental tumble over the edge, but this was as far as they could walk.

He peeked out over the edge, then turned to Lila and said, "We need one more Plan B".

"What do you mean? What do you see?" asked Lila.

Mathis smiled and said, "We're at the end of the tunnel, and there are about 450 people down there hoping that I'm still alive."

Lila picked up on his wording on asked, "How far is 'down there?'"

Mathis shook his head, "Fifty, sixty feet or so."

"Now what do we do?" asked Lila.

"Not much. It's up to them to help us. We're the ones up in the air. We can't jump from here, that's for sure. We'd kill ourselves from this distance. I don't think even dad has a Plan B for this one."

Lila disagreed. "This is Rex Templeton you're talking about."

"True, the man does have a plan. Let's let him know we're here."

"Mathis, I haven't seen him in years. What if he doesn't want us here?"

"Lila, give him a chance."

Mathis had no idea what her reception would be, but this was not the time to think of that. First things first: they had to get down there.

"Let me handle this," said Mathis.

Mathis maneuvered back to the end of the tunnel path. From down below he heard voices. Mathis dislodged a small stone from the edge of the tunnel path and it fell down, hit one of the tables, bounced eight feet off the ground, and landed harmlessly on the ground. Rex stopped cold in his tracks and looked down to the area where the stone landed. He tried to figure out the stones origin based on the trajectory. He used his finger to follow the sight line he had imagined in his head and when he reached the spot at the top of the old tunnel entrance, he saw the outline of a human head. Mathis stuck his head over the opening and yelled down at the assembled group.

"Hey, Dad, are we too late for dinner?"

A gasp ran through the crowd. Rex raised his hands and hushed the crowd. He cupped his hands around his mouth and said loud enough for all to hear. "Mathis, my boy, you certainly know how to make a grand entrance!"

CHAPTER 45

When they realized their beloved Mathis had returned home, almost everyone cheered with excitement.

Rex stood in front of the crowd, no longer concerned with laundry, food, or the impending destruction of the world. He focused on the people located above the conference room.

"Hang on a minute, Mathis. I'm tossing around a few ideas in my head to get you down. Is my granddaughter up there with you?"

"Yes, Dad, Sophie's here," shouted Mathis.

Rex didn't respond. He knew that if Sophie was there, the other two people with his son must be J.J. and Lila. That excited him, but he went into crisis management mode and told one of the Elders to go his dwelling and bring back the large green box in the corner of the bedroom closet.

He returned within minutes with the large container.

"What's in the box?" asked Buck.

"Rope. That's our family up there and I'm going to get them down and you're going to help me."

Rex opened the box and brought out the beginning section of a long rope ladder. The rope was several inches thick. Brown in color, it was a gift from General Taft years ago. Taft thought Rex should have it in case anyone had to escape out of a window. When Rex told him there were no windows in the tunnels, Taft laughed and told him to keep it anyway.

Three questions remained unanswered. Was the rope long

enough to reach the ceiling? Was the rope strong enough to withstand the weight of the people trying to use it? And lastly, was there a spot strong enough in the secondary tunnel path to affix the rope to?

The same men who retrieved the box prepared the rope for the first part of the plan. They began making a knot strong enough to withstand the pressure that would be placed on the rope while the people were descending from the ceiling.

"Rex, we're ready to give it a try," said one robed man. Rex grabbed the rope and did his own inspection. He made minor adjustments to the rope and gave the knot a final tug.

"Looks good to me," Rex declared.

"Dad, I can reach them. Let me do it," said Buck.

Lucas White had inched up to the front of the group and announced to anyone that would listen, "My arm is stronger and more accurate. Let me do it."

Ethan pushed through the crowd with reckless abandon and grabbed his son by the collar. Lucas pushed his father away with the ease.

"Dad, what are you doing?"

Ethan's wrath was apparent to those close to the scene. Bulging eyes, a single large vein engorged with blood protruded on the right side of his neck.

"What am I doing? Don't you have any pride? How many times are you going to be embarrassed by those Templeton kids? You might be able to stand there and take the humiliation, but I can try and stop it. That girl disgraced you. We don't need her back here. If she's so smart, let the fancy scientist figure out a way to get down here on her own. I'm not here to help and you shouldn't either if you had any sense. Now come with me back to our room."

Lucas held his ground.

"Dad, this had gone on far too long. Those were your battles, not mine. I'm not humiliated or disgraced. I thought Lila and I had something, but we didn't. I'm married to a wonderful woman. You must let it go, Dad. All of it."

Ethan wasn't ready for that. He took Lucas by the shirt, pulled him close, hesitated, and then pushed his son away in disgust and turned back towards the rear of the room, heading to his living area.

"Rex, I'm sorry you had to hear that," said Lucas.

"It's okay. Your dad's dealing with a lot of issues right now. Why don't you go and be with him? We'll get them down."

"I want to help."

"Fine, then let's get to work. The end of the rope is secure. We don't know if there is a spot for them to secure the rope on their side."

Rex cupped his hands around his mouth and gazed up at the waiting quartet. "Can you hear me?"

"Yeah. What's the plan?"

"Do you have a place you can attach the rope on your end that will support your weight?"

"I don't know, let me check. It's dark up here. Give me a minute."

A few minutes later, Mathis called down.

"Dad, I think we've got it."

Rex looked at Lucas and nodded. He knew nobody else in the village had the strength to toss the rope that high. Lucas spent a moment stretching his shoulder muscles. He swung his arms wildly in big circular motions, as if he was a helicopter turned sideways. Small beads of sweat began to pepper his forehead.

"I'm ready," said Lucas.He grabbed the knotted end of the rope with his right hand. The knot would provide weight at the end of the rope and allow him to propel the rope high enough for Mathis to catch it. "Just like when we were kids," shouted Lucas.

Mathis found that funny. A small nervous laugh popped out of his mouth. "Give it your best. I'll catch it if you can get it close."

Lucas swung the rope around his head a few times and before he let go, the rope nearly came out of his hand.

RICHARD FRIEDMAN

Elder Braham interrupted. "Folks, take a step back, give him room."

The second heave was better. Lucas launched the rope high into the air, but the weight at the end of the rope brought the twine too far to the left of the Mathis, who tried in vain to catch it, but had no chance at the errant toss.

"That was better, Luke, the next one ought to do it," said Mathis, trying to instill confidence in his old pal.

The force of the throw had given Lucas a sharp pain that ran through the tip of his right shoulder and spread to his elbow. He had grimaced in pain when he released the rope, but everyone was watching the brown twisted hemp soar upward and nobody noticed the young man's discomfort.

Lucas knew he had one more toss remaining in his arm. He rubbed his elbow vigorously in an attempt to relieve the soreness.

"Are you all right? asked Rex.

Before Lucas could answer, a chunk of the wall that Mathis had been leaning on gave way and sent a wave of debris hurdling toward the crowd below. The people scattered and barely avoided being hit by the largest piece that had fallen.

Mathis moved his hands backwards quickly as he felt the wall give way. Rex saw what was happening and didn't like the odds. He turned to Lucas and said, "Can you do it? If not, we'll figure out another way"

"I can do it," said Lucas. He moved back a few feet from the spot where his first two attempts had failed. He eyed the spot where he wanted the rope to go, and took several running steps to help build his momentum. He stopped short again, measuring his angles, speed, and release point. He gave Rex a wink with his left eye. He retreated to the spot where he had started a moment ago and repeated his efforts, but this time he released the rope. Lucas screamed in pain as the knotted end of the rope sailed upwards and carried higher and higher, appearing to defy the laws of gravity.

284

Mathis reached his right hand out with all of his length to meet the rope as it hung at its apex for a split second. His fingers mishandled the twine at first, but he recovered and grabbed it before it fell back down.

A huge cheer rose from below as Mathis slid backwards and found solid footing.

Rex went over to Lucas and patted him on the back shouting, "You did it! You did it!" With each slap, Lucas winced and shrank away. When Rex realized Lucas was hurt, he pulled back and looked for the doctor, who had observed the last toss and immediately saw the problem. Doctor Leber motioned his assistant to retrieve a bag of ice.

"Great toss, buddy!" shouted Mathis.

Lucas got to his knees and said, "You owe me big time for this!"

CHAPTER 46

J.J. fastened the rope to an outcropping in the wall. It was the first thing that had gone without a hitch in two days.

J.J. gave the rope a tug and felt it hold firm to the wall. "It's solid," said J.J.

Mathis grabbed the rope. "Lila, you go first, and then J.J. will help Sophie down. If that rope loosens at all, I don't want it to happen when the two of you are on it." Sophie started to cry.

"No, Mommy, I'm too scared! It's too high! I don't want to die. Please, don't make me, Mommy, please!"

"Sweetheart, I'm afraid it's the only way down. Daddy will carry you, it'll be all right."

Lila knew that if J.J. was going to lower himself down the rope and carry his daughter at the same time, he would need Sophie's cooperation. J.J. couldn't climb down the rope with a struggling and frenetic daughter tugging at his side or grabbing his neck in fear.

Sophie continued to whimper.

"Honey, please, calm down," JJ soothed. "I won't let anything happen to you. Haven't I told you that we're going to be okay? Remember when I promised you'd see Mommy again?"

Sophie nodded.

"Then I won't let anything happen to you now."

Sophie calmed a little, but she wasn't convinced that descending from the ceiling on a rope was an easy task. "Daddy, that doesn't make sense. What does before have to do with climbing down the rope?"

Lila finished the explanation. "What your dad is trying to say is that he will protect you. Being scared is rational, but you don't need to be frightened. That's a different thing. Just like at home; remember our big words, Sophie?"

"Yes, Mommy: all things can be explained."

"That's right dear, and this is an example of mass, gravity, tension, and various other scientific principles mixed together to get us down to the ground. I'm a bit anxious to get started. What do you think?"

"I think you're nuts. Scientific principles?" said Mathis.

"I'm scared, Mommy."

"I understand, but I promise Daddy will keep you safe. J.J., you should go first with Sophie. The rope is going to the strongest at the beginning and I don't know if I'm strong enough to hold Sophie. If you go first, then at least Sophie will be safe and sound."

"Don't worry," said J.J., "you'll be great. Stop trying to ascertain the probability of the rope breaking. Hold on the rope, go slow, and hold Sophie tight. You have to go slow or you'll start an uncontrolled spin."

"Thanks for the confidence," Lila said sarcastically.

"I'm serious. Take it slow. Come on, you can do this."

Mathis stood by the wall anchor, and prepared to use whatever strength he had left to relieve any tension on the rope when the Lila and Sophie were climbing down.

J.J. went back to the opening and glanced down one more time to the hushed crowd. Dozens of bed pillows and mattresses had been positioned at the anticipated drop zone. Even if the climbers could stay on the rope, the rope would only get them within twenty-five feet of the floor. This new "mountain" of bedding continued to grow and now reached six or seven feet high. If the climbers fell from thirty feet, they might suffer serious injuries.

Lila was ready to go. Sophie was terrified, but it was time to move. Lila grabbed her backpack and pulled out a hat and a pair of gloves. She strolled over to her daughter and caressed her hair. Lila second-guessed every decision she had made in the last two days. *What have I gotten my daughter into with this crazy idea?*

"Sophie, my sweet girl, I don't know what is going to happen when we get down there. I know for a fact we can't stay up here, and we can't go out the way we came in. That means our only choice is to go down. I'm going to go down the rope with you. There are a couple of things we need to talk about. I know you're scared. Everybody gets scared. Even mommies get scared. Did you know I hate snakes? Sometimes at work I have to touch them and I don't like those days. While we're on our way down to the ground, I don't want you to look down. In fact, I want you to use this hat that I brought with me to cover your eyes."

Lila demonstrated how she wanted Sophie to use the hat like a blindfold, preventing the girl from seeing how far from the ground they were.

"I want you to face me while we go down, and I'll be talking to you the entire way. I'll be right with you. You'll wrap your legs around my waist, and hold on to my back real tight. You should be able to wrap yourself around me and then I want you to link your hands together like you do when you and daddy do when you cross the street. Do you think you can do that for me?"

"Uh-huh," Sophie said quietly.

"That's my big girl."

J.J. peeked over the high drop and gave the thumbs up signal to the crowd below.

"She's ready," yelled J.J.

Lila positioned herself on the top rung of the rope ladder. She tried not to think about how much weight she would be putting on the rope as she descended. Lila waited at the top of the rope while J.J. escorted his child towards her mother. When J.J. placed her on the rope with Lila, she did as instructed and pulled the hat down as far as it would go over her head. She wrapped her hands around her mother's back and then with the help of her father, she took her right leg and moved it around her mother's left side and rested her foot on Lila's backside. The she did the same thing with her left leg.

Sophie had locked on to Lila with such force that the tips of her fingers were white from the pressure. Lila didn't dare say a word about relaxing her grip.

"I'm going to say 'one, two, three', and then I'm going to take the first step."

Sophie nodded, but was too scared to speak.

The rope was steady as Lila counted off the numbers and then away they went. The first two steps were uneventful as mother and daughter were linked as one.

The third step for Lila was ill measured, and her foot missed the cross bar of the rope and the pressure on the side of the rope forced the rope to sway to the right. Lila quickly adjusted her foot and found the toehold and steadied the rope. Mathis was lying on his back, feet pushed hard against the side of the wall, and his hands were trying to take the brunt of the weight that was starting to mount on the support piece sticking out from the wall. So far, so good, and Mathis was not wilting from the strain.

Lila was able to step down twelve rungs before her next mishap. This one wasn't her fault. She had planted her right leg down on the rope and as she lifted her left leg from the rope above the right one, the crossbar gave way and went limp to the side of the rope. The crowd gasped as Lila slid down to the next support piece and she landed on it with enough force to force all parties to stop for a minute and wait. Would the rope hold?

"Careful!" yelled J.J.

Lila felt her daughter's heart pounding through her shirt. "Easy, baby; Mommy is doing fine. I couldn't have ever done this without you. You're so brave. I'm proud of you."

Sophie was motionless as Lila reached the halfway point. More panic set in when another crossbar piece broke a few steps later. This time, Sophie landed on Lila with a jolt, and when Sophie adjusted her arms to re-tighten her grip on Lila, she bumped off the hat, and it fell harmlessly the ground. A little boy picked it up and started to put it on, but his mother grabbed from her son and stuffed it in her back pocket for safekeeping.

Sophie let out a sharp scream that startled Lila. She instinctively tried to turn and check on the girl, but her quick movement had forced the rope to twist. First to the left, and then slowly back to the right. Lila and Sophie were far from the top and J.J. couldn't help them. They were too far away to get any assistance from below. Lila was going to have to fix this on her own. All she could do was to try and keep moving lower as slowly as she could. She didn't want to spend any extra time elevated off the ground with her daughter than she needed to. She quickened her pace and in another minute, she had traversed the last of the ladder-rope and stood patiently as she waited for instructions from her rescuers.

"Lila, we're ready. I think you should help Sophie jump first," she heard Lucas say. "If you fall together, you could end up landing on top of her."

"Yeah, you're right." She turned to Sophie and said, "Sophie, now you have to do one last thing and then you'll never have to do anything like this ever again. I want you to jump off and land on all that padding. Pretend you're jumping on the bed and this time we're telling you it's okay."

Sophie, her head buried far into her mother's breast, wasn't buying that plan. "You tell me that if I keep jumping around on the bed that I'm going to hurt myself. This is a lot higher than the bed."

Lila couldn't help but smile. *My child's too smart for our own good. That's what I get for telling her not to jump on the bed.*

"Honey, let's put it another way. We have to get off this rope right now. If I let go of the rope, we'll both fall off and hurt each other. You have to jump first and then I'll jump right after you."

"No!"

"Sophie, this is hardly the time for an argument."

"I said no!"

Rex heard the commotion and tried his best to speed things up. "Lila, every minute you spend on that rope is time that J.J. and Mathis don't have. You've got to make your move now."

"Dad, we're jumping together. Like it or not, we're coming down together." She focused on her daughter. "Sophie, I'll say 'one, two, three' and then I'm going to let go of the rope and we're going to fall on the pillows and mattresses. First, you're going to have to climb around the rope. Here, let me help you."

Lila guided her daughter around the rope and placed her against her chest. Sophie clung to Lila's back tightly.

Lila fell backwards off the rope and as she dropped, she turned her body to the left and gently pushed Sophie away from her. In an instant, the two landed and spontaneous applause erupted in the room. The climbed down from the padded material and into the arms of well-wishers.

"Yeah!!!" shouted J.J. He pumped his fist into the air several times.

Mathis released his hold on the rope and wiped the sweat off his brow and his hands.

Old friends swarmed Lila and Sophie, and Rex parted the throng and made his way to them.

He reached his hand out to Sophie.

"Come, my dear. Give your grandfather a great big hug."

Sophie kept her head tight next to Lila's body. Lila walked towards her father and they embraced for the first time in years. She broke down in tears as they hugged.

"There will be time to get reacquainted, my daughter, but we have two men up there up there just as anxious as you were to get down here. Let's get them down too."

"Same old Dad," Lila whispered under her breath. It didn't matter that in this case Rex was correct.

"It's your turn, J.J.," said Mathis.

"I'm not going next," replied J.J.

"Look, don't argue with me. Get down this rope and go be with your wife and daughter. I'm coming down right behind you."

In his heart, J.J. didn't want to be the one left standing on the ledge alone if anything else went awry.

"Why don't we try to go together?"

"J.J., the rope won't hold. You must weigh at least 185 pounds and I'm at nearly that myself. No way. One at a time is the only way down."

"Fine, you win. Tell me, who is going to support the rope by the base of the wall while you climb down?"

"I have an idea. You let me worry about that."

J.J. inched closer to the ledge and moved into climbing position. He knew two people down there. The rest were strangers. Lila had become a stranger to these people, but she had been born here. J.J. was a true "outsider".

"Daaaaaddyyyyyyyy...Come down. I need youuuuuu."

Hearing Sophie's tiny voice, J.J. knew he had try. His head was even with the base of the tunnel opening.

"Remember, J.J., go slow," said Mathis with encouragement.

"I'll see you down there in a minute," said J.J.

J.J. moved down the ladder. His strong hands gripped on each rung. He was careful to circumvent the first cross bar that Lila had broken. J.J. had to take an unusually long stride to reach his left leg down to the next unbroken chain in the ladder. This awkward angle left his right leg much higher than it should have been, and J.J. saw the rope start to weaken at that point.

He moved his right leg down another notch, and this motion began to make the ladder swing violently to and fro. Mathis was doing his best to secure the rope at the top, and J.J. could feel a slight twisting of the rope.

Lila ran up to Rex with an idea. "Do you have another rope? It doesn't have to be as long as the first one. Any kind of rope will do. We can throw him that line and that will help steady him. He's not that high anymore."

RICHARD FRIEDMAN

"That's an outstanding idea. I'm sure we've got one. Braham, hurry, what else can we throw him for support? Quickly!"

Braham looked around the big room. Nothing caught his eye at first, and then he saw one of the electric cords that ran from the generator room to the master junction box that sent power to the individual sleeping rooms.

"We could cut the power, temporarily, and use the cable to—"

"Do it!" said Rex. "We don't have much time left."

Braham continued anyway. "Rex, there's a risk that we won't be able to re-connect the line perfectly."

"Do it, I said!"

Braham moved quickly and cut a fifty-foot section of the cable. The last half-inch was persistent and didn't want to let go. When it released under the force of the blade, it sent Braham flying backwards, causing the Elder to lose his handle on the knife and it flew out his hand and landed precariously close to his own daughter's foot. She screamed, but wasn't hurt. Braham gathered the cable and rushed it back to Rex, who handed the cord to Buck. He grabbed the three-inch thick cable and hit J.J. in stride as he held on to the ladder with one hand and made a nifty catch of the cable with the other. The men at the other end of the rope methodically tip-toed backwards, putting tension on the cable from below, and the line snapped at attention all the way up to J.J., who used that force to steady his ladder. Mission accomplished.

J.J. continued down the ladder. Sophie jumped in anticipation of her daddy making it down. As he lowered himself, the men holding the cable continued to step further away, this helped keep the tension on the line and eased J.J.'s descent.

J.J. fell into the bedding material. This caused more celebratory shouting from the crowd and Sophie rushed up to her father and jumped into his arms. "Ah, my sweet Sophie. You know I was scared up there. Then I thought of you and I said to myself that if my little girl can be brave, then so can I."

"Thanks, Dad. You were great too. But, Dad, I'm not a little girl anymore. Mommy says now I'm a big girl."

"I better get used to that," said J.J. with a glint in his eye.

Lila rushed up to her husband and they embraced. Then they turned back to look up at the isolated figure that was Mathis. Lila's brother had done his part to get them down.

There was no one left to help him.

CHAPTER 47

Rex stood at the bottom of the tunnel and yelled up to him. "What do you think? Will the rope hold on your end?"

"I'm not sure. The constant weight on the line has loosened the connection…I'm going to try and reinforce it before I try to come down. Don't worry if it takes me a couple of minutes."

Mathis went back to the spot where the end of the rope had been secured to the rock protruding from the wall. Where there had once been a solid circle of rock that enabled J.J. to tie the rope around, that circle had a small fissure in it. Had it been there all this time? Mathis had no idea. There were small rocks scattered around the base of the wall that held the circular rock. Would the wall hold long enough for one more man to descend down the line?

Mathis retreated back up the path and gathered a few large rocks and used those to build a new support wall that reached from one side of the tunnel to the other. He jammed the rope into this new collection of rocks as tight as he possibly could.

The wall was close to three feet in height when he realized that he had to get on the other side of this wall that he was building or he would completely block himself off from the cave opening. He laughed out loud at his own stupidity and chalked up the faulty choice to exhaustion and stress. Once he realized his error, he moved all the rocks to the other side of his wall and finished loading up the opening with large heavy stones that he trusted would stop the rope from sliding off the wall and sending him free falling to certain death.

"I think I've got it now." Mathis yelled down.

"Great. What can we do to help?" asked Rex.

"Well…come up with another Plan B?" Mathis said, only half-joking.

There was a lengthy silence. Then Rex said, "I…I'm sorry. I can't help you."

"That's a first. Figures, now of all times." Mathis muttered to himself, then he called, "Okay, then, here I come."

Lila called up to him. "Mathis, can you throw down my backpack? My computer is in there."

"It'll break from this distance."

"I don't think you want to carry it down with you from there. Yeah, throw it down. It's better padded than I am," said Lila.

Mathis fastened the latches on the backpack and sent it spiraling out over the edge. It tumbled end over end several times before landing on the bedding material with a louder-than-anticipated *thwack*. The straps of the backpack broke on contact and the force of the fall sent the hinges of Lila's computer flying off the pile of mattresses and landed a few feet away.

"Thanks. Now you've given me a reclamation project down here."

Mathis replied. "You said you wanted it! You got it! Are you ready for me now? Any more requests?"

"No. Come down."

"That's the plan. Have some faith down there."

Mathis grabbed the rope with both hands, inspecting his handiwork one final time. He couldn't see the end of the rope. It was wrapped around a potentially broken rock and it would have to bust through several hundred pounds of large rocks to cause disastrous consequences.

The two end pieces of the rope hung out from the wall of rocks Mathis had built and he began to climb down.

The rope felt solid. In fact, the rope held firm for the first twenty feet or so without a hitch. Then, he felt the rope slacken. He was convinced that the end of the rope had broken free of the wall and now only his makeshift pile of rocks was keeping the rope from sliding to him. He had to maneuver another fifteen feet lower before he would avoid serious injury from his fall. He hustled down that rope and with each step, he felt less and less confident that he would make it.

Would this be how it would end? All those years of preparation and countless hours of work and sacrifice and I'm gonna die because an old rope broke free after saving my sister? And worst of all, if I die here and now, it would be a horrific sight to witness. I'll forever be known as the guy that fell to his death.

As the ground grew closer step by step, he felt the tension on the rope fading. The ropes slid precariously close to busting through his make shift retaining wall.

Come on...come on...hold on, dammit...Thwap!

The rope broke free and began its slow motion chase to catch Mathis and meet him at the floor.

Then two things happened a split second apart. He heard the crowd gasp, and felt the electric pain of making contact. He was vaguely aware he'd landed on the bedding. It only kept him from dying, not being severely injured.

His legs were twisted in a sickening manner. His left foot was turned 90 degrees to the left while his left leg was turned the same degree to the right. He would never run again. Walking would be a minor miracle based on the initial view of his feet as he lay in a crumpled heap atop the pile of various bedding materials.

The crowd of onlookers rushed to his side. Buck was the first to get to him. "Mathis! Mathis! Are you okay?"

Mathis stared up at his older brother and fighting back the pain, he whispered to his sibling. "Do I look okay?"

"No, actually. But that's what you get trying to impress the ladies with your grand entrance," Buck joked back.

"Boys, boys, boys, that's quite enough," said Rex as he pushed his way through the crowd.

"Heh, Dad, I did it," said Mathis, each breath filled with searing pain.

"I'd say you did something remarkable. As I knew you would. How are your legs?"

"I didn't realize they were still attached to my body."

With that comment, the medical staff rushed in and placed Mathis on a gurney as gently as they could. They took every precaution to keep him safe, using a body board to secure his back and a neck brace to keep his head stable. Then they whisked him to the medical clinic. The doctors in Canamith didn't have medical degrees from traditional colleges, but their physicians had studied medical books, practiced medicine in the village and were prepared for any emergency. X-ray equipment, gauze, tape, bandages, and anything that the department required. It had all been accumulated throughout Rex's trips with General Taft.

Doctor Aaron appeared after a tension-filled hour waiting for news. Dr. Aaron was short, thin and his brown hair was flecked with gray at his temples. He didn't smile much, but he made up for that with a kindly bedside manner that eased his patient's nerves.

"Heart checks out, lungs are bruised, at least three broken ribs, two broken ankles, a possible fracture of the humerus bone, but his vitals are in surprisingly good condition," admired the doctor.

Rex, J.J., Lila, Sophie and Buck breathed a sigh of relief hearing the news.

"Don't get too excited, folks, he took a nasty fall. We're going to have to give him a few weeks to rest, but he's going to make a good recovery. Doctor Leber will be here in a minute to talk about the surgery on his ankles. You can come see him for a few minutes," Dr. Aaron guided the family into the surgical area of the clinic.

Rex moved closer to his son and grabbed his left hand and gave it squeeze. Mathis managed to give a small amount of pressure back and Rex held his hand until the "Bone Doctor" entered the room. The kids in Canamith gave him that moniker because of all the x-rays he had taken over the years.

"I've seen your x-rays. Heck, I think we have x-rays of your whole body. How do you feel, Mathis?" said the balding, middle-aged surgeon.

"Doc, you ever get run over by a herd of elephants?"

"No, can't say that's one of my life experiences thus far, but we'll see what happens when we get out of here someday. Maybe I'll take that trip where the elephants search for water. I've read about that. I'm going to prep for surgery in a minute. You don't have to memorize the Sanderell Book of Modern Medicine to see you've got issues. Dr. Aaron started your pain medication with the IV drip. Rex, if there's anything you want to talk to your son about, I'd do it now before he goes into surgery. He'll be in recovery for several hours. I'll see you in surgery, Mathis. Don't worry, young man, I'll take good care of you."

"Thank you, doctor," said Rex. Then he looked at Mathis. "You found the original entrance, didn't you? Very smart, young man. Very good indeed. We'll have time to talk about that later."

"Thanks, Dad. I'm getting a little sleepy."

"What in the world are you thanking me for?" asked Rex.

As Mathis drifted into sleep, he whispered, "Plan B…Plan B."

CHAPTER 48

While Mathis rested in the recovery room, Lila took this opportunity to re-acquaint with Rex. She found him waiting in the recovery room with Buck. They were thumbing through books trying to pass the time. Rex glanced up and smiled at his daughter. J.J. followed, trying to blend into the background.

"We have a lot of catching up to do," said her father.

"Yeah, I can't believe we're sitting here together."

"You better have the doctor take a look at your nose. I think it's broken."

Rex studied her, and caressed her shoulder-length hair.

"Lila, tell me, why did you come back home?"

"Dad, I've studied the stars in the sky. I learned all about the animal world. I read all the books I longed for. I saw mankind do great things, but I ran out of time trying to figure out what's going on out there and the logical thing to do was to live to fight another day. So here we are."

Rex shook his head in disagreement. "You won't figure out it with science. We're people of faith. We read the ancient scrolls and we adhered to their instructions. When I used to meet with General Taft, he would tell me about the world. He said that people would follow the rules that made their life easier, not better. We obeyed our rules in order to save mankind. And now, sadly, as it was predicted 2,000 years ago, here we sit. We're simply humble servants carrying out our destiny that was written long ago. When

Mathis is stronger, the village will gather to listen to the *The Holy Book of Knowledge*."

"What's that?" asked J.J.

"That is the original message from those who gave us our instructions long ago. It is the most sacred piece of writing in our long history. The text of that book has never been dislodged from its original case. Nobody in the village has ever opened the book."

Buck grew concerned as the conversation turned to the Holy texts.

"There are certain people in the village insisting that Lila and her family should not hear the sacred words."

"Then let those people deal with me. For now, I'm in charge and these people are my family. Are they not living here with us?"

Buck had struck a tender nerve and tried to retreat. "Yes, Dad. Don't be upset with me. I'm simply relaying what I've heard. Not everyone is pleased that there will be three more mouths to feed, and clothe, and shelter, and the Elder at the oxygen intake center was concerned about the amount of air."

"Oh, that's nonsense. Those are foolish people dealing with petty jealousy. We've factored in a safeguard. We have enough supplies to take in another few people if we had to. Now that the doors are sealed, I don't think three more is a problem. Tell the troublemakers to go drink herbal tea and relax. The people you speak of are probably friends of Ethan White. I'm sure he's responsible for this nonsensical chatter. I'll speak to him at a later time."

Ethan had entered the area and had heard the last few seconds of the conversation. "How about right now? Buck is right. I'm not happy about the recent events that have transpired."

"I see you changed the timing of the closing of the tunnel doors without my knowledge. I'm not sure how you did that, but I'll be calling a special hearing at the appropriate time. Your betrayal could have cost the lives of four people."

"I did no such thing! Your signature was on the bottom of that page! You are the Chief Elder, remember?"

"We'll see how that unfolds, Ethan. Seeing Lila must have been a shock to you and your son, but I thought Lucas handled it perfectly. That relationship was over a long time ago. If I can forgive my own daughter for fleeing from the village, can't you find it your heart to forgive her? Your own son has."

"It's not that simple. There are many issues to settle. Food, clothing, waste by-products, and more. You've said that contingencies were put in place for more people, but that was for unforeseen births that took place while we were inside, not for bringing in outsiders."

"You're talking about my family. Don't be like this. You and I have been through too much together for pettiness to sideline us from the bigger picture. You are not my nemesis. And I hope that after all these years you don't look at me that way either."

Ethan snarled, "Once your daughter left here she became an outsider. Just because her will to survive brought her back with a baby and another man doesn't change the facts. The real bigger picture is that this village agreed to a certain number of people that would be moving into the tunnels and you've taken those rules and thrown them out in order to keep your family intact. We have 453 citizens already and three more pushes us over the limit by one. I don't suppose you'd want to send your granddaughter back home to Sanderell? My own son put off having a child to maintain your sacrosanct population quota. I could be holding a grandchild if we allowed the kids to procreate freely. And now, you decide that three more mouths to feed are acceptable. And don't give me any of that 'I've got a plan for that scenario'. I'm not buying that logic either. You never thought you'd see Lila again. We all know that."

Rex was incredulous at his longtime foe, and wondered if Ethan's hostility was designed to incite trouble in the village. "Ethan, let's pretend for the moment that you're accurate. I don't think you are, but for the sake of this discussion, let's say you are right about everything.

What would you have me do? Throw them out? Lead them to the exit? We can't open the door anyway. It's sealed. We're not going to kill them, are we? We certainly can't raise them up to the ceiling and force them out the same way they came in? They're staying. Nobody here is kicking anybody out. We'll figure it out. Things have a way of working out. I don't want to discuss this issue with you. Every family has suffered due to our efforts to finish the tunnels. It's time to move on. Put away the past. Let it go. We're young enough that we may see the sunshine again in our lifetime. Let's think about the future. I'm done with the past. I've spent a lifetime preparing my future based on it. I'm ready to move forward. Now if you excuse me, there are people I haven't seen in a long time and I want to spend time with them. Then I'm going to sleep like a baby. Tomorrow is a big day. I suggest you get rest too."

"Dad," said Lila.

"Just a minute, Lila, we're almost done here."

"Dad, no, it can't wait."

Rex, irritated, raised his voice.

"What is it?"

"J.J. would like to see the water filtration systems."

"Now?"

Lila searched the room for support, but found no takers.

"Dad, where are filters located?"

Ethan shouted, "You can't tell her that! That information is classified!" With that, Ethan threw his hands in the air and let Rex have an earful. "This is an outrage! What's the point of having rules if the Chief Elder can't even follow them? This is absurd. You haven't heard the last from me, Rex Templeton!" Ethan stormed away.

Lila recalled her conversation with Aldo on the airplane heading to the Capital. She told him that certain individuals would consider her return to Canamith "contaminating" the village, and now here she was, causing a ruckus immediately upon her arrival.

"Dad, I'm sorry, I don't mean to be a pain."

"It comes natural for you," he said with a chuckle.

"Thanks, but that's not exactly the response I was hoping for. Dad, J.J. was a scientist back in Sanderell. What could it hurt? It'll keep him busy for awhile."

"Buck, go with Lila and J.J. show them what they want. If she's with you, then she can't bother me while I'm spending time with that grandchild of mine. Go see whatever you want. You live here now, whether Ethan White likes it or not."

While Rex told Sophie stories about her deceased grandmother, Lila, J.J., and Buck moved towards the back of the tunnel facility where the mechanical systems were located. They passed by the oxygen purification system, the waste removal operations and then arrived at their destination. Buck introduced his long lost sister to the director of the Water Filtration Department, a tall, thin woman named Sydney Jensen. Her long hair was tied back in a ponytail and she stopped the group at the door.

"Sorry. Can't let them in, Buck."

"Rex has authorized it. We're coming in. Sydney, this is my sister Lila and her husband J.J. They're new arrivals here from Sanderell and she—"

"I know who she is," retorted the director in an ice-cold voice.

J.J. tried humor to break the tension. "We decided to drop in at the last minute."

Sydney wasn't in the mood for jokes. Her eyebrows furrowed. A razor thin line separated the black hairs. "I know all about her. I married Lucas White, remember? I've heard the stories my entire life about you. What do you want from my filtration systems?"

"J.J. wanted to check on what type of system you have in place to check for MTBE's?"

"What are those?" asked Buck.

Sydney jumped J.J. with the explanation. "Methyl Tertiary Butyl Ether…In high doses, it's a possible carcinogen in water. What does he know about that?"

Buck still didn't understand what it was, but he knew a carcinogen wasn't good.

"My husband works in that field, and look, I promise we're not here to question your expertise, when people are placed in an environment for this long they can lose their ability—"

Sydney bristled.

"I haven't lost my abilities! Now if you'll excuse me, I'm busy and I don't have time for your—"

This time, Buck leaned in closer to the petulant director. "We're coming whether you want us to or not. So please point us in the right direction."

Stunned by his forcefulness, Jensen abruptly turned and uttered two words. "Follow me."

She led them into a dressing area where they all donned white anti-contamination suits and proceeded to the secure area of the department. Sydney swiped her entry key card twice as they passed through several rooms before entering the primary equipment that ran the ventilation system.

"You wouldn't even understand the systems we use. They are much different from what I've been told is used in your world."

Lila shot back, "I think you'd be surprised how much we've learned in—"

Buck interrupted the bickering ladies. "Can we get on with it please?"

"Sure, if that what Rex wishes. But I don't see the point in them barging in here and suggesting that I'm not doing my job."

"Nobody is suggesting anything of the sort. Your dedication is above reproach."

Sydney nodded slightly, offering a glimpse of a truce.

"Great. Lila, can you be more polite?" asked Buck hopefully.

"Who's not polite? She's the one getting defensive, not me," said Lila.

"I won't bite. I'm not a monster. I fell in love with Lucas too, but didn't let him go," said Sydney.

"I never told Lucas I loved him! Oh, this is so juvenile! Can you show us the systems please?"

"Fine."

They spent the next two hours reviewing the process how the water is filtered before it gets to the residents in the tunnels.

J.J. asked Jensen, "How have you dealt with any contaminated underground water?"

"There isn't any. We get our water from above ground."

"Perhaps, but what about seepage coming from Sanderell?"

"That hasn't been a concern. Our testing procedures have shown zero contamination levels."

"Were those tests taken after the new gasoline storage tanks were built last month? If you people are right, and with the fires I saw last night coming from Sanderell, I'm starting to become a believer myself… if those tanks rupture or the seals give out, our geographical research indicates that there may be a risk to the mountainous region here for underground contamination. If those contaminates head this way, that's bad news for Canamith."

"Are you talking about the plant located near Berkson Drive and the Highway?"

"Yes."

"We weren't aware any product had been placed in the containers yet."

"Happened the other night. They did it in the middle of the night so they could avoid any media coverage. The mayor was trying to get a restraining order to prevent the plant from opening. Part of his concern was my letter to him addressing BTME leakage. The company's lawyer convinced the local judge to dismiss the order and twenty-two million gallons of fuel are in those containers. Well, I should say the fuel was in there the other day…Now? Tomorrow? Next month? Who can say?"

Jansen flipped open her computer and ran a serious of equations. Two minutes passed and her facial expressions changed from anger to concern. "It what you're saying is true, there could be a problem down the line. We've got a few systems in place for that."

"If they weren't designed in the last year...they're antiquated. You've got to have several systems in place to assure the levels of contamination are within safe limits. We've used air-stripping, which wouldn't work in a tunnel. There's soil vapor extraction, advanced oxidation, but I think granule activated carbon would suit your...I mean *our* situation best."

"I see I've got a few things to brush up on. Let's continue this talk tomorrow. This isn't an emergency, but I'd like the rest of my staff to hear this too."

J.J. had shown an immediate benefit to the village. He and Lila headed back to find Sophie.

They found her sitting on a bench with Rex near the Library.

"Dad, I was wrong about what I said to Lila," began Buck. "There was indeed a problem that had gone unforeseen by everyone in the department. Sydney was stunned, but according to J.J., it wasn't her fault."

"It was nothing that you or anyone here would have caught until perhaps two years from now," added J.J.

"Buck, how could this happen? We've been careful. Every step of the way has been covered with a backup plan."

"Dad, not even your famous Plan B would have caught this. If J.J. hadn't been here, we could have had a serious problem later on. It's lucky they came back."

"J.J., can you please explain this to me?" asked Rex.

"First let me say that Sydney and her staff are amazing. Rex, are you familiar with Methyl Tertiary Butyl Ether?

"I'm afraid this is discussion is going to be way over my head. You lost me quicker than I thought. Methyl Turtle-Butter?"

J.J. laughed at the mispronunciation.

"All I really want to know, is everything working properly now?" asked Rex.

"In a word…yes," said J.J.

"Buck, I want a full report on this by the end of the week," demanded Rex.

Lila wrapped her arms around her father and hugged him tight.

Rex seemed bothered by her affection. He tried to gently push her away. She held on tightly, refusing to relinquish the firm grasp she had on the man.

"Lila, please, not now. Buck, are you listening to me?" Rex said.

She whispered in his ear, "Dad, does everything have to be explained? Can't you have a little faith?"

Rex smiled, pulled his daughter close, turned to his new larger family and said,

"Children, welcome home."

CHAPTER 49

Sanderell was burning. The gasoline storage containers that J.J. warned Jensen about exploded and killed fourteen employees. Millions of gallons of fuel spilled out of their containers and caused a rolling firestorm that ran for two miles. The fire split into two directions as the gasoline ran west and south from the plant. The southern trail moved into the Sanderell Trailer Park. The fires melted the aluminum homes like dominoes falling in a row, each home catching fire, propane tanks shooting into the sky, ripping apart and sending shrapnel raining down. Many of the park residents were trapped inside their trailers, succumbing to a combination of poisonous gas, smoke, and then fire.

The western trail of gas headed directly into the downtown district. Most of the stores were closed, but one building after another caught fire and within minutes, blocks of the city were aflame.

Days earlier, rescue squads would have been dispatched to the area immediately and first responders would have been on the scene within minutes. Those folks were long gone, abandoning their responsibilities to save their own families. City officials had secretly approved a plan for any government employees to avoid subjecting themselves to any further danger. The mayor and his family had commandeered three city-owned vehicles and had packed up their personal belongings and headed out of the town moments before the storage tank explosion. Their vehicles were caught in the inferno and all parties were lost. Firefighters, policeman, secretaries, probation officers, Judges, even the men and woman in the service department had fled. The unsuspecting citizens of Sanderell were left to deal with their horror without any government assistance. The city burned to the ground.

Civil servants throughout the country were doing the same thing. A complete breakdown of society was only hours away. President Griggs's biggest fear had come to fruition. The country, at least for now, was lost.

CHAPTER 50

Two Days Later

The Hall of Heroes filled with the adults from the village. The children had been instructed to spend this time in the playground, such as it was, with the teenagers supervising the younger ones.

The Elders were dressed in their finest ceremonial robes. A complete explanation of the tunnels' history would happen within hours. The ancient texts would be read aloud.

The texts were protected by one specially chosen citizen of Canamith. He was called The Guardian, a position that garnered the most admiration in the village. His job was to stay in the room where the text was stored. The current Guardian, a man named Orrick, never left his living quarters, known as the Dwelling of Honor. Orrick's living space encompassed 1,500 square feet. A large percentage of that was dedicated to protecting the *Holy Book of Knowledge*. Orrick guarded this book with his life. His oath forbade him from reading or touching the texts.

Orrick had been at his post for thirty-seven years. He was an old man now, closing in on his seventy-fifth birthday. The Elders brought his meals on a daily basis. He vowed to stay in the Dwelling of Honor until the Chief Elder requested the sacred books, or until he died. Orrick was not allowed to speak to anyone until the Chief Elder came to him and told him it was time to read the book. Orrick sensed his duties would soon be over. He had seen and heard the increased activity in the tunnels over the last twelve months.

Orrick heard a knock on the door.

He looked through the small hole in the thick wooden door that gave the Guardian a tiny glimpse of the man standing on the other side. It was Rex. Orrick knew this was serious business.

Orrick and Rex were casual friends years ago. His vow of silence didn't stop the Chief Elder from telling Orrick stories from the village or the status of the tunnels.

Rex spoke to his old friend through the door.

"You are Guardian of the Holy Book of Knowledge. Oh, Guardian, our dear brother who has sacrificed everything to protect and serve the village nobly, I am the Chief Elder and it is my duty to ask that you grant me entrance into your Dwelling of Honor so I may bring the Holy Book of Knowledge to the Hall of Heroes for the re-telling to the village."

Orrick's heart raced with anticipation. Thoughts of freedom from his tomb entered his head. He pushed those ideas back into the dark recesses of his mind and thought of his immediate task.

Orrick had prepared for this moment for a lifetime. He calmly remembered his training. He did not regret his decision to become Guardian, but he did wonder what his life would have been like from beyond the confines of this chamber. When he was a younger man he was able to suppress those thoughts easily, but as he aged, he thought more of missing out on fatherhood, friendship, and female companionship.

Orrick unfastened the four locking mechanisms on the door. *Click*, then *snap*, and then two more small *clicks* and the locks unhinged.

Orrick opened the door and gestured for his guests to enter the room.

Under dim lights, the thirteen Elders filed in one by one, Rex first. The Guardian had a small sleeping chamber located in the far north corner of the room. It housed a closet and a large bed with rich, dark wooded bedposts and full-sized mirror, now badly worn and faded.

Orrick seldom used the mirror. He hated the view. He entered this room as a strong young man and the image he saw in the mirror now was of an old man with sagging shoulders and a balding head. Next to the sleeping area was the dining room. It could hardly be called that. It consisted of a table and a single chair. It was the only dining room in Canamith with one chair. A bathroom and shower were to the rear of the suite. A sliding panel above the bathroom provided light through a series of reflector panels emanating from the Tunnel's main control room. The living room had a couch and a large chair with a worn-out cushion, its floral pattern long worn away by the passage of time. A tall bookcase filled with a vast collection of literature that spanned generations of authors, covering every conceivable topic.

The Guardian may have been restricted by space, but not in knowledge of the world around him. Books had been exchanged with Orrick when the Elders brought him his meals.

Rex had remembered Orrick as an average-looking man with dark hair. Now Orrick was gaunt, with the haunted look of a man who had done little exercise and received no direct sunlight. He was hardly the image of a man sworn to protecting the most sacred book in the known world. His life was extraordinarily lonely and Lila had called it "a wasteful excuse of a man's life" years ago before she left the village.

Orrick gave Rex a pleasant nod of his head when he entered the room.

"We have come for the Holy Book of Knowledge. You have performed your duties as instructed and I am instructing you to allow me access to the room."

Orrick paced ahead of Rex by a few steps and placed his trembling hands on the edge of the protective coverings and slowly snapped the lid that protected the Holy Book.

Orrick grasped the edge of the lid and used as little pressure as he could to pry the cover off. Sweat formed on his brow and he heard the steady breathing of Rex behind him.

Rex whispered softly to him, "Easy does it. Take it slow."
Clack.

The lid was off. Orrick held the lid in his left hand. Rex took the lid and passed it back to the hand of another Elder, who put it safely on the table.

Rex moved next to Orrick and used hand signals to move the Guardian out of the way. Orrick understood his cue and took several steps backward and one to the left to assume his proper positioning.

Rex gathered his thoughts for a moment. He wished Sara were at his side to witness this moment.

The Elders formed a perfect semi-circle around their leader as he began to speak.

"We are humbled to be in the presence of the *Holy Book of Knowledge.* Our ancestors gave us a monumental task and we have fulfilled our obligations. Our reward for that hard work is a mixed blessing. It is our duty to survive in these tunnels while Man suffers the consequences of his actions. When the time is right, we will emerge from our home and repopulate the world. Oh, Guardian, please place the book on the tray."

Orrick placed his palms face-down on the book. It felt cool to his touch. He picked up the book gently and rested it the tray. Rex lifted the tray and turned around to exit the Dwelling of Honor. The rest of Elders moved behind Rex and strode towards the door.

The Elders proceeded out of the door and when the last of them had cleared the exit, Rex turned to the Guardian, "You too, Orrick. Join us. It's time."

Orrick nodded. From his front door, he took a last look at his home. A tear formed in the corner of one eye, but he did not speak. He followed tight behind Rex as he exited the room, his room next to Elder Braham waited for him.

While the Elders marched to the hall, other members of the village lined both sides of the corridors to get a glimpse of the processional. Rex strode past J.J. and Lila. He acknowledged them with a slight nod of his head. Mathis sat next to Buck, watching the events in his wheelchair. Rex saw his sons, but didn't acknowledge their presence.

Grown men and women wept openly as Rex passed them by, the pent up emotion of the day overwhelmed them. Rex proceeded up the steps of the altar and placed the book on the podium.

The audience grew silent in anticipation of what they were about to hear.

He reached under the podium top for a glass of water that had been placed there thirty minutes ago. He drank slowly from the cup, finished the water, and began to address the gathered crowd.

"This is a historic evening in our people's history. We are aware of what is happening outside the confines of these walls. Death and destruction rain down on mankind as we speak.

"Fires from Sanderell could be seen prior to closing the tunnel doors. Reports from around the globe indicate our efforts were sagacious. It's not easy to stand here and wonder if there was more we could have done to help. We have heard the annual re-telling of *The Great Divide*. It is a staple of every childhood here in Canamith."

Rex shot Lila a glance when he mentioned this book.

Rex knew she had tried as much as any human to stop the madness of pollution and wastefulness that she had seen firsthand as a college professor. She had tried to help when she went to the capital and met with leaders from around the world, but none of that mattered now. The world was out of control and headed for disaster. There was nothing one person could have done or said that would have changed the course of history.

Rex scanned the crowd and made eye contact with as many of the villagers as he could before turning his head downward to read the Holy Book. He continued speaking.

"Generations have wondered how this place came to be and what secrets are in this book. Our ancestors left detailed instructions for us. We've seen the glorious illustrations throughout the tunnels and wondered about the origins of our people. The wait is over."

Rex turned his attention to the Holy Book. He placed his right index finger under the top right edge of the gold-bound book. His finger quivered a bit when he did this. Even Rex Templeton, the calm and cool one, Chief Elder of the Village of Canamith, battled his nerves. The angle of the podium prevented anyone in the crowd from seeing his finger hesitate ever so briefly, but Rex was overwhelmed by the moment as were many in the hall. He regained his composure and opened the first page, and began reading aloud.

"My name is Ellison Grant and I have been given the job of writing this epic tale with the hope that nobody will ever read it. That's a peculiar way to start a story. But it's true. It was our fervent goal that you never had been instructed to follow the steps necessary that led you to this day.

"You must have asked yourself why you spent generations building a series of tunnels in order to protect a few hundred people? Your question will be answered, but first, a short history lesson.

"Mankind. Who is Man? How did we get here? I live with people who believe that Man was placed here by a higher power, a 'God', if you will. The people call out to God for help, and all that has followed is more misery. The religious extremists say that we are on the threshold of 'Judgment Day'. They believe God will reward them in heaven.

"There are others here that think believing in a 'God' is foolish. Their contention is that Man evolved from other species and became a sentient being after millions of years of evolution. Throughout history, mankind has perpetrated violence against his fellow Man. That doesn't sound like the 'intelligent beings' we claim to be. Man ignored the harm he did to this planet and now we are the hunted and nothing in our vast arsenal of technology can help us.

"What has happened to us, you ask? Read on, friend.

Rex stopped reading and took a moment to absorb the first few pages of this ancient book. His pause unintentionally raised the tension in the room. He turned the page.

"The next page says 'Chapter Two, The end of our Civilization'.

"We began our civilization hunting for our food and dwelling in small villages. We evolved to build expansive cities with massive populations. The billions of people in our world squandered the gifts of this planet without any concerns for the long-term health of either themselves or the planet. Waves of death and destruction are afflicting the world and we believe it will not stop until Man is extinct. Our top scientists determined that the only explanation that made any sense was that our world had decided it had taken enough abuse from us.

"The chaos started in small ways. Ships mysteriously sank in the sea. Vast fields of grain were ruined by pestilence. The water became unfit for consumption and millions died from contamination. The air was filled with pollution. Our scientists couldn't develop technology fast enough to keep the air clean. Our senior citizens died from lung disease in great numbers. It was as if a plague had been set down upon Man.

"As these events grew in number and magnitude, it was clear that the planet was fighting back. How else could we explain different species of animals seemed to communicate and coordinate attacks on Man? Or swarms of insects attacking the food chain and causing catastrophic food shortages?

"Worse than all of what I have described—and deliberately left out—was Man's abhorrent behavior towards his fellow Man. I refuse to write of the injustices and savagery that is rampant here. My heart is filled with anguish. Perhaps it would have been best if we allowed our species to perish. Yet our instinct for survival outweighed that ideology and it is our hope that Man could learn how to co-exist with Nature and his fellow man.

"In response to these desperate times, our Government consulted with the leaders from the Arts and Sciences and established a way to preserve what we had accomplished before it was destroyed. This information was put into a series of books and preserved in perpetuity. In addition, we captured the DNA from all animals, insects, seeds, grains, and living creatures in a genetic sequencer. This device preserved millions of species for extraction at a later time.

"We loaded that genetic material on a space ship, which was part of the greatest space endeavor ever conceived. Hundreds of citizens from across the globe boarded Project Noah. When it blasted off and headed into space, we set our sights on a planet many light years away. Our scientists were confident that our technology would sustain the lives of the passengers during the long voyage.

"The also ship carried two books: one you are reading now, and the book that was used to teach your ancestors how to build the tunnels.

"We feared that even with the destruction seen here, Man would continue his hostile and irresponsible ways. Certain members of our space team were assigned the task of monitoring Man's behavior in this New World and determine if the lessons from our world had been learned. If the answer was no, that group was instructed to build a structure that would allow Man seek refuge on your planet. This structure would be needed if Man faced an ecological disaster similar to ours. Apparently our worst fears have been realized. This structure will permit you to live safely for eight years while your world heals itself and cleanses the damage from Man's destructiveness.

"Our efforts to preserve mankind were a valiant, but vain attempt to prolong the human race. Perhaps, given a third chance, mankind will flourish. We didn't have the wisdom to understand our symbiotic relationship with the planet until it was too late. Without the proper maintenance, our buildings will deteriorate. In a thousand years or so, there won't be any evidence left of our existence here at all.

"Have we done anything worth saving? There are books written by magnificent storytellers. I used to take my children to the movies and eat popcorn. My favorite football team used to get fans to bark like dogs. That must sound funny to you. It was. In the future, space travelers from another solar system may find this place and build their own world. I wish them well.

"May God bless you…

Signed: March 8, 2123, in New York City, The United States of America. Planet Earth"

THE END